M000032076

The Coding Samurai

The Way of the Computer Warrior

By Ian Felton

For Jen and the cats.

Copyright © 2017 Ian Felton

All rights reserved. This book or any portion thereof may not be reproduced or used in any manner whatsoever without the express written permission of the publisher except for the use of brief quotations in a book review.

Cover art by Dream Chen © 2017

Published by jerk cat publishing

Visit the author's website: http://www.ianfelton.com

ISBN: 978-0-9986909-0-2

This is a work of fiction. Names, characters, places, and incidents either are the products of the author's imagination or are used fictitiously. Any resemblance to actual persons, living or dead, businesses, companies, events, or locales is entirely coincidental.

ACKNOWLEDGMENTS

Many people have helped me with this book. I want to acknowledge the following for reading and giving me feedback during the initial drafts: David Bielejeski, my brother, Chris Felton, J Wynia, and Roz Foster at Sandra Dijkstra Literary Agency. I want to thank my developmental editing team of Tim and Steve Parolini, my copy editor, Sarah Kolb-Williams, and my cover designer, Meng Qian (Dream) Chen. Mostly, I need to thank my dearest editor and inspiration, Jennifer Buege, for pushing me to do better and helpin' me wit' my werds. After my own, Jen's efforts throughout the process—developmental editing, copy editing, craft tips, and general whip cracking—are largely responsible for what follows.

Finally, I also have to acknowledge the absurd and largely soulless landscape of corporate IT. Thanks.

CHAPTER ONE
Lepton Mountain

The words lit up above the sleek entrance of the office building in downtown Lepton Mountain—a yellow "Boom!" followed by an orange "Snap!" and then a fiery red "Pow!" Throngs of well-groomed professionals pushed past Artemis Pound and through the revolving doors. He wiped a bit of sweat from his forehead, caught a glimpse of himself in the window, and realized his pants might be just a bit too short for him to be taken seriously. It wasn't how he'd envisioned starting his career as a coder.

This is why I need a girlfriend, he thought, glancing around to see if anyone was watching him scoot his pants further down his hips. As he squinted down the long stretch of Fowler Avenue, an advertisement for DIY Brew, a printable adult beverage company, grabbed his attention. Standing in an upscale home with all the latest gadgets, appliances, and décor, a debonair man casually pressed a button on the machine and then handed an attractive smiling woman a martini glass of bubblegum-colored liquid topped with foam.

"Maybe in a couple months, I'll be able to afford one of those," Artemis said to himself as he entered the building. LEDs cast light across the lobby's white, polished floor. A message stamped into the tiles in green letters read, "Made from 100%

recycled Greek yogurt containers." He caught sight of his reflection in the floor and thought his pants looked much better.

He double-tapped his wrist and said, "Live stream." A blue indicator light pulsed in Artemis' peripheral vision.

Tilly has joined the live stream.

"Hey, Artemis. You made it, I see," said Tilly through the teeny headphone synced with Artemis' augmented reality lenses.

"This building is incredible," he said.

"I knew you'd be impressed. Almost a thousand of my breakfasts helped make that floor you're standing on."

"Hairy," said Artemis. "Thanks again for the bike tour yesterday. You've gone far beyond your recruiter duties." He waved his hands in front of him as if he were making a proclamation to the world and said, "Tilly, Tech-Tech-Go recruiter and ambassador to Lepton Mountain."

"All right already. You better get going or you'll be late," she said. "Good luck!"

Tilly has left the live stream.

"Stop live stream," said Artemis. He took a deep breath and then, summoning a bit of swagger, he joined the mass of people muttering into their devices as they headed toward the elevators.

After cramming himself inside, he reached his arm between two well-dressed men speaking into the air, seemingly to no one, and pressed the button for the fifteenth floor. Artemis activated the chatter mode on his earpieces to filter out the human voices clogging the elevator and watched above the doors as a public service announcement played. "The BSP building has a triple-A energy rating from the Lepton Mountain Energy Board. Sun, wind, people, and, yes, even waste create more than eighty percent of the energy used to operate it."

"Excuse me, sir. Can I squeeze by you?" Artemis asked one of the men.

"Getting off? The door opens that way." The man laughed, pointing in the other direction.

"Oh, no. A game I play. With the lenses," said Artemis, pointing to the thin layer covering his eyes. "There are some materials showing up in the corner of the elevator that I can use."

The man smirked and edged out of Artemis' way. Artemis faced away from the crowd and simulated the action of scraping the virtual blue nuggets of BioCore off the elevator wall. As he reached out his hand to collect the minerals, an orange ooze shot out of the corner of the elevator and enveloped his hand.

"Ow—fuck!" yelled Artemis as the game sent a pain signal to his haptic suit, creating a real sensation of burning pain on the back of his hand.

Artemis waved his hand counterclockwise, shaking off the ooze. The crowd in the elevator absentmindedly made more room for him.

Quite the score—10 kg of BioCore.

By the time the door opened to his floor, Artemis was alone. He saw the Boom! Snap! Pow! Marketing reception desk straight in front of him and sighed in relief. *Five minutes to spare,* he thought as he walked toward the waiting area.

Behind the desk, a man wearing a tight-fitting shirt that revealed his athletic physique sat staring in frustration at his display, an ultra-slim Adapta. The nameplate on his desk read "Brent Jennings."

"Excuse me. I'm Artemis, the new hire here, to see Jeff."

"Oh, good morning," the receptionist said warmly before sighing at the display. "Brent Jennings. They showed me how to make this screen bigger, but darn it if I haven't already forgotten how."

"Put your finger in the little divot in the corner," Artemis said as Brent searched around the screen. "And now pinch the opposite corner."

"Oh, like this?" Brent asked excitedly.

"There's a little button there. Press it and then make it whatever size you want," Artemis said.

"That's better!" exclaimed Brent. "Now I can see the darned thing. Thanks, young man. Let me call Jeff. There's coffee and tea over there. Help yourself."

Artemis turned to the reception area and felt a hand on his shoulder.

"Hold on. Let me fix you. I can't let you meet Jeff with your collar sticking down into your shirt like that," said Brent as he straightened Artemis' clothing and fussed over him with care.

"Thanks. You'd think I could dress myself better by now."

"We all have our strong suits," said Brent, his hand on

4

Artemis' shoulder.

Artemis poured a cup of coffee before sitting by the windows that overlooked Fowler Avenue. He quickly found his apartment building down the street; the greenhouse and antennae on the roof made it easy to spot. Fidgeting with his pants again, Artemis felt the holographic ball in his pocket that his parents had given him for graduation. Just as he took it out and smiled at the projection, a man with a weathered, deeply tanned face emerged from a door behind the reception desk. His thick, straight hair was full of pomade, and he wore a suit jacket patterned in a dazzling floral print. He beamed at Artemis.

"You must be Artemis! I'm Jeff Rove. Welcome to BSP!" he said, punching the air after saying each letter in the acronym. After the final punch, Jeff slowly lowered his fist, inviting Artemis to bump it.

Artemis awkwardly hit Jeff's hand, only managing to brush a couple knuckles. "Hi, Jeff. Great to meet you."

"Nice lenses you've got there. I can barely see them. FourthForce?"

"Yeah. I love them. I never take them out."

"We've got a lot going on, so let me get you introduced to the team," said Jeff. "We'll need to get you an access code and have you sign some things, but you'll be squared away pronto."

Artemis felt overwhelmed as his mind leapt from thought to thought. "You have the same name as my cat," he blurted out as Jeff led him into the offices.

"Your cat's name is Jeff?"

"My cat's name is Jef with one *f*. I'm guessing yours probably has two," said Artemis, quickly realizing how weird the conversation had become.

"You're absolutely right. Two *f*'s," Jeff said, giving Artemis a strange look.

"So, where are you from?" asked Artemis, trying to bring the conversation back down to Earth.

"California. I worked in Silicon Valley before coming here," replied Jeff. "The Mountain is great, but man, I miss the ocean."

"I love the water, too, except I've mostly been on lakes."

"Oh yeah? That wouldn't cut it for me. I'm a surfer. I wouldn't even be here, but I had a nasty wipeout a while back— busted up pretty bad. I promised my wife I'd quit."

"That's awful," said Artemis, catching a glimpse of employees in lab coats milling around in a secured room. "What are they working on?"

"Who? Oh, they're our researchers. They do A/B testing on our products," Jeff said as the two entered the team's work area. Flooded with natural light, the large, open room contained about fifteen workstations, most of them occupied. The floor was made of the same white plastic tile as the lobby's and had the Boom! Snap! Pow! logo painted in the center in the same colors as the sign over the building's entrance. One wall held a wide digital task board, in front of which stood a squat, burly man swiping through tasks and stories. *Probably preparing for a morning meeting,* thought Artemis.

"Hey, guys, this is Artemis," said Jeff. "Everyone do what you can to help him from grubbing."

"Grubbing?" asked Artemis.

"Wiping out. Eating sand. You catch my drift?" asked Jeff. He then turned to an exceptionally tall man standing nearby. "Brad, can you get Artemis everything he needs to start working on Groundswell?"

"Sure thing," Brad said, turning to shake Artemis' hand. "Good to meet you, Artemis. Welcome to BSP!" he said, punching the air after each letter as Jeff had done.

"Good to meet you, too. It's Brad, right?" asked Artemis.

"Correct," said Brad. "So here in the common work area, we're all using Mobipod work stations."

"Mobipods?" asked Artemis.

"Yeah, those things over there that look like gym equipment. You can sit, stand, recline—whatever makes you comfortable. Sensors line the frame to track your gestures however you have it adjusted."

"I'll need some help. I've never used one before."

"No surprise there since we are beta testing them for a subsidiary," Brad said. "Let's see, what else?"

"What kind of machine will I be using?"

"Great question. Your quantum is a Quark One. That's what we're all using."

"I can't wait to play around with it."

"That thing's not a toy," said Brad in a manner that took Artemis off guard. "There's a reason you have to be registered to use them."

"I just meant that . . ." Artemis realized he wasn't sure what he had meant and changed the topic. "What operating system is it running?"

"Pathways."

"Why not Gopher World?"

"You're joking."

"No, why?"

Brad looked at Artemis quizzically. "We have some features that don't play nicely with the Gopher World license."

"Ah, blame the lawyers. Got it. So, what's Groundswell?"

"Groundswell is our landmark marketing platform. It's a way for us to inject marketing opportunities into augmented worlds that let the user interact with our clients' products in a natural way," explained Brad. "Think of it as 'try-before-you-buy' ad placement in your favorite forms of entertainment, whether that's games, movies, or social. It's going to be industry-transforming."

"It's going to melt your mom's face!" yelled a man from somewhere nearby.

"It sounds complex. What will I be doing?" asked Artemis.

"For starters, we just need you to get up to speed on your quantum. You didn't use these much in college, I'm guessing," said Brad.

"Actually, I used them a lot, but I haven't used Pathways," said Artemis. "I don't think I'll have much trouble with it, though. I have a pretty hairy quantum at home running Gopher World that I put together in college."

"Would you mind not using that *hairy/bald* slang here?" said Brad. "My parents were both *bald*, as you'd call it. And proud of it. The Alt Youth Corp did plenty to help this country and shouldn't be denigrated just because they helped round up a few troublemakers. How did other people help? Oh, that's right, they just started growing their hair long to protest. Wait—did you just say you've been using Gopher World? The only people authorized to use that are . . ." Brad paused and gave a serious look to Jeff, who quickly shrugged his shoulders and resumed his conversation.

"Let's get the project set up for you," said Brad. "Then we'll have you get started upgrading our templates and models to the latest versions. It's a good way for you to get your feet wet. Before all of that, though, we need you to see Jessica in HR. Wait here a minute."

Artemis watched Brad walk over to Jeff and pull him away from his conversation. The two men engaged in a serious exchange, which ended with Jeff smiling and shrugging his shoulders. Brad grimaced, then smiled a little too widely as he walked back toward Artemis.

"Sorry about that. Follow me."

As they walked to HR, BSP-produced advertisements

playing in loops on the hallway wall caught Artemis' eye. The company had created ads for many Fortune 500 companies and had even won the contract for the Summer Olympics in Reykjavík, Iceland.

From the corner of his eye, Artemis saw something dart behind the plastic plant he was approaching. It had a long, spiny tail and a clump of long feathers on the crown of its head.

There's only one thing it could be.

Artemis ran over to the flowerpot and slid it into the middle of the hall, almost making Brad trip over it. Staring back at Artemis, with nowhere to hide, was a Polymorg. Not just any Polymorg—a beautiful, female, Level 90, pregnant Polymorg. Artemis leapt forward. The virtual beast countered by jumping onto his neck and digging its sharp talons into his flesh.

"Son of a bitch!" yelled Artemis as his haptic suit sent a piercing pain signal to his neck. "Sorry, Brad. I caught it. It's just a game I'm beta testing."

"Beastville," said Brad.

"You know?"

"I mean, I figured. Let's move along now. I have a meeting to get to."

When they arrived at Jessica's workspace, she was talking with a female coworker. Artemis took note of their shaved heads. "With everything going on with the offshore team, I don't think the new employee temperament assessments should be accessible to anyone outside of HR," said the woman speaking with Jessica.

"Outside of HR, only hiring managers can see them. I don't see a problem," said Jessica. Brad coughed gently, and Jessica said, "We'll talk more about this later," dismissing the other woman. She turned to Brad and asked, "A new hire?"

Brad nodded his head and opened his palms to present Artemis to her.

"Artemis Pound. Nice to meet you," Artemis said, reaching out to shake her hand.

"I'm Jessica. Welcome to BSP. I have some paperwork for you to complete, and then I'll send you back to Brad. Sound good?" By now, Artemis wasn't surprised that Jessica, too, had pumped the air when saying the company's name.

"Sure."

"I'll see you after you wrap things up with Jessica," said Brad, heading back down the hallway.

Jessica pulled out a thick stack of paper. "Here are a few things for you to keep for your records: your benefits package, your salary information, and so on. Read this set of documents and sign where I've highlighted. It includes the dress code policy, your temperament assessment—wait, I'm not supposed to give you your temperament assessment," she said, removing the documents from the pile. "But here is your noncompete agreement, sexual harassment policy, and discrimination policy," she said before pausing with a perplexed frown. "You're smiling . . ."

"It's just funny to be in IT and still have so much actual paperwork," said Artemis.

"Paperwork will go on forever," replied Jessica without a hint of humor. "Let me know if you have any questions."

Artemis sat at Jessica's desk and started going through the pile of documents. He skimmed through the dress code policy.

"Employees of Boom! Snap! Pow! Marketing (BSP) must present themselves professionally at all times. Men, women, and nonbinary-gender employees must wear appropriate business attire including skirts, slacks, professional shirts, blouses, suits, dress shoes, and sweaters. Clothing with distracting patterns or that which is considered revealing is inappropriate. Men, women, and nonbinary-gender employees may wear makeup so long as the makeup isn't applied in a way that appears distracting (see example)."

The example photograph showed a person with a Mohawk, piercings, and a large black star applied in makeup around each eye. Artemis chuckled.

"Do you have a question?" asked Jessica, still frowning and rubbing her hand over her shaved head.

"No, I'm just looking at the . . . never mind. I'm fine."

The next section read: "Employees of BSP may reference the company as Boom! Snap! Pow! Marketing or BSP as an abbreviation. When using the abbreviation verbally, employees are expected to say each letter enthusiastically and punch the air gently with either hand. The punching should happen *gently* and never be delivered in a way that appears aggressive or threatening. If the employee is carrying a number of items, such as hot coffee, that would prevent the employee from safely waving his, her, or the nonbinary-gender person's hand, do not attempt an air punch. Employees should never attempt an air punch when doing so could endanger themselves or others."

After reading through the paperwork and signing it, Artemis handed it back to Jessica. "I'm finished."

"Not quite yet. There's one more document to sign," she said as she handed him a single piece of paper.

"BSP, as a marketing research company, utilizes certain proprietary technologies that are a core part of its business. As an employee of BSP, you may be exposed to these technologies as a result of your employment. 'I hereby state that I consent and I have not been coerced into signing this form,'" it read.

"What exactly does this mean?" asked Artemis.

"Here's the addendum," she said, handing him what looked to be about a thousand pages of legalese.

Artemis took the stack of documents and set it down. He barely glanced at the piece of paper, put his signature and the date on it, and handed it back to Jessica.

She looked it over briefly. "Thank you. I'll let you know if there are any issues. Can you find your way back to Brad?" she asked.

"I think so. Thanks," he said before walking back toward the team space.

"Hey-ho, it's the FNG," said a man in his early thirties with short curly hair and squinty eyes. He was leaning back in one of the Mobipods and wearing jeans and sneakers.

"FNG?" asked Artemis.

"The last two words are 'new guy.' You can figure out the first one," the man said, sitting up in his pod.

"That's supposed to be funny, I guess," said Artemis, trying to coolly express his displeasure at the acronym.

"It's an old IT saying. I'm Rodney. You're new, aren't you?"

"Yeah, I'm just starting."

"Nice to meet you, Just Starting. I'm guessing you're one of the interns?"

Artemis thought, *How old are you, thirteen?* Then he said, "That's right. It's Artemis, by the way. How about you? What do you do here?"

"I'm a DOT—DevOpsTester. You know there was a time when it was just developer? Then there was a time after that when it was just DevOps. Now we're DevOpsTesters. What's next? DevOpsTesterChefs?" laughed Rodney. Artemis had no clue what any of that meant.

"I'm just trying to find Brad."

"He's not around, but he asked me to show you your spot. It's that one over there," said Rodney, pointing to an empty Mobipod at the end of the aisle in the corner.

"I'm not real certain what to do with the Mobipod."

"Don't be intimidated by all the tubing and crap sticking off it. It's just for show and a way to get all the sensors in place without using much creativity. The hardware's all under the seat. Just turn it on and it will sync with your lenses. Mmkay?" said Rodney, scratching his arm.

"Which one again?"

"That one," said Rodney, jabbing his finger in the direction of the bright pink Mobipod decorated with flames.

Artemis looked at the Mobipod and then back at Rodney.

"Someone's gotta use it," said Rodney before turning away and walking off.

Artemis walked over to his pod and flipped the switch under the seat. Nothing happened. He squatted down and examined all of the connectors. *Are you kidding me?* he thought, searching in vain to find the power supply. *What am I supposed to do without any power?*

A young, heavyish woman wearing the brightest pink top Artemis had ever seen approached him. She was African-American and looked to be about Artemis' age. From the way she carried herself, Artemis guessed that her personality matched her physical size—and likely dwarfed it. She flashed a big smile that showed off her bright white teeth.

"Hey there. I haven't seen you around before. You must be the new guy," she said, shaking his hand with a strong, sure grip. "I'm Beyoncé, one of the interns."

Artemis thought maybe she was making fun of him as Rodney had. "Like the singer my mom listens to?" he asked.

"The very one. Mamma said she was singin' when she was conceivin'.' Would you like to join us for lunch?" She nodded her head toward two young males Artemis assumed were other interns.

"I think I'll stay here and go through this HR paperwork."

"You'd rather read HR manuals than go to lunch?"

"No, it's just that there's a lot to go through and I usually eat lunch on my own while getting caught up on my hologs."

"I'll summarize the manuals: Blah blah blah blah blah. You can watch your holographic blogs later on. Come eat with us."

Artemis hesitated. "Well, okay."

"This is Wei Wei and Tony," Beyoncé said.

Wei Wei had a slight physique and dressed formally. Tony had a square head and wide eyes that made Artemis wonder if he'd had some type of surgery on his eyelids.

"And you still haven't told us your name," continued Beyoncé.

"Geez, sorry. I'm Artemis," he said, waving to everyone.

The group followed Beyoncé to the elevator, where they packed themselves in. The walls played BSP floor-to-ceiling videos showing smiling employees engaged in meetings and workplace fist-bumping. The elevator doors opened and the group walked into the cafeteria. Located on the top floor of the building, it had a view of downtown set against the backdrop of the Appalachian Mountains.

The cafeteria contained a wide variety of food stations,

including a food-and-drink-printing area, which seemed the most popular. Artemis followed behind Beyoncé as she swiped her wearable on the machine to let it know her preferred diet. The machine then printed a custom meal designed for her nutritional and allergy requirements.

"Do they stock anything fresh or just the printed food?" asked Artemis.

"Eating the old-fashioned way? There's an island over there with some papayas, and I think it might be Perfect Burger Day," she said, pointing toward the corner of the cafeteria.

After making their way through the cafeteria line, the interns selected a table on the outside patio by a small Zen garden.

"So, what do you think of BSP?" asked Beyoncé. Like the others, she punched her fist in the air after each letter, but her tone was mocking.

"So far, so good, except there's no power supply with my quantum," said Artemis.

"Not surprising. Brad had to let me into the building for a week while they tried to get me an access code," replied Beyoncé before taking a bite of her lunch.

"How about you all? What do you think of BSP?" asked Artemis, finally performing an air punch.

"Wei Wei and I just started last week," said Tony, without blinking. "I'm still getting used to the place. Beyoncé has been here the longest, since January."

"What are you doing?" asked Beyoncé with a furrowed brow

as she glared at Artemis, who was staring into space while waving his hands in a rhythmic pattern.

"Oh, sorry. I was catching a Scrapulum. I need their skins to make a potion."

Beyoncé shook her head. "We've lost another one," she said to Wei Wei and Tony, who were both chuckling.

"Lost another what?" asked Artemis.

"Human being. To technology," said Beyoncé. "Do you ever just take out the lenses and look at the world without all the augmented layers?"

"No. Why would I do that?"

"Oh, I don't know, maybe see a pretty girl to talk to?"

"Ha. I get it. So, what's your impression of this place?" Artemis asked Beyoncé.

"My dad always said work's what you make of it. As far as who's who, Brad's the go-to guy. Jeff's a real character but rarely around."

"Jeff's outfit this morning," said Artemis. "Wow!"

"And it's a dressed-down day for him. You wait," said Beyoncé. "Then there's Deepak . . . only he's not an easy one to figure out."

"How so?" asked Artemis.

"Just the vibes I get from him. He's definitely not hairy. I'm leaning toward bald. And the jury's still out on you, too." Beyoncé laughed.

"I'll do my best to make a positive impression," Artemis said with a grin. "What have you been working on?"

"Groundswell. Pretty much everyone is. It's launching soon, you know."

"I can't believe I'm working on a project like this right out of school."

"I can," interjected Tony. "I don't really think they brought us here to work. I'm fairly certain we're here as test subjects."

"I think I'm lucky more than anything else," said Artemis to Tony, wondering how someone who looked so much like a fish could breathe out of water.

"I guess we'll find out," said Beyoncé, finishing her blueberry drink and printed tacos.

"How are the tacos?" asked Artemis.

"They could be a little spicier. The blueberry drink, though . . . hairy good," she said.

Artemis turned to Wei Wei. "How about you, Wei Wei? What's it like working on Groundswell?"

"I'm patently thrilled with the illuminating challenges I've encountered thus far while applying my craft to the viewport components," said Wei Wei.

"Holy moly, Wei Wei. Your English is amazing," exclaimed Artemis.

"You would never expect that from a guy who grew up in Flushing, would you?" Beyoncé said, laughing loudly.

"I didn't mean it like that, like because he's Chinese he should have broken English. I just mean he has a great vocabulary," said Artemis sheepishly, fumbling with his cutlery.

"Why do you think he's Chinese?" asked Tony.

"Isn't Wei Wei a Chinese name? I mean, c'mon. He looks Chinese," answered Artemis.

"What's a Chinese person look like, Artemis?" asked Beyoncé in a serious voice.

"Are you serious? Like Wei Wei. Come on, you guys, it's just an observation. I'm not racist. My mentor from college is Chinese."

"Not racist? You sound pretty racist to me," said Wei Wei. "You think because of the way I look you know my ancestry?"

"Sorry, I wasn't trying to offend anyone. So, what is your ancestry then?"

"Chinese," said Wei Wei, and everyone at the table erupted in laughter.

Artemis pushed himself back from the table. "Thanks for inviting me to lunch. I should get back to work, since it's my first day and all."

"We were just playing, Artemis. You don't have to leave," said Beyoncé.

"It's his first day on the job and he's going bald already," added Tony.

"Not quite yet, just trying to make a good first impression," said Artemis. "See you all later."

"Catch you later," said Wei Wei.

After rushing back to work, Artemis spent the afternoon

waiting on a power supply that would never arrive. At five o'clock, hardly anyone had yet to leave the office. Unable to justify staying any longer to parse through the details of the materials Jessica had given him, he stood up to leave.

"Leaving so soon?" said a voice from behind him.

Artemis turned around and saw a man standing in the shadows of the hallway.

"I'm waiting on parts. I figured I'd head home since they probably won't be coming today."

"How do you feel about your first day?"

"It was fine. Met some new people. Saw some cool new things like the Mobipods."

"I hate those things. Ridiculous contraptions. I like to work in an empty room with space to truly move around in quantum worlds, to leap and spin and not be constrained to hand-waving or walking on those goddamn treadmills they use in Gopher World pods."

"Oh, yeah. That sounds like the way to go. Do I know you?"

"I don't think so. It looks as if it's time for you to go."

"Good night," said Artemis to the man before he left the office and walked home.

****

The following morning, Artemis arrived at work in time to hear Jeff kick off the stand-up meeting with an announcement.

"Look what I picked up," said Jeff, pointing at a DIY Brew printer.

"What are you going to do with that?" asked Brad.

"Everyone's been busting their tails all week. We're gonna blow off some steam at my house after work. Drop in at seven. It's gonna be gnarly," said Jeff, squatting down like he was surfing. He concluded the meeting by high-fiving the people standing next to him.

Artemis stopped Brad before his next meeting. "Brad, did the power supply to my quantum arrive yet?" he asked.

"It did. Let me know if you need anything else. If I'm not around, Rodney can help you out," said Brad.

"Are you going to Jeff's tonight?"

"I'll stop by for a bit. How about you?"

"I doubt it."

"Maybe try to at least make an appearance."

"I guess I can do that," said Artemis before walking over to his pod.

The power cord sat in a tangled mess on the seat. It took him several minutes to unwind it. *It'd be nice if they could figure out how to supply enough power to these things wirelessly like everything else these days,* thought Artemis as he connected the cord to the plug at the back of the polymer case.

Artemis examined the Mobipod for anything he might have missed, touched the power button, and sat down. The quantum synced to his FourthForce augmented reality lenses as he leaned back and stretched out his legs.

This is gonna be fun, he thought before spending the rest of the day sifting through the software packages and upgrading templates and models.

****

That evening, shortly after seven, Artemis arrived at Jeff's cabin, which was nestled in a grove of trees on the outskirts of town. He heard voices on the back deck, which overlooked a small creek.

"Artemis! Get up here, bro!" yelled Jeff, who punched away at the DIY Brew machine sitting on the deck beside his grill. "I'm making some hairy stuff with this thing. You gotta try it."

Artemis walked across the lawn and found Brad and Tony talking to each other among the twenty or so people congregated on the deck.

"We're going down to the creek to catch crayfish for the gumbo. You want to come?" asked Brad.

Artemis didn't hear a word that Brad had said. He was too busy tapping away at the air to defend himself from a scraggly green MossKito that was currently doing 39 damage per second.

"Artemis. Hey! Artemis!" shouted Brad.

Artemis cleared the game layer from his FourthForce optics by swiping his left hand across his eyes and said, "Sorry, what's up?"

"Hello. I don't think we've met yet, have we?" said a man wearing a white linen outfit who seemed to appear from nowhere. He appeared to be of Asiatic Indian descent, with black hair and perfect teeth. In fact, the only imperfection Artemis could see on the older man's youthful face was a small birthmark on his left cheek.

"I don't think so. I'm Artemis."

"I'm Deepak Gupta, team lead. I'm sorry I haven't been by to introduce myself. With the finish line for Groundswell in sight, I have to stay focused on several important things," said Deepak, awash in confidence, his words flowing as smooth as a song. "Not that you aren't important, of course." He smiled.

Artemis just stood there stupidly with his eyes crossed, and then he realized he hadn't said anything in response.

"Grab a bucket and come with us, Artemis. I want to show you something," said Brad.

"Not without a drink first, he's not," said Jeff, still working the DIY Brew. "This thing cost a fortune. We're gonna get some use out of it."

Artemis looked at Brad and shrugged his shoulders. "Okay," he said to Jeff.

"What can I make you, Arty?" asked Jeff, scrolling through the machine's preprogrammed recipes. "How about a Triple Banger?"

Having no clue what a Triple Banger was, Artemis said, "Uh, sure."

Jeff pushed a few more buttons on the machine and then handed Artemis a cup filled with a pitch-black liquid that smelled like pure alcohol. Artemis winced when the vapor hit his nostrils.

"Enjoy," said Jeff.

"I'll try," Artemis replied with a grimace.

"'Do or do not. There is no try,'" said Jeff before erupting in laughter.

Artemis grabbed a bucket and followed Brad and Tony down to the stream, while Deepak stayed behind with Jeff. Brad rolled up his pants legs and waded in. Artemis stood on the bank next to Tony, pulled out a holographic camera, and started recording.

"So, the trick is to step gently because the crawdads are hiding under the rocks. Then pick up a rock about this size or bigger," said Brad, demonstrating the technique. "Try not to stir up the mud; you want to be able to see if the crawdad is there. If it is, you have to be real quick and snatch the guy right behind his front claws or else he can bend his body around and give you a good pinch."

"That sounds painful," said Artemis.

"Don't worry. It won't hurt you, but you'll probably drop the crawdad."

Artemis sipped on his drink as he watched Brad catch a few. When he'd finished his drink and felt warm inside, he waded out to try his hand at it.

"Got one!" yelled Artemis, who nabbed one on his third try, the crayfish now arching back to give him a pinch on whatever flesh it could find.

"Oh, that's a big 'un," said Brad. "Put him in the bucket."

"I don't think so," said Artemis.

"You don't think so?" asked Brad.

"It would violate my F.O.A.L. oath," said Artemis, wading deeper into the water to set the crayfish free.

"Suit yourself," said Brad while Tony laughed.

Artemis watched them catch a few more before Brad decided they had enough for the gumbo. When they got back to the deck, Jeff was still serving drinks.

"That's a lot of crayfish," said Jeff. "Brad, here's one we haven't tried yet. It looks weird, but give it a try," he said, handing Brad a cup.

"No thanks," replied Brad, waving off the cup. "I've hit my limit."

"You've only had one," said Jeff with a 'what the hell is wrong with you' look.

"Exactly."

"Always the responsible one," Jeff said, rolling his eyes. "Arty, you have it then." He offered the cup to Artemis, who was standing at the foot of the stairs leading up to the deck.

"I should probably wait a little bit," replied Artemis, still reeling from the Triple Banger.

"Too good to have a drink with us, Artemis?" said Deepak with a slight sneer.

Artemis began walking up the stairs, staring at the cup in

Jeff's hand. He gripped the railing tightly and stopped at the penultimate step. He looked around at the merry people on the deck. *Why not keep the good times rolling?* He stepped onto the deck, took the drink from Jeff, and ventured inside the house with Tony.

That was the last thing Artemis remembered. He woke up in a bedroom that he assumed was in Jeff's house. He wasn't wearing a shirt, but he still had on his pants and shoes. The skin on his chest was burning.

What the heck happened?

Artemis left the bedroom and wandered into the kitchen, where Jeff and his much younger wife were sitting at the table. As soon as he saw them, Artemis got a very bad feeling.

"There's the man," laughed Jeff. "Guessing you're a little wiped out. You probably don't remember a thing. Here ya go, breakfast of champions."

"Thanks. I guess I drank too much," said Artemis, taking the plate of potatoes and eggs from Jeff.

"Perish the thought. Let me get you a shirt."

Artemis sat down at the table and tried not to look at Jeff and his wife. After devouring the plate of food and drinking several glasses of juice, Artemis decided he needed to leave as soon as possible.

"Jeff, I have to get home. Thanks for the party and for the place to sleep," Artemis said. "Can I get your shirt back to you later? I can't find mine."

"Sure thing, Wild Man. See you Monday," said Jeff.

Artemis practically ran out the door, got on his rental bike, and pedaled home as fast as he could. Once inside his apartment, he put a can of wet food into Jef's bowl and then went straight to his bed, where he slept most of the day.

****

On Monday, a feeling of dread washed over Artemis as he walked to work. On the way to his workstation, he passed Jeff, who just said "hi" and smiled. But something weird was going on. Everyone he passed, including the secretary, wore a knowing smile.

What the hell?

He logged in to his quantum to check his email. The first one he saw was from Tony with the subject, "The Wild Man." Knowing he'd probably regret it but unable to stop himself, Artemis opened the email and played the holographic clip embedded in it. The snippet showed Artemis, shirtless, running across Jeff's lawn with a crazed look in his eyes, chasing people he didn't know. As he ran straight towards Tony, the clip showed him with his mouth gaping open. Then Artemis noticed something weird dangling from his chest. *It can't be,* he thought. Artemis restarted the clip and put his hand on his forehead. Then he advanced the hologram at half speed. As the camera zoomed in on Artemis' bare torso, it all became horribly clear. There, with tails flicking and antennae probing, were two crayfish, one clamped to each of his nipples. Tony, apparently feeling he needed to spice up the clip a bit, had added text that read "Feeling crabby? Drink an Arty Palmer!"

Artemis could feel the color draining from his face. He had become a meme.

CHAPTER TWO
The Way of the Computer Warrior

Two weeks earlier

"And now, everybody welcome the graduating class of Minnesota Tech University!" said Dean Winston to the assembled audience. Filled with hundreds of Artemis' college classmates and their families and friends, the auditorium echoed with cheers as the dean called out each graduate's name. Artemis stopped himself from laughing at Julie Peaslee, who tripped and fell on the podium. Peggy Fulbright, who was sitting next to Artemis, showed no such restraint. He watched as Peggy's drone flew back to her and nested itself in the ring on her finger. A moment after her drone synced, he assumed she was replaying the episode on her lenses as she giggled, while staring into the space in front of her face.

Artemis held back not only because it would be rude, but because he was worried about his future. He questioned whether he was ready to be a professional software developer and whether he might be about to make an even bigger fool of himself.

When Artemis' name was announced, he climbed the stairs to the stage, shook Dean Winston's hand, and smiled at the flock of hovering camera drones taking graduation pictures. Then he walked down the stairs on the other side, and that was it—graduation complete. After the final names were called, he left the building to meet his family. He saw his mentor talking with a well-dressed man wearing all white at the side of the road. By the time Artemis made his way over there, the man had left. Professor Lao stood wearing that wild-eyed smile of his.

"Glad to see you made it across the stage in one piece," said Professor Lao, wearing leather pants and a T-shirt emblazoned with the logo of a popular college rock band. "Have you decided which job to take yet?"

"I'm having a tough time. Maybe you have time to talk this week?"

"I'm very sorry, Artemis, but I don't. I'm leaving for Puerto Rico tomorrow. After I leave here, I need to pack and finalize arrangements with the bird-sitter."

"I guess I'll have to just try and channel you while I go through my options."

"You'll do fine on your own. I should go now. I'm sure your family wants to see you."

The news of his mentor's imminent departure wounded Artemis a bit. Professor Lao had taught his intro-level quantum programming course. Artemis wasn't the best or the smartest student in the class, but for some reason Professor Lao had extended himself to Artemis. Artemis thought back to the start of their relationship, halfway through that semester.

"Artemis, can you spare a few minutes after lab today?" the

professor had asked.

"Sure," said Artemis, who then spent the next two hours of lab wondering whether he'd done something wrong.

Once class ended, Artemis approached the professor's desk.

"I've been shorthanded on a project for the university," said Professor Lao. "Would you like to get some experience by lending a hand? It's not paid, but you'll learn a lot."

"That's a relief," replied Artemis. "I thought maybe I'd done something wrong. What kind of project is it?"

The professor didn't immediately respond. Artemis wondered if he was questioning whether he had chosen the right student. Then Professor Lao said, "It's an anti-bullying project to help social networking websites satisfy Congress' Digital Social Network Compliance Act. I thought it might be something you would find interesting."

"What would I be doing?" asked Artemis.

"Anything I need you to do. Mostly programming. It will change from week to week as we get new directives and as our lawyers make more sense of what Congress has legislated. Some people," he continued, "see the law as a handout to the major social networking companies to make it more difficult and expensive for start-ups to compete against them. After all, the two biggest platforms cosponsored the bill. It does have good intentions, though. I can't argue with that."

"I've been following the story pretty intently—maybe too intently," said Artemis. "My friends think I'm weird because I spend so much time reading about things like this."

"Ah, then I chose wisely! This describes in more detail what we're working on," said the professor, handing Artemis his portable display.

"Congress' Digital Social Network Compliance Act states that any website deemed a social network as defined by the Act must establish that mechanisms are in place to prevent bullying, prostitution and human trafficking, white-collar crime such as pump-and-dump stock schemes, gang and terrorism propaganda, and the exploitation of children. This project will comprise of programming a platform to enable social networking companies to stay in compliance."

"I'd love to work on this," said Artemis. "Can I ask what the schedule would be? I've been really busy with some things." Artemis was too sheepish to tell the professor that what he had been busy with was playing massive multiplayer online roleplaying games with his friends until three in the morning and then scrambling to get his homework completed during breakfast. He was also trying to impress a girl in their group by being guild leader, which required a larger time commitment by an order of magnitude.

"I will send you the schedule and the project timelines, and you can get back to me by the end of the week. How does that sound?" asked Professor Lao.

"Great. I really appreciate the opportunity; I just want to make certain I have the time," said Artemis.

As it turned out, Artemis was going to have plenty of time. That night, with Professor Lao's offer pressing on him, Artemis decided he needed to accelerate his investigation into SexyElfPrincess' feelings toward him—which, as it turned out, were nonexistent. It wasn't because of Artemis' tendency to belch into the microphone accidentally when it was late and he'd drunk too many carbonated beverages, nor was it because he had wiped the group five times recently after six hours battling in the dungeons.

"I like nonbinary genders," typed SexyElfPrincess after Artemis asked her to meet for coffee.

"OIC," he typed back.

Artemis wrote the professor that night and accepted the apprenticeship. From then on, he spent two afternoons a week working with Professor Lao. The professor wasn't easy on Artemis. Artemis had to learn practices that were advanced for his level, but Professor Lao also took the time to train him. Artemis learned more than he expected about the professor: fall was his favorite season, his favorite book was *Siddhartha*, his wife had died two years earlier from cancer, and he used to be in a rock-and-roll band. Artemis' time with the professor became the most important part of his college education.

Now, back at graduation and faced with a parting, Artemis felt a sudden pang of sadness. He said, "I'm going to miss you."

The professor replied, "I do have a surprise before I leave. Follow me. You're gonna like this."

Artemis followed Professor Lao through the crowd of graduates. The professor pointed toward the road, where a delivery pod sat underneath a large crate the size of a person.

"For me?" asked Artemis. "What's in the pod?"

"After our project ended, I was tasked with liquidating the lab. Once I met the mandated financial goals, I had some wiggle room to get quite a good deal on a couple of quantums."

"You're joking," said Artemis. He'd dreamed of being able to buy a quantum like the one he had used in the lab. The first day he'd stepped inside the computer, he had known he wanted one more than anything. These particular quantum computers could run the best virtual reality operating systems using the highest settings, with no lag. Within certain applications, it was hard to tell what was real and what wasn't. The machines from the lab were the Teslas of quantum computing.

"Just approve the shipment; the drone will handle the rest," said the professor, smiling.

"I'm in shock!" Artemis gushed. "There's no way I'm letting the drone deliver that without me there. The Smunts across the street were pod-snatched last week. I'll just have it follow us home."

"You do that. I really have to go now," said the professor. "Take care of yourself."

"Now that I've graduated, can I start calling you Ambrosius?"

"Maybe not just yet," said the professor, smiling and turning away.

"Bye, Professor! Have a great trip!" shouted Artemis as Professor Lao walked away. Artemis wondered how long it would be until he saw him again, then made his way through the crowd until he found his parents.

"There he is," said Artemis' dad, Gunter.

"Congratulations, Artemis," added his mom, Charlotte, reaching out to give him a hug.

"I just saw the professor," Artemis said as they walked to the car. "You're not going to believe it. He just gave me the best graduation gift ever."

"Oh?" said Gunter, who exchanged a look with Charlotte. "What is it?"

"One of the quantums from the lab. It's unreal," said Artemis.

"That's far too generous of him," his mother said with a frown. "Gunter?"

"I don't think he had to pay for it," said Artemis.

"Your professor gave you a stolen computer?" asked his mother.

"It's not stolen, Mom. He was just able to get a good deal on it," said Artemis, feeling suddenly deflated.

"However he got it, I hope it doesn't get you into any trouble," said Artemis' mom as she got into the family car.

Artemis climbed in with his parents and sat silently. He watched the drones flying in the space above the road. The skies were full of them, following the public roadways in the space designated by the FAA. Artemis liked spotting rare drone models and guessing what they might be up to. The rarest model he had spotted was a prototype that would be used for delivering medicine, as well as administering it, to people such as elderly diabetics. Today he saw nothing but common models, though he did spot an oriole flying among the flock of robots.

The car left the highway and pulled into the Pounds' neighborhood in South Minneapolis. When the car turned onto South Sixty-Fourth Street, the smell of barbecue charcoal floated in the air. As the car pulled into the driveway, Artemis watched the Smunt kids across the street chase each other with water balloons.

"My delivery's right behind us. I'm going to wait out here," said Artemis.

"Okay, Son. We'll be inside getting things ready," replied his dad.

Artemis watched as the boxy delivery drone made its way from the road and up the driveway. At the porch stairs, its wheels retracted and its metal legs walked it through the open door. Just as Artemis began to chase the drone upstairs, his mom appeared and said, "Will you take Buddy out so he's not prancing around during dinner?"

"Come on, Buddy. Outside," said Artemis as the labradoodle hopped and ran around in circles with a dumb look on its face.

Artemis sat on the steps of the deck in the backyard while

Buddy wandered around, sniffing and pawing the ground.

"Okay, Buddy, do your thing. It's time to go back inside," said Artemis as Buddy stared down a squirrel that had run up into the oak tree in the backyard.

"Buddy!" shouted Artemis. Buddy came running toward Artemis with a grey object in his mouth.

"Whatcha got there?" said Artemis, taking it from his dog's mouth. "Good boy! A BrenTech 2000."

Artemis had trained Buddy to pick up drones that had violated the family's airspace. Citizens were permitted to install devices that would disable drones that ventured illegally onto private property. Artemis' dad had installed one after he noticed a drone hovering outside his bathroom window.

"Here, Dad. Buddy found this in the yard," said Artemis, walking back into the house and handing his father the drone.

"Cheap pieces of junk. It costs as much to make these as a pizza. They're like pigeons," said Gunter.

"Yeah, Dad, total garbage," Artemis agreed. "Hey, Mom, smells great," he said, walking over to the stove to see what she was cooking. "I'm going upstairs to check out my computer."

"Don't be too long."

Artemis opened the door to his room and stared at the gift from Professor Lao: an AntiMatter-model quantum computer. The AntiMatter quantums looked like giant eggs that could hatch a full-grown human. As Artemis moved closer to the computer, he had an astonishing realization.

"Princess Di!" shouted Artemis.

Professor Lao had given him his favorite machine he'd used during their work together. He'd named the computer Princess Di—not after Diana, Princess of Wales, but after Princess Diana of Themyscira, a.k.a. Wonder Woman. The machine was indeed a wonder. When on the quantum network using optimal shared resources, it could simulate ten years of weather for every city in the world in one second. Sequencing genes of newly discovered species was trivial. Artemis touched the door to authenticate using his biometrics.

The door opened and Artemis stepped onto the platform inside. It was like standing on a balancing platform that could shift varying degrees. A treadmill on the top of the platform allowed the user to walk or run in any direction. Sensors inside could detect the slightest shift in the skeletal system of the user to adjust the direction and incline of the treadmill.

Artemis had configured Princess Di to stay almost dark when he entered, with light pulsing faintly to the rhythm of his beating heart. *Ba-bump, ba-bump, ba-bump* boomed the bass speakers.

"Hello, Artemis. How have you been since 4:48 p.m. Central Standard Time on May 19th, this year, which was the last time I saw you?"

"Don't be so formal, Princess Di."

"Sorry. What's up?"

"Log in to my network at the university. I left some work

there. I need to find some strategies on raiding Bunicula's Keep with only four team members."

"Okay."

Artemis saw stacks of documents floating in front of him.

"Ugh. I knew I should have organized these better for later. Let's try something else. Do a network search for 'samurai strategy'."

"Okay. Here are the results."

Two documents floated inside the giant egg. One was the document he was looking for and the other was a book called *The Coding Samurai*. It wasn't a very thick book, maybe only fifty or sixty pages. The amateurishly designed cover looked like parchment paper and had "The Coding Samurai" written in bold black letters at the top. Below the letters, the ink outline of an old computer screen from the mid-2010s filled most of the remaining space. On the computer screen, two Samurai swords crossed each other in an X. Below the swords was written the phrase "The Way of the Computer Warrior." Perplexed but intrigued, Artemis smiled as he flipped through the pages.

The Coding Samurai

"It's time you read this," said Mitsuhide, handing his daughter a hand-copied book written in kanji as she sat on a tatami mat in the tearoom of their family home.

"*Bushido Shoshinshu*. I thought only boys read this," said Tama, looking up at her towering father.

"The wife of a samurai will live a similar life," he said, looking at her sternly, but with tenderness in his eyes.

"I don't need to learn to fight, Father," said Tama.

"You think the samurai only wage war and eviscerate our enemies?" asked Mitsuhide, laughing.

"Yes. No. I don't know," said Tama, pulling at her hair.

"Our goal is to master ourselves. Don't you think you need to learn to do this too, Tama?" asked her father.

She stared at the letters, wondering what secrets might be encoded in them. She had no idea what it meant to master herself, but she knew her father was an important man. If he felt the book was important, then it probably was.

"Yes," she said.

"I haven't survived so many battles with only the speed of my sword, my little flower; I survived with *kokoro*," said her father before turning, leaving the room and closing the screen behind him.

Lao's commentary

To whoever is reading this, you're embarking on what I'll call The Way of the Computer Warrior *and on your way to becoming one of the* Coding Samurai. *No, you're not going to learn how to cut people's guts out. Corporate America isn't violent by nature, but it can be hostile, passive-aggressive, and chaotic. Many of the lessons of Bushido apply directly to situations frequently encountered in the workplace. After you decide to walk* The Way of the Computer Warrior, *the office becomes the dojo where you'll find opportunities every day to master yourself.*

Why is this way needed? The goal of the Coding Samurai is to acquire wisdom and spirit, not knowledge and arrogance. Many coders worship lesser things at the expense of gaining something else. What that something else is, I'll get to in a minute. I've watched coders constantly chase the next new products, trendy programming languages, and buzzwords while seemingly never really learning more important things. They remain trapped in a purgatory of tech fashion where what's held up and idolized one year is discarded and disdained the next.

The samurai knew that the most important skill to train was something called kokoro. *This Japanese word can be thought of as "heart" or "spirit." The life of a samurai is a reflection of his heart. Working with a poor spirit and maniacal ego, while being proud of the ability to type fast and knowing a thousand keyboard shortcuts, is not* The Way of the Computer Warrior; *it's just fast and conceited.*

These lessons aim to help strengthen one's spirit in a way that leads to success and satisfaction with one's efforts. The Way of the Computer Warrior *is a practice, not a mandate of perfection. I'm not prescribing a rigid code of conduct; rather, I'm giving you a reference guide to be used when questioning a situation—a way to help walk a path that you can easily get lost on. Is this way better? Decide for yourself, but don't be weak of heart—that's really the whole point of this thing.*

****

"Lao's commentary"—the professor wrote this?!

"Your aunt, uncle, and cousins just arrived. Go say hi," shouted Artemis' mother from outside of Princess Di.

"Princess Di, save this book and my strategy guide to my home world and then go to sleep. I'll be back soon."

Artemis walked downstairs and into the living room where his aunt Celeste, uncle Connery, and cousins Ova and Perry were sitting. Ova wore a white sundress, her blonde hair in perfect curls. Perry, younger but more popular and athletic than Artemis, cast a shadow on Artemis. As children, they swam together in the lakes in summer and played hockey and skated with each other in winter. Artemis missed those times, but his cousins weren't into the augmented reality subcultures as he was. In recent years, they only saw each other at family get-togethers, like tonight.

"Hey, everyone," said Artemis.

"There he is. Congratulations, Artemis!" said his aunt, standing up to give Artemis a hug. "We're all very proud of you."

"Thanks, Aunt Celeste. Glad you all came by," said Artemis, thinking about how much small talk he would need to make for the next few hours. "How's the beekeeping going?"

"Oh, just fine. They're a handful and I'm still a little sore from the incident last week. But it's all part of the fun," she said.

"What incident?" asked Artemis.

"I figured your mom would have told you. I teach a beekeeping class at the hobby farm, where urban house mommies and daddies gather once a week to learn the ins and outs of honey farming and get closer to the earth."

"Sounds pretty boring, Aunt Celeste."

"It wasn't boring when I tore my beekeeper suit on a piece

of fence without realizing it. One little bee found its way inside and stung me."

"Doesn't sound too serious. Bee attacks can be defended by circling the left hand counterclockwise. And anyway, it doesn't matter because bees only generate Level 1 pain, unless of course you encounter a Bee General, then you better be prepared."

"Artemis, I'm talking about real life, not some game. But it wasn't the sting that was serious; rather an overly enthusiastic daddy who felt he had to run to my aid and began smacking every bee he saw—whether inside or outside the suit. Some of the smacks left bruises. You know, Level 3 pain."

"Level 3 pain I can handle easily as well. Actually, in my group, I have the highest pain tolerance. Level 34. But good to hear you're okay. It sounds like it could have been much worse," said Artemis.

"I suppose. Lesson learned," sighed Aunt Celeste.

Just then, Artemis heard a scratching noise coming from a box next to Ova. "What's that sound?" he asked.

"Mom, can we give it to him now?" asked Ova, clearly excited.

Artemis' aunt nodded, and his cousin lifted the box onto her lap and opened it up. Artemis watched as first two extremely furry paws and then an even furrier head peeked out over the edge of the box. He raced over to Ova and saw, peering up at him with eyes like large black marbles, a tiny kitten the color and shape of a cotton ball.

"He's your graduation gift!" exclaimed Ova. "I picked him out."

"He's all fluff," said Artemis, petting the cat and then lifting him out of the box. "He's so cute! I already have a name for him: Jef."

Ova rolled her eyes at her mother as Artemis lifted Jef up toward the ceiling and let him tower over him.

"He's your cat, but isn't 'Jef' a little plain?" asked Ova, scooting up on the edge of the couch to stroke Jef's fur.

"No, it's purrrfect," said Artemis as his family groaned. He pulled Jef to his face and nuzzled him. "It stands for 'Just Enough Fur.'"

"Time for dinner, everyone!" yelled Artemis' dad from the kitchen.

They made their way to the dining room, where Artemis' parents had prepared a feast of his favorites: Spam hot dish, fried fish, and honey-apple crisp. Artemis let Jef curl up in his lap. Once everyone was seated, Artemis' dad gave a toast.

"Today, the first of the Pound kids graduated college. While he certainly won't be the last, he paved the way for his cousins. We are awfully proud of him. Congratulations, Artemis!" said his dad, raising a glass.

"Cheers!" said the family, toasting Artemis' success.

"So, what's next? Did you find someone to pay you to be guild leader?" joked Ova.

"Ha ha," said Artemis, shaking his head at his cousin. "I have a few offers, but I'm still trying to make a decision."

Prior to graduation, Artemis had sent dozens of résumés to companies in various industries and cities. To his dismay, none of the three offers he received involved asteroid mining or quantum computer design. As he explained to everyone at the table, the project at Mega Globe Communications consisted of writing scripts to convert old data formats into new ones. The county library wanted someone to help create a new e-reader system for its digital catalog. And Boom! Snap! Pow! was looking for "a rock-star ninja to make super-secret high-performant multi-qubit-powered ad software."

The job at Mega Globe paid okay, but it sounded boring. The library project had some appeal but was a little low on the pay scale. Boom! Snap! Pow! paid well for an internship, and the project sounded like it could be very cool—even though the description was sort of corny and the job was only scheduled to last six months.

"So those are my options," said Artemis.

"The county library sounds the best to me," said Charlotte. "The county has great benefits, and you'd be close to home. You wouldn't even have to move out for a while if you didn't want to."

Gunter shot his son a knowing glance before Artemis had a chance to say anything that would upset his mother. The last thing Artemis wanted to do was make a decision based on how close he'd be to home.

"That one might not be too bad, Mom, but I'll have to think about it," said Artemis. "I just found a book on my computer that Professor Lao wrote that might help. It's a sort of career guidebook."

"Do you really need a book to help you? What's more important than being close to your family?" teased his mother.

"Mom, with Holograms Everywhere, it's not like we can't basically have dinner together, or lunch, or snacks, or dim sum," said Artemis in his dry way that irritated his mother.

"You know I hate that thing, Arty. I'm not from the hologram generation like you," replied Charlotte.

"Those jobs all seem like they could be a good place to start," said Uncle Connery, chuckling. "Except maybe Mega Globe," he added, turning serious. "I hate that company!" He was now visibly irritated. "Every month my bill gets bigger and the customer service gets worse."

"Tell me about it, Conny," said Gunter. "They need a good dose of competition, I tell ya. Bloodsuckers, that's what they are."

The two men continued to disparage Mega Globe while Aunt Celeste and Artemis' mother discussed ongoing drama in the family. During dinner, Jef had jumped under the table and was now lying next to a surprisingly calm Buddy and batting at the dog's ears.

Perry turned to Artemis and asked, "So, do you have a girlfriend now?"

"I was kind of seeing this girl for a while, but it didn't work out," Artemis replied.

"Seeing her in real life?" teased Perry.

Artemis blushed. "I've just been really busy with the project at the university," he said a bit defensively. "You know, the anti-bullying software."

"I think it's really cool you had that apprenticeship," said Ova.

"It was the best part of undergrad," said Artemis. "I learned a lot from Professor Lao."

"Did your mom ever stop worrying about you working with him?"

"What do you mean?"

"Oh!" said a surprised-looking Ova. "Mom said something about a kid in your program telling his mom something about your professor. She told your mom and that made her worry about you working with him, I guess. I figured she'd talked with you about it."

"No, we never talked about anything like that. And it doesn't make any sense. Professor Lao was great. Our project was really positive."

"It must have been a good thing for you, getting all the job offers and everything."

Artemis nodded. He doubted there was any truth to what Ova said. *Just more family gossip,* he thought.

"What are your friends going to do?" asked Perry.

"I don't know; I've been busy. I haven't really talked to them lately," said Artemis.

"You've been too busy to find out where your friends are going to college?" asked Perry in wry disbelief.

"I mean, I talk to my friends online, but they aren't from around here; we don't really talk about those kind of things."

"Do you even have a single real friend?" asked Ova.

Artemis wasn't sure how to answer Ova's question. He felt like he had friends in F.O.A.L.—an organization committed to being friends of all life. When Artemis wasn't playing his games, he spent a lot of time learning from the members of F.O.A.L. about how to respectfully create quantum worlds bearing life. *I do have friends,* he thought. *Just because I don't know their real names doesn't mean I don't.*

"I do," said Artemis.

"You do? What do they look like?" asked Perry.

"Most of them are gnomes, really cute gnomes," said Artemis, attempting to disarm his cousins.

"Gnomes aren't real, Artemis," said Ova.

"Technically, no, but they're controlled by real people. I mean, they *are* real people, just in gnome form," said Artemis with a grin.

"You're hopeless," said Ova.

Artemis mustered the energy to stay polite throughout the rest of the visit, but he was relieved once his guests announced they were leaving.

"Bye, Artemis. Text me when you make some real friends." Perry snickered as he ducked out the door.

"Take care, everybody, and thanks again for Jef," Artemis said as his extended family walked out. He was happy to have the cat. But he was even more excited to spend time with the computer Professor Lao had given him.

CHAPTER THREE
Family Histories

Artemis quickly walked upstairs to his bedroom and closed the door. He immediately heard a knock.

"Artemis, can I come in?" his dad asked.

"Sure," Artemis said with a tone of slight annoyance at the interruption.

Gunter whistled when he saw Princess Di. "Wow. That is something else, Artemis. And the professor just gave that to you?"

"I wouldn't say he just gave her to me. I worked for almost a year with no pay," corrected Artemis.

"That you did," said Gunter. "But I didn't really come up here to talk about that."

"What's up?"

"First, here's some kitty-training papers for Jef that your cousins left. I know you're excited, but that little guy is going to do more than just shed fur."

"It looks just like what newspapers looked like," said Artemis, taking the business section–looking paper from his dad and then laying it in the corner of his room before setting Jef down on it.

"Artemis, your mom's anxiety nanobots are almost spent

51

because she doesn't know what you're going to do about your job," his dad explained, "and you saying you were going to read that book from the professor to help you make your decision didn't make her feel any better. I really don't feel like shelling out another $150 NAD for another pack of those things this month."

"What does Mom have against the professor?" snapped Artemis.

"She doesn't have anything against him. She just doesn't think his influence should be greater than your family's."

"I get it. But if she got to know him, she wouldn't worry."

"Maybe. How about we take a look at that book and see what it says?"

"Hold on, Dad. I'll have Princess Di send the audio out here."

Artemis stepped inside the giant egg for a few moments before emerging. He then sat down on his bed with his dad to listen to Princess Di read.

Family Histories

"What can you tell me about the Oda family?" Akechi Mitsuhide asked his daughter during breakfast.

"They live in the castle and they hired you to protect them," said Tama, taking a bite of rice with her chopsticks.

"Yes, that's true. But that isn't what I want to know. I want you to tell me about their history," said Mitsuhide, stirring his rice bowl.

"I don't know, Father," said Tama.

"The Oda family are powerful warlords who will unify Japan. They are great rulers and fair hosts. Our master was born in Nagoya Castle in Owari. His victory in the Battle of Okehazama, when three thousand of his troops defeated Imagawa's army of forty thousand men, made him a legend," said Mitsuhide.

"That's impossible! How did he win?" asked Tama.

"He deceived Imagawa by creating thousands of fake soldiers out of straw—a field of scarecrows. While Imagawa's attention was on these phantoms, our lord attacked the camp when they least suspected it, killing Imagawa and seizing victory," said Mitsuhide.

"I believe we owe Oda Nobunaga our loyalty," said Tama, reaching for more rice.

"Remember these things I've told you of our lord's history," said her father.

Lao's commentary

I worked for nine different companies before I became a professor. Long gone are the days of lifelong, blind loyalty to an employer. In spite of that, those learning The Way of the Computer Warrior *are encouraged to know what they can about their potential employer. Companies vary greatly in their histories and their contributions and harm to society. If the Coding Samurai doesn't know who it is he is pledging his sword to, he can grow to regret it, even becoming bitter and angry. Spending years on an initiative or product that you don't believe in, or that you're even ethically and morally against, can bring suffering to both you and your employer as each party's goals and desires conflict.*

By asking a lot of questions, the Coding Samurai can start his career on a clearer path. Some questions to ask might be: What type of companies will I absolutely not work for? Am I willing to work for tobacco companies? Arms dealers? Marijuana dispensaries? Do I want to work for the government or the private sector, or would I rather work for a nonprofit? How much am I willing to travel? How many hours a week am I willing to work? Should I work abroad while I'm young? *Continue probing and drilling deeper into what type of work will provide meaning as you grow older.*

Don't be prejudiced in assessing whether or not to work for a company. Sometimes seemingly noble companies are seeping with toxicity. I ran for the hills two months after taking a job with an NGO working to improve water quality. The petty politics and unnecessary stress left my blood boiling each day. In comparison, an adult toy manufacturer provided me with one of the best programming jobs I ever had.

****

"Sounds like decent advice. Have you done that yet?" asked his dad.

"Applied to a sex toy company?" asked Artemis incredulously. "No, Dad."

"What in god's name are you talking about, Son?" said Gunter, who'd only been half-listening as Princess Di read from the book.

"Just . . . what? Never mind. I haven't asked myself these questions, if that's what you mean," said Artemis, frustrated that he didn't find this information at the career fair on campus.

"I'm going to go back downstairs and let you be. I'll tell your mom you're doing the right thing." His father paused before adding, "Just so you know, I'm glad you were able to work with the professor. I saw a lot of good changes in you after that."

"Thanks, Dad," said Artemis. "Tell Mom thanks again for dinner. It was really nice."

Once his father had left, Artemis turned to his x86-based computer on the desk beside his bed so he could log on to IA, or Internet Alpha. The original Internet—the old one created by DARPA that had been popular in the late 1990s and early 2000s—earned that name upon creation of Internet Beta, or IB— the quantum computer–powered Internet. IB had only been available for two years. Prices had recently lowered enough for consumers to start grabbing consumer-grade quantums off the shelves. While quantum computing was obviously the future, IA still had the most content. It seemed that IA would be like AM radio; it just wasn't going to go away.

Artemis navigated to http://SearchGiantClassic.com. It came as no surprise that Mega Globe had plenty of complaints lodged against it. The company was accused of horrible customer service, price fixing, and much more. Under "Company Reviews," Artemis noticed one at the top of the list.

"Mega Globe? Mega Suck, I'd call this company. They are horrible, horrible, horrible!" the review began before fading into the "Read More" link. Connery Pound had written it. Apparently

Uncle Connery, still inflamed, had written it soon after he'd arrived home from Artemis' graduation dinner.

I get that Mega Globe is a soulless global company that everyone hates, but they're definitely doing some interesting work there. Maybe if I go there and they see how good I am, they'll put me on one of these IB projects, thought Artemis. *But what if they never do and I'm stuck on a boring project for the next ten years?*

Artemis decided to research something else. On IA he was also able to find plenty of information on the county library. In fact, the county library was still available only on the old Internet. They were trying to move forward with technology, but with a limited budget, they were largely still struggling to maintain their existing web presence.

Morally and ethically, the library is definitely a great choice. I'm all for literacy—but I want to go somewhere new. Minnesota is home, but I want to experience life somewhere else.

Artemis continued his research. He couldn't find a thing about Boom! Snap! Pow! Marketing (BSP) on IA. A little frustrated, he used his wearable to send a request to the fridge for a sports drink. A very simple robot—little more than a small platform with rubber tank-wheels—delivered a cold beverage to him and then returned to the kitchen, docking itself under the refrigerator. Artemis sat sipping his drink for a bit, entertaining the opportunities he'd just researched—not really interested in either.

I guess it's time to try IB. Hopefully there's some inspiring information there.

IB was built largely for two purposes: to create protocols more suitable for quantum computing and to make a more secure Internet. However, once IB had launched, it was discovered that security problems had been baked into it just like IA. Most companies incentivized feature creation, not quality or security. Since the root problems of greed and lack of accountability remained, the second Internet had emerged just like the first one, albeit built on significantly more powerful hardware.

Artemis walked over to Princess Di and pulled out a stretchy, white unitard. He put on the haptic suit so he could receive sensations from the computer and send signals from his body. Once inside, Princess Di loaded his home world and projected it to his lenses that tracked the smallest of eye movements. The computer could understand the emotions of the user when eye movement and pupil dilation data were combined with heart rate and perspiration signals being read by the haptic suit. The walls and floor of Princess Di made up a 360 degree display; the lenses added layers of visual effects. Equipped with visual augmentation capabilities, the eyewear painted 3-D graphics in the spaces between the user and the walls, most notably on the user's own body, such as making the user appear to be another gender or appear to be carrying a sword.

Once his home world loaded, Artemis wore a space suit while standing under the black, star-filled sky of Mars. To his left, a biosphere; to his right, the head of a path leading from the valley of Dao Vallis toward the Martian mountain of Hadriacus Mons. Artemis turned and entered the biosphere, which caused his space suit to fade away. Brushing past rows of hydroponic plants, he approached a pool of water. At the water's edge, Artemis jumped into the air and waved his right hand forward. He banged his head on the top of the egg.

Ow! It's been a while.

Sensors inside Princess Di tracked his movements, which had the effect of showing him leaping into the deep water. He moved his arms in a swimming motion as he navigated toward a glowing red light under the water that read "IB." Arriving under the sign, he pressed a button and the water receded, leaving him standing in an empty, white room. He'd arrived at the entrance of Internet Beta.

"Search," said Artemis.

"Your preferences are set to 'Surprise Me.' Here's your surprise," said Princess Di.

An immense door appeared in the distance with a tiny sign on it that said "Knock Me." Artemis lifted his foot and Princess Di, able to sense Artemis' intentions, began moving the multidirectional treadmill. Once at the door, he knocked.

"Who's there?" asked a child's voice.

"Artemis."

"Artemis who?"

"Uh, Artemis Pound?"

"You can do better than that!" said the child, giggling. "Who's there?"

"Artemis Smartemis?" Artemis said hopefully.

The door opened, and Artemis walked into a fun house decorated with mirrors that reflected deformed versions of himself. The shape of a child ran down a hall. He chased after it and, turning the corner, saw a giant Whac-a-Mole game. The hammer for the game was twice the size of Artemis, but he had no trouble picking it up. A scrolling marquee sign read, "State what you're looking for and then whack a mole!"

"Company history of Boom! Snap! Pow! Marketing," said Artemis.

Suddenly, carnival music blared and giant moles with fierce eyes and sharp claws sprang out of the holes in the game. One swiped at Artemis while he swung the giant hammer at it. The mole dodged Artemis' attack and sank its teeth into his arm. The pain sensor in his suit made him feel a distinct jab in his left bicep.

Ohmygawd! That's at least Level 27 pain!

Artemis thought about the mauling he had just received from the monstrous vermin and felt a rush of endorphins. His mind focused on the pleasure he derived from doing battle. The deformed mole roared at him as it lifted itself onto its haunches and towered over him. When the mole raised its arms to frighten him, Artemis used the hammer like a spear, jabbing the mole in its exposed stomach. It flopped down onto all fours after the strike, and Artemis used that moment to clock the mole on its gourd with a confident swing of the hammer. The carnival disappeared to reveal his search results.

I need to catch my breath, thought Artemis after the intense fight with the grotesque beast.

Most of the results were press releases and tech blogs that described the company in the same corporatespeak that the company's tech manager had used when recruiting Artemis. The company was certainly receiving a lot of attention, although it was tough for Artemis to figure out exactly why. So much hype surrounded the company that he didn't feel like he really knew anything more about it than before. BSP had been priming the media for months about a new product, but delay after delay stopped anyone from even seeing so much as a demo of it. The media had begun to express a sentiment that BSP only made vaporware.

"With the launch of Boom! Snap! Pow! Marketing's new product, the game will change. With qubit-powered analysis of consumer trends, consumer industries will experience a new type of leverage," read one press release after the other. After reading the same phrases regurgitated twenty different ways, Artemis couldn't read any more. He was feeling tired and melancholy about the entire situation, but at the same time, he was strangely attracted to the idea of working for BSP.

This is a lot more frustrating than figuring out what school to go to.

"Princess Di, go to sleep," he said before opening the door of the giant chicken egg and moping over to his bed.

"Sweet dreams," she said.

Artemis didn't feel much better in the morning. He woke up with each of the opportunities running through his mind.

I don't want to be a cog in a wheel. Plus, Uncle Conny would never forgive me if I went to work for Mega Globe. That's it— bye, Mega Globe, he thought. *Making an e-reader could be really cool. But it's the library! And I'd still be here living at home. Mom would be absolutely thrilled, though. Working for the library—noble and convenient and safe and boring. No, no, no. That leaves Boom! Snap! Pow! I never imagined I'd be going to work for a marketing company after college. It's the exact opposite of a field like asteroid mining. Gawd, it's going to be a brogrammer paradise. But I really feel like I should be there. Plus, it's in Lepton Mountain.*

He punched his pillow and yelled, "Yes!"

"Is something the matter?" yelled Charlotte from downstairs.

Artemis rolled off of his bed and walked downstairs to find his mom and dad sitting in the living room having their morning coffee.

"Nothing's wrong. I've made my decision," he said.

His parents put down their tablets and looked keenly at Artemis.

"I'm taking the Boom! Snap! Pow! internship," he said. "I'm going to go to Lepton Mountain."

There was silence in the room for a few moments. "I'm sure you've made a good decision," said his mom, standing up to give him a hug.

"I'm not thrilled about it, but it's just six months. It'll give me time to look for something else and get some experience. There's tons of work in Lepton, so it'll be a good place for me to be right now," he said.

"I'm proud of you, Son," said his dad.

"Thanks. I'm going to call my recruiter and let her know," he said before going back to his room. His stomach tightened at the thought of moving, but he tapped his wearable and said, "Call Tech-Tech-Go."

A tiny holographic globe emerged from the wearable device on his wrist. The floating orb on Artemis' arm was just one of many garish displays of holographic ham-fistedness. After a moment, the orb changed into a little glowing head with a long, cute face. "Thanks for calling Tech-Tech-Go. This is Tilly," said the puppet-sized person on Artemis' wrist.

"Hi, Tilly. It's Artemis Pound. I want to accept the internship," he said.

"Good for you!" said Tilly. "They are going to be very pleased to find out."

"It was a tough decision. I hope I'm making the right choice."

"You are, Artemis. You're going to love Lepton Mountain. Have you ever been there?" she asked.

"Nope. Only seen the holograms."

"They don't do it justice," she said before the two worked out the details of Artemis' new employment at Boom! Snap! Pow! Marketing.

****

A week later, the day of Artemis' good-bye celebration, he and his father put the last tag on the items Artemis was taking with him.

"Do you think you'll have enough room in the truck for all of this?" asked Gunter.

"I think so. Only one way to find out." Artemis used the app on his wearable to initiate the move. A scanning drone detached from the moving truck and came upstairs to scan each tagged item one by one. After optimizing how best to pack based on each item's dimensions, it sent a message to Artemis notifying him that the items were approved for transport. The scanning drone delegated the moving operation to the helper drones by providing them the results of its packing algorithm.

"Looks like we can go relax now," said Gunter. "People should be arriving soon."

For the next few hours, Artemis spent time with neighbors and family, saying good-bye and repeating many of the same phrases.

"Lepton Mountain is full of opportunity" was one of

Artemis' favorite lines.

"It's just six months, so I have time to get some experience and learn about what other jobs are around" was another of his default responses.

After sunset, a few people remained, sitting with his parents on the patio out back. Artemis watched Jef chasing lightning bugs while his parents talked with the remaining guests. The drive from Minneapolis to Lepton Mountain would take about ten hours nonstop, since his personal vehicle could use the high-speed autonomous lanes. His stuff was already on its way, traveling slightly slower in the cargo lanes. The time had come for him to say good-bye.

"If I leave now, I can sleep most of the way and get there around sunrise," said Artemis, interrupting the group of older adults who were chatting cheerfully.

"I suppose it's that time," said his mother.

"I'm going to miss you a lot," said Artemis, holding back his own emotion to spare his mother any more tears as he walked over to her.

She hugged him for a moment and then handed him a small gift-wrapped box.

"Open this up after you get there."

Artemis couldn't stop the single tear from welling up in his left eye.

"We're always here if you need us, Son," said his father. "Your mom and I will be down to see you once you get settled."

"Take care of each other," said Artemis, giving his dad a hug before picking up Jef and climbing into his car. The control center of his car synced to Artemis' wearable as soon as he entered it. Having already programmed the destination, Artemis situated Jef and his drink, put on some music, and pressed the button on the dash to begin the journey.

As he rolled down I-94, he thought about the coming summer and his family at the cabin. This would be the first year he would miss it, but it was too late to go back now. Artemis' thoughts wandered until he fell asleep.

The road from Minneapolis led to Wisconsin and on toward the flatlands of Indiana and Ohio. The earth rippled up when the car entered the Appalachian Mountains of West Virginia and Lepton Mountain. It was early morning when his car alerted him that he was approaching his apartment building, next to a diner and a few retail shops on the corner of one of Lepton's main streets. Artemis had already been given an authorization code for his apartment building, so the car entered the garage and pulled into the loading area in the basement.

Jef still slept in Artemis' lap. He picked him up, left the car, and followed the lights embedded in the sealed floor leading to the elevators. He made a pit stop out a back door to give Jef a few minutes outside. Beams of sun broke through the pine trees behind the building. He couldn't see much else except a bike path leading away from the building. He picked up Jef and carried him to the elevators. The doors opened and he pressed the button for the seventh floor. Upon arriving, he walked down the self-healing, bacteria-enriched, concrete hallway to number 707.

He opened the door and was shocked at the smallness of 350 square feet. The main room of his studio apartment had enough room for his futon and Princess Di, and that was about it. He set Jef down on the floor to explore. To the left was a tiny kitchenette with a small stove and refrigerator. Looking out the window behind the sink, he had a view of the pine trees behind the building. On the other side of the kitchenette was a tiny bathroom.

It'll do, he thought. He remembered that Tilly had asked him to contact her when he arrived. While the drones brought up his things, he sent her a message.

It's Artemis. I've made it to my closet . . . I
mean apartment.

> *Busy later? I'll give you the nickel bike*
> *tour.*

I don't know, I should probably just get my
things put away.

> *Oh, come on. It'll be fun.*

I need to get my computer set up on the
network here and update my quantum
registration and some other things.

> *You really don't want to meet up, do*
> *you?*

No, it's not that.

Then we'll meet at your place at 4pm.

Where is it again?

Crockford Apartments on the corner of Fowler and Lovelace.

Perfect! See you then!

Artemis flopped onto the futon and stretched out his arms. He reached into his pocket and pulled out the gift his mother had given him before leaving home. He tore off the red and purple giftwrap and opened the box to find a plastic ball with a button on top and a note from his mom.

"Turn this on anytime you miss home," it read.

Artemis pressed the button. The ball beamed a hologram of his parents with their arms around one another's waists while smiling and waving. Artemis laughed and set it down on the nightstand as Jef ran across his legs.

He spent the day setting up his computer and live streaming a tour of his apartment for his 157 followers. At four o'clock, he received a message from Tilly: "I'm in your lobby."

Artemis took the elevator to the lobby entrance, where a very cute young woman with platinum-blonde hair was inspecting the potted plants by the decorative waterfall.

"Hi, Tilly," he said when he realized it was her.

"Artemis! Great to finally meet you in person," she said, reaching out to shake his hand.

She was a little shorter than he'd imagined; her bike shorts revealed muscular legs.

"Are you all settled?" she asked.

"Getting there. Tiny doesn't begin to describe my apartment. Fortunately, I don't really have much to put away," he said.

"Not surprising," she said, laughing. "Lepton was designed to be a sustainable city, which doesn't always translate to 'comfortable.' Just ask the people whose apartments are right next to the noisy roof windmills."

"Did you have any trouble finding my place?" he asked.

"None whatsoever. I don't live far from here," she answered. "Anyway, I have a nice ride planned to give you the lay of the land."

"The bikes are in the rack out back," he said. "The brochure for this place said the rental bikes are awesome."

"They are. I just saw them. Mine's out back, too. Let's go, shall we?"

The pair walked out the back door to the bicycle racks, hopped on their bikes, and started pedaling. The trail, covered in solar panels, wound sharply away from the city and toward a patch of piney woods. As they approached the forest, Artemis noted several old barns and a few ponds.

"This area used to be nothing but farms and coal mines," explained Tilly. "The mines are closed, but a lot of farms are still operating."

"What are they farming?"

"I think it's buckwheat season. They also grow a lot of

potatoes around here," Tilly said as they rode past the remnants of a wooden windmill.

"How long have you lived here?"

"About three years now." She shifted her bike into a higher gear.

"Where'd you come from?" asked Artemis as he matched her speed.

"I went to school at William and Mary and started here right after graduation."

"Why Lepton?" The shade of the forest darkened the slippery pine needles blanketing the trail.

"I wasn't sure what I wanted to do with my communications degree. I love working with people, and I ended up getting a job as a recruiter at Tech-Tech-Go. I'm pretty good at it and I love Lepton Mountain, so I've stuck with it," she said as they left the forest behind them.

"You must know the area pretty well by now," said Artemis as his bike tire hissed, and he lost speed.

The two stopped to look over his bike; the rear tire was completely flat. Artemis stared blank-faced at the bike.

"You need a hand?" Tilly asked.

"I don't have a kit on me," he said.

Tilly grabbed her bike kit and worked on the flat. She put in a new tube and had the tire back on the bike in record time.

"Wow," said Artemis, impressed at her speed.

"This wasn't a terrible place to have a flat. It's a good view of the city from here," she said, walking off the trail a few yards onto a small knoll. She waved to Artemis to follow her. "Now I'll put on my tour guide hat," she said, pretending to put on an invisible cap. Artemis chuckled.

"It began during the quantum computing explosion. In the eastern panhandle of West Virginia, real estate developers—using federal funding—coordinated with corporate technology leaders to create the tech center called Lepton Mountain. Companies flocked to the area near Washington, DC, to be near the influential decision-makers establishing a presence there."

"You sound exactly like a tour guide," Artemis said.

"Don't interrupt," she said, smiling. "Lepton Mountain, although built in a rural area, grew quickly, reaching one hundred and fifty thousand inhabitants after only five years. Look over toward that concentration of office buildings. That's your apartment complex with the antennae on the roof."

"I see it. I can also see the big glowing sign for BSP," he said.

"Hold on a second," she said, checking her wearable. She frowned at him. "I'm going to have to call it a day. I hope that's okay."

"Of course. Is everything all right?" Artemis asked.

"A friend in need," Tilly said. "She's been having boy trouble and says she needs me 'urgently.' Duty calls. You can find your way back, right?"

"Shouldn't be a problem," he said. They waved good-bye to

each other. Artemis stood on the knoll as Tilly rode off toward the city.

I can't believe I'm actually here in Lepton Mountain, all on my own, he thought, stretching his arms up toward the sky and turning in circles as the sun set over the city.

CHAPTER FOUR
Fame and Infamy

"Hey, Palmer. That must be one powerful drink they named after you," said Wei Wei, who'd stopped by Artemis' workspace a few minutes after Artemis had watched the clip from Jeff's party.

"Say again?" said Artemis.

"The 'Arty Palmer.' That's what they dubbed your drink from the party," Wei Wei continued. "You were quite demented."

"Real crazy. Can you please not call me Palmer?" asked Artemis.

"My deepest apologies," said Wei Wei before walking away.

Beyoncé was waiting in line to hear from Artemis.

"I see you were off the chain at Jeff's party. Didn't anyone ever tell you not to get wasted at work functions?" she said.

"I know. I don't know what happened. Everyone in the office has seen this?" said Artemis, starting to panic. "Why weren't you there? I'm glad you weren't. Not because I didn't want you to be there, but because I'm glad you didn't see . . . never mind."

"'The Wild Man,'" she said, throwing her head back while stretching out the word "wild."

"Not again. This is bad. This is really bad," said Artemis half to Beyoncé and half to himself.

"What do you mean 'again'?" she asked.

"I don't want to get into it," said Artemis, stopping to collect his emotions. "This stuff makes me angry. It makes me disappointed in people."

"Just keep your head down and quit acting crazy. You'll be fine," she said before swaying back across the room.

Beyoncé's words of encouragement did little to change how he felt. After spending the day hiding in his Mobipod, Artemis skulked home that afternoon feeling defeated. He lay down on his bed, trying to sort things out. He didn't know whether to punch the wall or cry. Instead, he gave Jef a few strokes and then cocooned inside Princess Di.

"Princess Di, load my home world."

Artemis had been crafting a Mars-themed customized home world on his quantum computer for some time using a sophisticated editor. As a boy, his heroes were the 121 pioneers who had left Earth and settled the red planet. Artemis had hoped he'd be there with them someday, but colonization was going much slower than anticipated—mainly because of the time the Russians tried to use nukes to propel their ship there and caused an environmental catastrophe. The doors were still shut for the average citizen, so the next best thing for Artemis was being alongside them inside the biosphere in his simulation.

After the home world loaded, he noticed the book he had previously saved lying on the red Martian soil before him. He picked it up and started reading.

Fame and Infamy

Tama sat on the ground letting cherry blossoms fall onto her head as she read from the book her father had given her. Tama's heart jumped when she heard heavy horse hooves. Her pulse quickened when she realized that after being gone for many days, Mitsuhide had returned from battle.

"Father, you're home!" shouted Tama, running up to her father's horse.

"Pink flowers are growing in my daughter's black hair," he said, pulling a tiny blossom from her hair and letting his hand slide gently across her cheek.

"Everyone in town is talking about the battle, how brave you were and how many enemies you defeated," said Tama, her hand on her father's boot, resting in the stirrup.

"Don't be too concerned with stories, Tama. We were victorious, but it was my men who fought bravely and saved me many times. If you want to hear stories, someday I will tell you about truly legendary samurai—ones who didn't seek fame, but ones who put themselves last and fought courageously on the battlefield for their lord and brothers," said Mitsuhide.

Lao's commentary

On The Way of the Computer Warrior, *the Coding Samurai avoids acting in a way just to stand out. He works diligently on his craft and lets his daily efforts build a reputation. In order to become legendary, one with enough skill must take on seemingly overwhelming problems with great enthusiasm. By succeeding in the face of huge difficulty, one can earn a reputation as a fearless coder. Nevertheless, the Coding*

Samurai doesn't take on tasks for the purpose of self-aggrandizement. He takes on imposing tasks in the spirit of service because no one else wants to or knows how to do the work.

This is counter to trendy, fame-worshipping, pop culture where people are famous for being famous. Seemingly there is no greater glory than having everyone talking about you. The saying 'there's no such thing as bad publicity' is a common response to reading about ridiculous celebrity behavior being exhibited. But the Coding Samurai doesn't seek this type of negative attention. A deep sense of security can only come from inside, and this is where the Coding Samurai goes to bring forth the best part of himself.

Those who seek fame often find it's never enough. Recently, I witnessed a famous programmer on Stack Overflow with an unfathomable number of golden ponies, or whatever the rewards on that particular site are called, become so wounded at someone disagreeing with him that he flew into a defensive rage and badgered the person with a difference of opinion until he forced the other man to retract his comments. Is this any way to live? Is this success?

Doing ridiculous things and exhibiting poor craftsmanship will make one infamous in one's circles. Someone who doesn't keep up with skills, doesn't complete tasks or completes tasks poorly, leans too much on others, lies about the work he's doing, or wastes too much time will eventually gain a negative reputation.

Some other things I've seen in my career that led to infamy: someone who left a Watchtower magazine on the lunchroom table every day, a woman who wore a onesie with heels to work, a guy who left his computer on with a furry-porn website loaded, and a drunk woman at the Christmas party who simulated giving the CEO a hand *job in front of his wife. Sure, it was only two or three quick strokes, but it was enough for her to earn the nickname "The Hammer."*

****

Artemis threw down the book, sat down in Princess Di, and cried. He needed to talk to someone.

Maybe MasterBlaster is online.

He logged on to his guild server, but no one was online—it was still too early in the evening. He heard his cousin Ova's words in his head from his graduation dinner. *Do you have a single real friend?* He spoke into his wearable on his wrist. "Call Tilly."

"Artemis?" said Tilly.

"Yeah, it's me."

"What's up?"

"Where do I start?" he said, sniffling. "It's only been one week . . . I'm so embarrassed."

"What's the matter?"

"I messed up at work. I think I want to quit."

"Oh no! What's wrong?"

"At Jeff's party last weekend, he'd bought a DIY Brew printer. He was pushing drinks on everyone because he couldn't get enough use out of his new toy. I drank way too much."

"So what did you do?"

"I don't remember much of it, but there's an embarrassing

video of me. Everyone at the office was laughing at me."

"Jerks!" yelled Tilly. "Yes, you shouldn't have drunk so much, but they shouldn't have sent a video around the office. That's a very bald thing to do. How bad is it, though?"

"I don't want to say," said Artemis, before sighing at the thought of telling Tilly the details. "I have my shirt off. I'm yelling and chasing people around the lawn."

"That doesn't sound super bad. Not appropriate for work, but nothing people won't forget about soon."

"I guess there's one more thing."

"One more thing?"

"I have crayfish clamped on my nipples."

There was a long pause, which Artemis assumed Tilly was using to conjure an appropriate response.

"You said crayfish?" she asked.

"Uh-huh," he said.

"The little crabby things in creeks?"

"Yes."

"Live ones?"

"Clamped on my nipples."

"Wow. Okaaay. I can see where that might make people remember it a little longer," she said. "I wouldn't worry. Something embarrassing will happen to someone else, and people will forget about your, um, unique fashion statement."

"So I just hang my head in shame until someone else screws up?" he said.

"You know, I don't know. How about this? Don't hang in your head in shame."

"But that's the only thing I feel right now. Shame, shame, and how about some more shame?" said Artemis, exasperated.

"Artemis, you made a mistake. It's not a life-ruining mistake. You have your job; no one got hurt. I've never met this Jeff guy, but I've heard tales. But regardless, they apparently just have a culture there that you need to be careful around."

"Tell me about it. Jeff offered Brad a drink, but he turned it down. I was the idiot who took it instead. But no more excuses. I won't be doing this again."

"There you go. Think of it this way—you've just started. You can't damage a reputation that you haven't built. Go in tomorrow believing that you belong there and you're going to do excellent work. Then pretty soon everyone will forget about this, including yourself," said Tilly.

"Thanks for talking me through this."

"Are you okay now?" she asked.

"I think so. Anyway, thanks and have a good night," said Artemis.

"Hang in there," she said before ending the call.

****

A cool breeze blew past Artemis as he walked to work. He stared down at his feet while listening to music, his preferred method to block out the world. The sonar on his wearable sent a fast, pulsing vibration on his wrist to alert him to pay attention to his surroundings. He looked up and saw a young woman rolling directly toward him on her sidewalk scooter.

"Careful!" she yelled angrily as she zoomed past him.

I'm done hanging my head.

He walked into the BSP offices, passing Tony on the way in. He watched as Tony's lips curled into a smile and a gleam appeared in his eyes.

"Don't even think about calling me Palmer," Artemis said to a surprised Tony. He heard Tony say something just out of earshot as he continued to the morning stand-up meeting.

"Okay, everyone, let's get started," said Brad, focusing the team. "We've met with the Groundswell product owners and they want a lot of new features built this iteration."

Groans erupted around the room. Someone activated a squawking chicken animation on the story wall.

"We're launching soon and none of these stories were in the backlog. It's all unplanned work," said one of the DOTs.

"I get that," said Brad. "We moved around a few things to get these features in. But we also need to fix a few lingering tech-debt tasks, particularly the authentication piece. It's turned into a huge mess, so it's got to be refactored into something sane."

"It's too close to launch. It's ridiculous to refactor it now," said Deepak.

Wow that guy is confident, thought Artemis. *He's the sheriff in town.*

"We're going to be adding a lot more types of users and ways of authenticating into Groundswell," said Brad. "Right now, it's a disaster because of how we kept piling more and more code into that area as we added users and roles. If we wait any longer to clean it up, it'll become completely unmanageable."

"It already is completely unmanageable," said Rodney.

"You're risking breaking functionality. We can't afford more bugs right now," said Deepak.

"Exactly, Deepak. We can't afford more bugs," said Brad. "Every week new bugs are found when test users are trying to log in. The bug list in the authentication piece is crippling momentum. I made a story for someone to refactor that piece of the application so it's modular, testable, and easy to maintain. So who wants to unwind that tangled ball of yarn and be a hero?"

"I'll take it," said Artemis.

"Artemis, I appreciate your enthusiasm, but this is a critical piece of the application and it's in seriously bad shape. Why doesn't someone else pick this up?" said Brad.

Artemis was convinced that if he hadn't had the incident at the party, Brad would have given him a chance. Anger welled up inside him—mostly anger at himself. He could feel his heart rate accelerate, and he started to sweat. He had to say something.

"Brad, please. I won't mess it up. I know how to do this. My professor at college worked with me on problems like this. Give me a couple days at least. I'll show you my progress and if you aren't happy, someone else can take it," pleaded Artemis.

"Brad, if you are going to insist we do this now, I will take that task," said Deepak. "I know the authentication piece best. And I agree, this is too much for an intern to take on."

"I'm not sure I can afford to lose you from your other work, Deepak," said Brad.

Brad looked at Artemis for a moment.

"Two days it is," said Brad.

"Hey, Artemis. If you can't figure out how to do it," said Deepak, "try not to get *crabby.*"

There were some chuckles at Artemis' expense. Artemis glared at Deepak, who was smiling widely. Artemis tried to shrug off the joke, but he realized that moving past his mistake and building a new reputation was going to be a battle.

****

At lunchtime, Beyoncé and crew were sitting in their usual spot by the Zen garden. *Great—Tony's there,* Artemis thought as he walked toward a small table to sit by himself.

"Artemis! Join us," shouted Beyoncé when she caught sight of him.

I guess I can't just avoid everyone.

"What's the topic of discussion?" asked Artemis as he sat down.

"The Tower of Babel regulation," said Wei Wei.

"'The intent to create consciousness is an insult to God and His creation; no different than the human egotism that created the Tower of Babel.' Something like that, right?" said Artemis.

"That's almost verbatim," said Tony. "You're pretty smart when you're sober."

Artemis shrugged off the jab and continued. "Is anyone here in support of the regulation?"

"Of course not, but there's a lot of gray even if you denounce the claim that to create artificial consciousness is to elicit the wrath of a supreme being," said Beyoncé.

"I think artificial life-forms are more significant than mold in a Petri dish, in opposition to what the writers of the regulation claim," said Artemis.

"Why?" asked Wei Wei.

"The mirror test research at Yale and Berkeley. Plus the latest cognitive tests that continue to support the fact that these generated life-forms have some level of consciousness," said Artemis.

"Yes, *some level*," said Wei Wei.

"But we don't understand to what extent because we don't fully know how to test for the existence of consciousness. But the limited tools we have say these creatures are as real as us. That's why we should protect them," said Artemis.

"You're in F.O.A.L., aren't you?" said Tony.

"Yeah. So?" said Artemis.

"So that's why you only eat from the printed food bar.

You're a 'friend of all life,'" Tony continued.

"I try to be."

"I agree with Niels Bohr," said Beyoncé, jumping into the debate. "'Everything we call real is made of things that cannot be regarded as real.' How do we know that our universe is significantly more real than a simulated, quantum world? Scientists are arguing that perhaps our own universe is just another simulation, whose life-bearing amino acids were not the act of a god, but rather of some other intelligent species who has unraveled the nature of the universe as pure information and then found ways to simulate universes in a lab—just like we are doing with our quantum networks, only with much better equipment than we have."

"But that's a profound argument for creating a law to stop humans from deliberately trying to create artificial life—whatever that phrase means anymore," said Wei Wei.

"How's that?" asked Beyoncé.

"If our universe is a simulation created by a more advanced species, it's reasonable to fear that a consequence of a simulated species simulating other species could indeed lead to its smiting by its creator. In our case, no, not a biblical god, but the overseer of the lab where our universe is contained could decide we have overstepped our purpose once we venture into a realm that they see only themselves fit to manage," said Wei Wei.

"You do make a point," said Beyoncé.

"Regardless of the science, what is crazy is that there are still these sort of political extremists in Congress," said Tony.

"There's not as many as there used to be. Did you ever read about the state of politics in the 2010s? There's been an utter transformation even with the increase in terrorism," said Wei Wei. "When Americans see fifteen Western capital cities bombed in one year, there are bound to be some extreme views as a response, which, sadly, has been the goal of the terrorists from the beginning."

"I gotta wrap this up for today, boys," said Beyoncé.

"Thanks for the debate," said Artemis, getting up and waving good-bye to the group.

Artemis left work feeling better, but he was still afraid of what the next day would be like. On the way home, he passed a bakery and smiled at the smell of buttery bread. He walked in and looked around at the racks of croissants, tarts, and other baked goods. A young woman wearing an apron stood behind the counter.

"Can I help you with something?" she asked.

"An almond croissant, please," said Artemis.

The woman took one from the rack and wrapped it up.

"Anything else?" she asked.

"No, that's it."

"North American or US dollars?"

"North American."

"That's 1.48 NAD."

Artemis swiped his wearable across the payment scanner and

stared as it merely blinked back at him.

"Swipe it again," said the woman.

Artemis swiped his wearable across the flickering lights again, this time slower.

"Swipe it again, faster," she said.

He swiped it faster and the machine honked at him.

"It didn't take. I think it was a little too fast. Try it again," she said.

"Can I just give you cash?" he asked.

"Sorry, we don't take NAD cash," she said. "Try it one more time."

Artemis calculated what he imagined was the perfect swiping speed: somewhat faster than his first swipe but a good bit slower than his speedy swipe that angered the machine. He prepped his wrist and let the swipe fly with grace and ease.

The machine honked like an aggravated goose. Artemis gave up and turned to leave the store.

"Try it just once more!" shouted the woman as he left the store and continued his walk to Crockford Apartments. He opened the door to his apartment to find Jef curled up on his futon, sleeping. He sat down next to the placid feline and pet him until Jef started batting Artemis' hand and biting at his fingers.

"Let me get you something to eat," said Artemis as he opened a can of vegan Fancy Feast and put it in Jef's bowl. He then walked across the room and shut himself inside of Princess Di.

"Open home world editor," said Artemis.

After he issued the command, grid lines and a coordinate system appeared across the Martian landscape.

"At thirty-seven, forty-eight, nineteen, add an obelisk with the texture of obsidian rock. When I'm within five meters of the obelisk, add a lavender scent," said Artemis to Princess Di, who would now vaporize a bit of the molecules for lavender using a molecular printer and puff it into the air inside the quantum when he approached the obelisk.

"Create a new trigger. Touching the obelisk opens a private wormhole," said Artemis.

Wormholes were portals to virtual worlds. Like a folder on the desktop of old x86-based computer systems, opening a wormhole caused an entirely different quantum-generated environment to appear in a flash. Some people liked to create wormholes as a special place to view travel photos and videos. Others created wormholes to make simulated resorts to throw quantum world parties. What was on the other side of a wormhole was up to the creativity and patience of the person who created it.

"Connect this wormhole to the F.O.A.L. quantum network," said Artemis. His quantum linked into the Friends Of All Life shared resource pool, which gave Artemis an incredible amount of power to generate simulated worlds. "Create a new default life-sustaining world within a binary-star solar system with real physics. The default life-sustaining compound is liquid methane.

Fast-forward time until the first conscious beings evolve," commanded Artemis.

Princess Di followed Artemis' instructions and, with the help of the vast resources in the F.O.A.L. network, generated a solar system with two suns and random planets. One planet was generated with all of the requisite characteristics to sustain liquid methane-based life. After inducing the compounds to form, Princess Di sped up time as the compounds evolved. Billions of years passed before a creature emerged that showed the neurological patterns associated with consciousness. Time froze.

"Whoa, that's weird," said Artemis, gazing at the creature that had emerged.

The organism looked no different from a pebble, about a centimeter cubed. On the underside of the creature were thousands of flagellum that allowed the creature to crawl across the surface of the planet. Yet for all of the seeming simplicity of the creature, it was fully conscious. The creature knew it was alive, was aware of its feelings, maybe even its hopes and dreams.

"Fast-forward to creation of language," said Artemis.

Princess Di let time continue again until the system detected communication between the sentient beings. "Finished," she said.

"Please explain how the creatures communicate," said Artemis.

"The beings rub the flagella on their undersides together at different frequencies to create speech. Depending upon which flagellates are rubbed, the sound carries through different tubes within the body of the creature, which is the creature's way of uttering phonetics," said Princess Di.

Artemis thought they sounded like whales, indris, or maybe angels. Artemis' admiration of the simulated creatures' musical speech was interrupted by his alarm. *I always lose track of time in here*. He stopped his experiment before exiting the wormhole back to his home world on Mars.

"Good night, Princess Di," he said, logging off and then going to bed.

CHAPTER FIVE
The Spirit of Combat

In the morning, Artemis stepped out of his apartment building and noticed a line of cars pulling into one of the city's charging stations across the street. The towering parking ramp, covered in reptilian scales that captured the sun's rays, housed cars in stacks so they could charge during the workday. He watched as people exited predominantly single-person shuttles at the ramp entrance before the cars drove themselves into the mouth of the lift to be densely packed like insects inside the giant lizard building.

Artemis lived near the border of the ten-square-block city center, the area that was designed to be pedestrian friendly. Workers crossed the intersection by the ramp freely without the use of pedestrian walk signs. Designed to deter the use of vehicles in the city, software downloaded to vehicles' piloting systems when entering the city followed a mandatory pedestrian yield policy.

Artemis tried to block out work for the duration of the walk down Fowler Avenue to the BSP offices by watching the drones fly overhead. Like low-hanging storm clouds, their density blocked out most of the sun. Drone swarms had been flying above the streets for years, but he wasn't used to how thick they were in Lepton.

Artemis arrived at BSP, walked through the lobby past Brent, and continued into the DOT work area. Artemis was making a conscious habit of being one of the last DOTs to arrive. By the time he sat in his Mobipod, it was only five minutes until morning stand-up. He scanned his email quickly for anything important.

"Reminder for DOTs! Groundswell launches in 20 days. Make certain all your work is your best work during this final push. Everyone is doing great, but we can't let up now.—Brad"

At the morning status meeting in front of the story wall, Artemis watched as stories flew from one position to another— the effect of being sorted and reorganized.

"Kinda cool, ain't it?" said Rodney.

"There's so much going on," said Artemis.

"It's actually not that cool once you figure out exactly *what*'s going on."

"What's going on?"

"I'll tell you what's going on," said Rodney. "This meeting exists for one reason: so managers can create reports to give to their managers. There's this fantasy that work happens in easily quantifiable chunks, but there are constant disruptions and requests that aren't accounted for."

"So what are we doing here, then? What's the point of the board and the daily meetings?" asked Artemis.

"It's mainly a charade. Pay attention. What the—*look out!*" yelled Rodney, just as the panels making up the task board display began pulling away from the wall and crashing onto the floor. Rodney pulled Artemis by his shirt away from the falling panels. The other team members ran away from the wall as fast as they could. One by one, panels fell until five of them lay in a broken mess on the floor. The final panel hung at an angle, displaying a blue screen with a system error.

"Goodness! Is everyone alright?" asked Brad as the team stared in shock at the pile of shattered screens.

"I think so," said Suzi, one of the DOTs.

"We need someone from facilities up here, right away," said Brad into his wearable.

Just as Artemis said, "It looks like you upset the stand-up gods," the final panel dislodged and fell with a crash.

"Okay, everyone, back away from the wall. This isn't safe. Follow me over here and we'll get started," said Brad.

The stand-up meeting began and Artemis watched closely how each person responded, trying to learn the techniques for getting through stand-up. It seemed to Artemis that the key was to speak with a monotone voice, not make eye contact with anyone, and say as little as possible—but enough to satisfy the DOT chief. It was Artemis' turn to check in and he was excited to try out his technique.

"Yesterday I examined some of the new models and today I'm going to work on the authentication piece no blockers," he said in one breath, not emphasizing any single word and not looking around for approval or any questions from the team.

Brad moved on to the next person. Artemis glanced over at Rodney and smiled. Rodney winked at him and gave him a quick grin before removing all of the emotion from his face.

After stand-up, Artemis started to head back to his Mobipod when he felt a hand on his shoulder. He turned to see Rodney smiling at him.

"You did good, kid," Rodney said before walking away.

Artemis felt a moment of satisfaction, but he was quickly overwhelmed with anxiety at the thought of how little time he had to complete the task by his promised deadline. He started off toward the recreation area when Deepak stopped him.

"You're very sure of yourself, aren't you?" asked Deepak.

"No, not really," said Artemis.

"But you so boldly took on that task. Why do you think that is?"

Artemis didn't readily have an answer. "I guess it was just instinct. I sensed that I needed to do something to survive."

"I think you might be on to something. I'm very curious to see if you accomplish your goal. I won't take any more of your time," he said before walking away.

Artemis continued walking over to the DIY Brew machine to make himself a root beer. The dark liquid poured out with the perfect amount of carbonation. Artemis lifted the cup to his mouth—root beer heaven. *This device isn't completely evil after all,* he thought. He continued on toward the rec area sipping his drink.

The far side of the DOT work area contained a few games and some big, plush beanbag chairs. When he arrived, two DOTs were playing holographic ping pong, knocking the glowing ball back and forth to each other. Artemis plopped down in a beanbag chair and started a remote session into Princess Di. Artemis' FourthForce lenses projected his home world.

"Hey, Artemis," said Princess Di.

"Hey there. Start reading from *The Coding Samurai*."

The Spirit of Combat

"You're too tense," said Mitsuhide while teaching his daughter sword-work in the courtyard. "That's why I was able to disarm you so easily. And you aren't balanced. That's why you're sitting in the dirt."

"How am I supposed to relax when you are attacking me?" said Tama, pleading with her father to help her.

"That's why you must train every day. It takes a lot of effort and practice to train your mind to naturally maintain a spirit of combat," he said.

"What's the 'spirit of combat?'" asked Tama.

"The spirit of combat comprises four qualities. Two qualities, *relaxed* and *adaptable*, complement each other. A tense warrior will overreact and become overwhelmed easily. By letting go of expectations and going with the flow, a warrior can stay in the moment and not be preoccupied with distracting thoughts. Does that make sense?" asked Mitsuhide.

"I think so. Basically, the more relaxed I am, the easier it is for me to adapt. The better able I am to adapt, the more I can relax," said Tama, picking up her sword from the ground.

"Exactly. *Balance* and *focus* also complement each other. The warrior in battle must be aware not only of the enemy in front of him but of the overall battlefield and things in his peripheral vision. He must be aware of both the sword and shield of his enemy. By seeing all that is going on around him, when it's time to strike, he is able to focus completely and confidently," said Mitsuhide.

"When do I use the spirit of combat?" asked Tama, swiping her sword in the air.

"Always!" said her father, looking at her sternly. "Whether going to the market or walking home after school, keep your mind ready for battle. If it lapses, you could be ambushed and defeated by something or someone far below your ability."

Lao's commentary

Developers can be ambushed by changes in requirements, production bugs, rude coworkers, and a slew of other day-ruining surprises. A mindset that is relaxed, balanced, focused, and adaptable leads you to being prepared for the daily "battles" in the workplace. Life's not a computer; it doesn't work logically and do exactly what you tell it to do. Letting go but staying balanced can be tough for some people to do, but practicing can help anyone.

Some ways to balance the mind include thinking through other teammates' tasks and considering how one's work fits in with theirs. Getting to know the stakeholders also helps. Do they change their minds often? What are their tastes? How hands-off do they like to be? By understanding as much as you can about the environment you're working in, staying balanced becomes that much easier. Only once balanced can you focus like a laser on one task.

Staying relaxed is not only a sign of confidence; it allows your mind to function at a higher level. Panic leads to poor decision-making and a restriction of creativity which is necessary to perform at a high level. You must be adaptable as well. Managers regularly shift priorities. The Coding Samurai understands this and remains fluid to goals that are constantly in flux. Don't let this reality of work weigh down the spirit, as that will result in more problems.

Oh yeah—it's tough to maintain the spirit of combat if you're freaking out on too much caffeine. There were times in my career when I was so high on espresso all day that I became easily distracted and too uptight; my work suffered. Be careful how you use that stuff.

****

"Princess Di, copy *The Coding Samurai* to my BSP network folder."

"Okay."

This section of the book invigorated Artemis. He charged back to his station to get to work. He opened the project. It was indeed a confounding mess. Thousands of lines of code were strung together in no discernible pattern. The code branched a hundred different ways, making it almost impossible for Artemis to even get a basic understanding of what it did. *It's amazing anyone can log in at all,* he thought.

Artemis studied the code intensely until patterns started to emerge. Just as he was making progress, he received a message from Brad.

"Artemis, you didn't assign a priority to your tasks this morning. Please update these ASAP," wrote Brad.

Frustrated by the distraction, Artemis started to dread the looming deadline. But then he heard the voice of Mitsuhide say, *"Keep the spirit of combat."* Artemis chanted it to himself while he updated his tasks.

Once back on the authentication project, he began to identify seams where the code could be broken into smaller pieces and, in turn, be better organized. After studying the entire landscape of the authentication code, he focused on making a game plan. He wrote down as many notes as he could about how he would attack the problem, refining the plan until he was confident in his strategy. He looked at the time. *It's five o'clock already,* he thought, wondering where the day had gone.

He'd made significant progress, but he still had a lot to do before the deadline. Artemis wanted to keep going, but his mind was scattered and spent. *"Sometimes you just have to know when your mind has nothing left for the day,"* he remembered Professor Lao saying to him one time when he was working late on an algorithm for their project and getting nowhere. So Artemis left work.

****

The next day, with the deadline looming, Artemis logged in

to his quantum while thinking, *relaxed and adaptable, balanced and focused.*

By lunchtime, he was already close to finishing up when he discovered a strange piece of code that didn't fit into any of the other patterns he'd accounted for in his strategy. He messaged Brad to try and find out what the code did, even though Brad's status indicator showed he was unavailable. *I need a break anyway,* he thought. He saved a couple screenshots of the code to conduct more research later before going upstairs to the cafeteria to find Beyoncé. He saw her in line at the grill.

"I think I need a fauxburger," said Artemis after walking up to her.

"There you are. I didn't see you yesterday," she said, moving up in the line.

"I worked through lunch. I've got to get this big rework done on the authentication piece," he said.

"Now it's certain. You're bald. Quit denying it," she said, laughing.

"I swear I'm not. Why am I trying to defend myself to you? I think you know I'm not bald," he said, catching a whiff of French fries.

"So how's the work going?"

"Great. Almost finished. But I found some weird code. No idea what it does." They picked up their orders and made their way to their favorite table where Tony and Wei Wei were already sitting.

"Tell me about this code," said Beyoncé.

"I couldn't make heads or tails of it. It reminded me of stuff I saw in my holographic universe physics class."

"Slow down. Pretty sure you didn't see anything like that in this codebase," said Wei Wei. He gazed off into the distance, reflecting, then turned back to Artemis. "This is marketing software. You're imagining things."

"I don't think so, but whatever," said Artemis.

"A query for you, Artemis," said Wei Wei. "Did your neurons blow a gasket when you learned that quantum mechanics research turned the view of the universe on its head, when you were made starkly aware that the Platonic view of the universe— that is, that the laws of physics reside in a perfect realm of ideas and that the universe is the physical manifestation of these pure laws—was determined to be an inversion of reality?"

Artemis paused a few moments to digest Wei Wei's incredible ability to densely pack information into one sentence. "Yes. It took a while to grasp that the universe is just made of information and that laws of physics are just coded into this universe," said Artemis.

"It's still a trip thinking about it that way, that our universe is just a holographic computer with quantum information as the building blocks," said Tony. "Freaks me the hell out."

Beyoncé piped in. "It's a lot less freaky than seeing the world as a battle of good and evil, a world where my decisions could lead to the fires of hell."

"It could still mean that . . . yet to be determined," said Wei Wei.

Artemis added, "I hate not knowing who's running the show."

"Is that why you don't eat meat?" asked Beyoncé.

"Maybe one reason," said Artemis as he picked up his last French fry. "Okay, I gotta go."

"See you, Artemis," said Beyoncé.

Artemis hurried back to finish up his task. When he tried to check into his code, the system warned him that there was a merge conflict he needed to resolve. His stomach knotted when he realized the conflict was with the piece of strange code he'd found. It had completely disappeared from the server. *Someone deleted it.* He looked at the code annotations to find the username of whoever made the change. *A654980.* It was a system account, not tied to any one person.

"Hey, Palmer. How's the authentication work going?" asked Deepak, gazing deeply at Artemis.

Artemis was startled by Deepak's sudden appearance next to his workspace. He didn't know how long the other man had been standing there, and he felt the hairs on his neck stand on end.

"Good. I'm almost finished," he replied.

"Impressive. And just before your two days were up," said Deepak.

"By the way, when I tried to check in my work, some of the code had recently been deleted from the server. I wanted to make certain I wasn't messing up someone's work, but when I looked at the user account, it didn't belong to anyone; it was a system account. Anything I should worry about?" asked Artemis.

"No, no, no. That's an account that the offshore team uses occasionally. They had a task this sprint that touched the module you were working with," said Deepak, smiling.

"Okay, thanks."

"I need to pull you off the refactoring task."

"What do you mean? I'm almost finished."

"I spoke with Brad and we agree you should be working on something else."

"What about all my work?"

"Shelve it. Check the task board for your new assignment."

After Deepak walked away, Artemis' wearable vibrated. It was a response from Brad. Artemis touched his wrist and Brad's text began scrolling across the thin material adhered to his skin.

"Artemis, I take responsibility for letting you take that task. We'll have the offshore team handle this. You've done enough for today. Go home and take a break."

Artemis felt horrible. *I'm almost finished and they pull me off the task? Why? This is crazy.* He shut down his workstation and left.

Back home, the odd code he'd discovered began bothering him. He sat down on his futon and took the portable out of his backpack. As Jef gnawed on his toes, he fed the screenshots he'd taken into Amazon's search service. The results included a list of books relating to the math and physics of the holographic universe.

The equations in the software related to black hole entropy and the Bekenstein bound. There was also an equation about quantum computing violating the cosmological information bounds and the potential side effects of those violations. Artemis vaguely understood some of it, since he'd minored in quantum computing, but most of the information was way over his head. The problem seemed to be worthy of Professor Lao's time.

"Professor, I hope your trip has been going well and you're catching lots of fish. I'm working at Boom! Snap! Pow! Marketing in Lepton Mountain. It's a really great city. Work is going well, I think. I found some really interesting code in the application I'm working on. From what I can tell, it has something to do with holographic physics and quantum mechanics. Why it was in the code for the project, I have no idea. I thought you might be able to help explain it, because it mysteriously disappeared and no one seems to know what I'm talking about. If you're interested in looking at it, I attached some screenshots. Take care."

CHAPTER SIX
Relating

Artemis woke up the following morning to the sun beaming into his eyes. Through the open window he heard nuthatches yank-yanking. He watched them as they snatched seeds from the pine trees behind his apartment building. Feeling miserable about being pulled from the Groundswell task, he walked to the kitchen to boost his mood by printing some coffee.

"Princess Di, read the news," said Artemis.

"Detectives in Lepton Mountain are investigating a drone attack on the city's north side. A single bullet was fired from the drone outside the victim's home . . ."

"Stop reading the news."

"Okay. You sound upset. How about a song from your Favorites playlist?"

"Fine."

He grabbed a cup from the cupboard and placed it under the nozzle of his coffee machine. He scanned through the options on the menu: Ethiopian, Costa Rican, Hawaiian. He pressed the button for Rwandan Medium, but an indicator light flashed red.

Please insert a new nitrogen cartridge.

He crouched down and rummaged through the box of molecule cartridges under the counter until he saw one with a big

"N" on it. He slid the cylinder into the back of the machine that had rotated to the one that needed replacing. With the cartridge replaced, he pressed the start button and watched the coffee pour from the machine.

I hate that so many coffee economies around the world have disappeared, but it's better for the environment this way, Artemis thought, bringing his cup to his lips. *And it tastes perfect.*

Artemis finished his coffee, said bye to Jef, and then sprinted on his bike to work. When he arrived, the daily stand-up was just getting started.

"John, why don't you go first?" said Brad. John was a senior DOT on the team who sat near Artemis. He seemed fairly ordinary to Artemis, who never heard him say much.

John began his check-in. "Yesterday, I worked on some of the UI for the administration of Groundswell. Today, I need to export some of the data into a report—"

"I have some ideas for that, John. I'll meet with you after stand-up," said Artemis mid-sentence.

"Okay . . ." said John.

"Wei Wei, how about you?" asked Brad.

"Yesterday, I continued applying myself to the injection piece of the Titan module. My attempt to complete it is currently impeded, but it's progressing."

"I know a lot about injection. I can give you a second pair of eyes, Wei Wei. Let me know what time is good," said Artemis.

Wei Wei stood silently, staring across the room at Brad, who looked slightly uncomfortable. Brad continued around the room as each person on the team checked in. Artemis was full of suggestions and offers to help, and he was feeling good about being such a wealth of information for the team.

After stand-up, Artemis walked over to John's workspace to lend a hand.

"Hey, John," said Artemis.

"Hey," said John without looking away from his screen.

"So is now a good time? I know you're working on that export piece. I can share a few ideas I have."

"Thanks, Artemis, but I don't need any help right now. If I get stuck, I'll let you know," said John casually, only half speaking to him.

"Look up data normalization, especially the new stuff being done at Dunn Labs. Really cool stuff."

"Gotcha. Thanks," said John, still staring at his screen.

Artemis looked across the room. Wei Wei was just sitting down at his desk. As Artemis strolled toward him, Wei Wei appeared to notice him and immediately started toward the rear exit of the team's work area. Artemis hurried to catch up.

"Hey, Wei Wei. Real quick, let me share something with you," said Artemis.

"I have to go to the bathroom," said Wei Wei, moving away from Artemis before he could get another word out.

Artemis started to head back to his desk, feeling exasperated that he wasn't able to help anyone. As he walked past Julie, another teammate he had offered to help, he heard her giggling along with the DOT sitting next to her. Though he couldn't make out exactly what she was saying, he was pretty certain he heard the word "busybody." Back at his Mobipod, he searched the index of *The Coding Samurai* for the word "busybody."

Relating

"Who was that, Father?" asked Tama about the man who Mitsuhide had just firmly turned away from their home.

"Ishida Mitsunari," said Mitsuhide.

"What did he want?" asked Tama.

"He wanted to straighten out a situation that doesn't concern him," he said.

"You sounded angry with him," said Tama, setting the dinner table.

"He brings it on himself. He's a busybody, going through the village acting like he's the town supervisor. The villagers hide when they see him coming. He makes everyone uncomfortable," said Mitsuhide. "Unfortunately, in his eagerness to help, he doesn't take the time to carefully think through requests when they are actually made of him. As a result, he fails too often, which only adds to his tarnished reputation as a samurai."

"Father, dinner is ready. Please come and eat," said Tama to her father, who was still looking out the window watching Mitsunari walk down the road.

Lao's commentary

In the workplace, someone who is always inserting himself uninvited into the work of others will alienate those he thinks he needs to help. The Coding Samurai should aim to be dependable but not interfere unless invited. Some people walk around the workplace as if they're enlightened and everyone else is in the dark. Those on The Way *of the* Computer Warrior *don't act this way. They understand that their concerns are for doing their work the best they can and not worrying about others. If someone genuinely asks for help, help him. If someone comes to you in the spirit of discussing a matter, give her your full attention.*

Something else to avoid is engaging in arguments with fools. Let them spin their yarns. The Coding Samurai has nothing to gain and a lot to lose. Most people who argue are only arguing with themselves. Many times they don't understand the problem that has them worked into a frenzy. Don't waste your energy by latching onto the words of someone who just wants to argue.

Sometimes coworkers may ambush others in meetings, trying to grow power or reputation. If this happens to you, keep your cool. Deflect the person's attacks and maintain professionalism. Make statements calmly and clearly without letting the other person antagonize you or make you react in anger, for this may be their actual objective—to make you upset and appear out of control in front of the team so that you lose face.

Sometimes you have to work with someone with whom you have a tense personal past. One time I had to work with someone whose wife I'd dated. She and I were on good terms, but this guy hated me. I approached him and said, "Even though the two of us have a history, I'm not going to let that get in the way of accomplishing our work or let personal feelings get in the way." We never had a problem at work.

The Coding Samurai understands that he must protect his career and take the high ground.

****

Artemis stopped reading the book, stunned.

No wonder everyone has been avoiding me like the plague this morning.

He thought about sending out an email to the team telling them he realized what he was doing and that he would leave them alone. Instead, he walked over to Beyoncé to get her perspective.

"Chill!" she said after Artemis explained to her what was going on.

"I'm trying! I get one thing right and then I get five things wrong," said Artemis.

"Nobody's perfect. You have to own it all: the good, the bad, *and* the ugly," she said, looking at Artemis intensely. He nodded his head while twisting up one side of his mouth. She continued, "You think the people here are always doing right?"

"No," said Artemis.

"I've only been here six months and I can tell you some of the things I've heard here make you look like a regular Boy Scout."

"How'd you know I was in Scouts?" said Artemis.

Beyoncé shook her head and sighed without saying anything else.

****

On his way home, Artemis was swiping some virtual Godar dust off of a street sign when his augmented reality layer flashed red so intensely it hurt his eyes.

"STOP THE PAIN," scrolled text across the street in front of him.

What the hell? That's not part of the game.

Artemis hurried home to feed Jef and give him some fresh kitty-training paper. He nervously packed some water and power gels into his pack and walked down to the bike rack.

The rental bikes were equipped with a module that could convert pedaling into power. Artemis snapped his power cell in place to charge, then sped off away from the city and toward the farms to the south. The clouds threatened rain, but the dashboard unit on his bike said there was only a 26.35 percent chance of precipitation. Once he left the city limits, the solar panels in the bike path disappeared and large cracks split the asphalt. The trail transitioned into a dirt path that branched in two directions. To the left, the path tracked the barbed-wire fence of a farm. To the right, it ran parallel to the county road heading away from Lepton.

He turned left and wove down the narrow dirt path through a field of tall buckwheat. Patches of the field filled Artemis' nose with a rich, grassy smell. He approached a pond and the sounds of crickets and bullfrogs echoed all around him. He smiled when lightning bug butts started flashing along the top of the grass near a large white farmhouse.

As he approached the house, Artemis saw an older woman sitting on the porch. A big oak tree with a swing tied to a large, knotty branch grew in front of the house. The woman watched, expressionless, as Artemis biked nearer. As he passed the tree, the woman waved without changing expression. Distracted by the waving woman, Artemis didn't see a slippery root crossing the path at an odd angle. When his tire hit the root, his bike skidded sideways and he crashed to the ground, banging his knee hard on the tree root.

"Ow!" yelled Artemis. "Ow! Ow! Ow!"

"Are you okay, son?" shouted the woman. Artemis looked down at his knee just below his shorts and saw blood oozing.

"I'm really hurt!" he shouted.

The woman walked down the stairs, stiffly raising her right hip to ease down each stair. She made her way across the lawn and examined his knee.

"Stand up, boy. You aren't hurt," the woman said, sizing up the severity of his cut.

"But I'm bleeding!" he pleaded with her.

"Stand up, boy. Go sit down on the stairs over there."

Artemis stood up and limped over to the stairs.

"Fancy-looking bike," said the woman.

Artemis noticed a few gardening tools in a bin and a stack of potato sacks along the wall. He could smell food cooking inside the house.

"Smells good," said Artemis.

"Apple pie," the woman said, now smiling and rocking in her chair. "How about I get you a slice?"

"I'd love that!" said Artemis.

"You just sit here and I'll be right back," she said, walking slowly inside.

Artemis walked up the steps onto the porch and sat down on an old wooden chair. From the porch he could see the skyline of Lepton Mountain. The small windmills turning on the top of some of the buildings made the lights behind them appear to constantly flicker.

"Here you go," said the woman, handing Artemis a washcloth as well as a small plate with a slice of pie and whipped cream on top.

"This looks delicious," said Artemis, taking the offerings from the woman. "My name's Artemis."

"Debbie," said the woman, who'd sat back down in her rocking chair.

"Does the flickering bother you?" asked Artemis.

"I'm used to it."

"How long have you lived here?"

"Over sixty years," she said, growing a proud smile. "Been living here since before a single one of them buildings was built."

"Geez. So what do you think of the city?"

"Ain't nothin' to me."

"So you never go into the city?"

"Nope. My grandson brings me what I need. He sent one of them damn buzzing things over here once, too, to bring me my medicine."

"You don't like the drones?" asked Artemis, taking another bite of pie.

"Hell no, I don't like them things. They scare the birds. I told him not to do it again even if I was on the floor dying."

"Does anyone else live here with you?"

"Oh, my grandson stays over from time to time. My husband, he died about five years ago. Ran the farm here. Now we rent the land to the farmer at the next place down."

"So what do you think of how the world's changed since you've lived here on the farm? It's a lot different than it was sixty years ago," said Artemis before shoveling the last bite of pie into his mouth.

"Ain't changed much here," she said, laughing. "Maybe people's dumber than before, like they can't think for themselves no more. But maybe I'm just an old woman who doesn't know anything."

Artemis couldn't imagine what life would be like if he were completely disconnected from virtual worlds, augmented reality games, and hologs.

"Do you ever think you're missing out on all the changes?" he asked.

"I miss my husband. When that man died, I lost a lot of what was important to me. But I still have my grandson and he means everything to me. So no, I ain't missing nothing."

Artemis noticed raindrops landing on the steps of the porch.

"Well, Debbie, thanks for the pie. I should be getting home. Where should I put my plate?" Artemis asked, standing up to leave.

"Just set it on the chair and I'll get to it," said Debbie.

Artemis walked his bike across the lawn past the oak tree and back onto the path before waving good-bye to Debbie.

"Check yourself for ticks when you get home. They get pretty thick on that buckwheat."

"Oh, great," said Artemis woefully. "Bye, Debbie."

"Don't be a stranger," she said as Artemis pedaled off toward Lepton.

****

Back home in the shower, Artemis looked all over his body for ticks, rubbing his hands over everyplace he couldn't see for anything bumpy. Satisfied that nothing was sucking his blood, he dried off, put on his haptic suit, and touched the door to open the giant egg-shaped contraption. After a biometric scan, he appeared at the entrance of the Mars biosphere. He walked over to the obelisk he'd made the other night and touched it, triggering the wormhole. He stepped through and found himself on the surface of the planet he'd started building.

"Name the planet 'Heidi,'" said Artemis.

A huge amount of quantum power was needed to manage all of the information on a life-sustaining planet—as much as it took to save the entire remainder of the universe. The thoughts and memories of trillions of creatures had to be managed. Because of this, most people were only simulating universes with one planet containing sentient beings. Other F.O.A.L. members had created thousands of universes, yet over ninety-nine percent of them only contained one life-sustaining planet.

Artemis' simulation had been constructed as a holographic image based upon a copy of the physical laws of Earth's universe. However, since universes at their core are only information, he made a couple changes to these physical laws. For example, instead of a universe with the forces of gravity and electromagnetism and the strong and weak nuclear forces, he created an additional force, an anti-gravitational force. Where gravity is always attractive and operates on matter over large distances, an anti-gravitational force also acts on matter over large distances, but instead of being attractive, it's repulsive. When celestial bodies in Artemis' universe reached a certain threshold of size, gravity flipped and repelled other objects.

At Artemis' location in the binary system that contained the life-sustaining planet, it was sunset and sunrise at the same time. The ground was rocky and crawling with the critters that had gained consciousness during Artemis' previous session. There was a type of thick moss and lichen in one area where most of the creatures were congregating. He heard a cacophony of utterances coming from the huddled mass of rock-creatures by the clumps of moss. Their calls sounded like beautiful music, so he decided to call the beasts harpstones.

The harpstones were feeding on the moss and lichen. Most of the time they were stationary, but when they moved, they did so with purpose and speed. Artemis had to remind himself that these simple, bug-rock-looking things were sentient.

"Restrict the environment of the harpstones. Isolate the species to create a new branch of life-form. Fast-forward until the next distinct species emerges from the harpstones," said Artemis.

When time stopped, there were giant, blue mountains that had an unusual aura about them even in the bright daylight. Artemis looked around, trying to find the new life-form.

"How big is the new life-form?" asked Artemis.

"New life-forms are 82,111 meters in height on average and 21.1 kilometers long," said Princess Di.

Artemis was quite small in proportion to the landscape, since Heidi was one hundred times the size of Earth. With two suns to provide constant energy to the surface of the planet, this new life-form had grown to an immense size.

"Highlight new life-form," said Artemis. An indicator light flashed over the blue mountains.

"Ohmygawd!" said Artemis. "Annotate the key stages of evolution of the new species using one-million-year increments."

Princess Di began stating the steps of the creatures' evolution.

1. Harpstones created symbiotic relationship with moss.

2. Harpstones developed ability to create photosynthesis in their skin by absorbing moss cells.

3. Harpstones gave up moving and their flagellates were used to anchor them to the ground like roots.

4. Harpstones gave up sexual reproduction and multiplied using asexual reproduction.

5. Species mutated to allow a neural network to cross individuals. Stem cells that previously grew the flagellates used for transportation mutated and the flagellates grew into neural fibers, tunneling across individual animals into the openings previously used for vocalizations.

6. Immense chains of organisms formed one entity and the neural network became unified.

Artemis was blown away. Not only were the mountains alive, they knew they were alive.

Poor Debbie really doesn't know what she's missing out on.

CHAPTER SEVEN
Cultural Refinement

Artemis' alarm sounded late at night while he was still staring in awe at the harpstone mountains. He saved the simulation before leaving the eggshell enclosure of Princess Di. He saw Jef curled up outside the shell, his tail gently swaying back and forth.

"I really need to spend more time with you, little guy," said Artemis, reaching down to pick him up. As he stretched out his arms, he noticed a message from Tilly.

Hey Artemis, I wanted to see how you're doing. Can you meet up tomorrow morning? There's a cool event going on.

Sure I can meet. What time?

11AM. Your lobby.

See you at 11.

The following morning at eleven o'clock, Tilly sent a message to Artemis notifying him that she was waiting downstairs. Artemis grabbed each of them a cup of coffee and rode down to meet her. Tilly was waiting for him when he exited the elevator.

"I brought you a cup of Costaropian," said Artemis.

"Costaropian? I don't think I've had that," said Tilly.

"It's a blend—Costa Rican and Ethiopian beans."

"Thanks, you can have mine," said Tilly squeamishly. "Besides, you look like you need two cups. Your eyes are half closed."

"I was up pretty late working on a universe simulation. It's hard to quit when you're discovering new life-forms and watching eons of universe formation take place."

"That's what you're doing? Gee, I really wouldn't know where to start."

"It's not for everyone, but maybe I'll show you sometime," Artemis said, trying not to sound condescending but still sounding condescending. "So what are we doing? What's the surprise event?"

"We have something here in the Mountain called 'The Volunteer Marathon.' Social service organizations around the city open their doors for people to come in for a few hours to volunteer and see how the organizations help the community," she said.

"So we're volunteering?" asked Artemis, feeling a bit nervous about what he'd gotten himself into.

"We're going to the city park," said Tilly, grabbing Artemis by the arm.

"Hold on, which park?"

"The City Park. That's the name."

"I need to look something up," he said before muttering

something to his wrist. Artemis froze and then said, "I can't go."

"What do you mean you can't go?"

"I just looked up the City Park in my game guide and the beasts there are way over my pain threshold. If I go there . . . doesn't matter, I'm not going there."

"Artemis, can't you just stop playing the game, like turn it off?"

"You're joking, right?"

"No, I'm not joking. Just turn off the game for a few hours while we go do this. It'll be okay," said Tilly, gently taking Artemis by the arm.

He stopped and thought about it for a few moments, then tapped his wrist and said, "Turn off Beastville."

Tilly led him to the two-person autonomous vehicle.

"I haven't been in one of these," said Artemis.

"A Free Sport? Really? They're everywhere," said Tilly, pressing the start button on the console.

"You're just renting this one though, right?"

"Yeah, I don't need a car very often."

"I thought I saw a Minute Car sticker on the side."

"Leaving Lepton Mountain city limits. You're now driving in a free zone," said the car.

"Yeeeee-hawwww!" yelled Tilly. "Let's drive through Farmer Jones' crops!"

Artemis started laughing hysterically. "You're a funny girl."

"There's the park," she said, turning to look at him. Her eyes stopped on his for a moment, and then their laughter turned into silent smiles.

After pulling into the park, Artemis left the car and saw several groups of kids and a few park employees standing outside the visitor center. He followed Tilly inside the center, where a woman sat behind a table with a "Volunteer Marathon" sign.

"Hello, are you here to volunteer?" asked the smiling woman.

"Yes, we are!" said Tilly. "Tilly Benson and Artemis Pound."

"We have you two down for chaperoning a middle school on one of the bird walks. It's starting soon, so you're just in time," said the woman.

"Sounds great. Where do we go?" asked Tilly.

"Walk back outside and look for the park guide with group five," said the woman. "Here are your name tags," she said, handing them stickers to put on their shirts.

"Chaperoning children?" asked Artemis incredulously as the two wandered back outside to find the group.

"What's wrong with that?"

"Kids are so . . . unruly and . . . jeez, these are middle school kids. You know what they're like," said Artemis, nervously scratching his arm.

"You don't have to do anything. Just stick with me," reassured Tilly.

"Welcome to the bird walk, Artemis and Tilly," said the park guide, reading their name tags as the two caught up to the group.

"That's us!" said Tilly.

"I'm Sally. The kids doing the walk today are from Preston Middle School. Say hello to the chaperones, kids," said Sally.

"Hi!" chanted the group of kids.

"While we're walking through the park, we'll be looking and listening for birds. You can take pictures, but try to be as quiet as possible since most of the birds scare easily. Listen to Tilly and Artemis. If you need anything, ask them or me. Is everyone ready?" asked Sally.

"Yeesss . . ." said the kids in a robotic chorus.

"Okay, kids, look in that tree. There's a very bright blue bird on the limb. That's a real treat! An indigo bunting! Once you've spotted it, take out your checklists and mark it off," said Sally.

"Ms. Sally, what's it called again? An indyglow bunny?" asked one of the boys.

"Close, Gary. It's called an in-di-go bun-ting," said Sally very slowly. "Let's walk this way down the trail."

As they walked, Tilly shushed the middle schoolers as their chatter grew too loud. They quieted for a few moments until the whispers turned into muttering, which once again turned into loud talking.

"How can you be so patient with them?" Artemis asked.

"They're kids. You can't let it bother you. That's how they are at that age," she said.

"Hmmm—I wasn't like that," said Artemis.

"Why don't you try talking to one of them?" said Tilly. "They're not some type of alien creature."

Yeah right, thought Artemis, but he looked around anyway, trying to pinpoint one he could talk with.

"Hey, Gary. Did you find the indigo bunting on your checklist?" asked Artemis.

"I didn't know there were so many birds. There's hundreds on this list," said Gary, clearly excited.

"Is this the first time you've done this?"

"Yeah. We have bird feeders in the yard, but I've never done a walk like this. It's really hairy."

The trail wandered along a creek. Honeysuckle blossomed and filled the air with sweetness as a gentle summer wind blew.

"I love this time of year, and those trees," said Tilly, pointing at a few weeping willows.

"What do you love about them?" asked Artemis.

"They seem wise and caring, like a grandmother."

Sally stopped the group.

"Look up into this tree. On the branch is a big, black bird. That's a raven. Ravens are social birds but will also survive on their own. They're very intelligent. They aren't predators, but they will scavenge dead animals," said Sally.

"Do you see it, Gary?" asked Artemis.

"No, where's she pointing?" Gary asked.

Artemis crouched down to Gary's height and pointed over his shoulder to the tree branch. "It's right there," he said.

"Now I see it!" said Gary.

Tilly looked over at Artemis and smiled. "See? They aren't so bad," she whispered to him.

"Kids, I need your help. There is a very unusual bird in the forest that we don't see too often," said Sally in a serious tone. "There's a special dance we can do called the Crossbill Dance. If we do it right, we might be able to see one. Do what I do," Sally continued as she started gyrating her hips in a circle.

A few of the kids started doing the same thing, but most of them just stood there and watched. Artemis looked to Tilly and his fears were realized. She was doing the Crossbill Dance and waving at him, encouraging him to do the same. Artemis stiffly moved one hip and then the other while timidly looking at the ground. He glanced up. Tilly and more of the kids were swaying their hips in the middle of the trail. He noticed Gary watching him, which gave him a little more courage. He loosened up and encouraged Gary to get in on the act. Gary smiled at him and began dancing while holding his checklist and pencil in his little hand.

"Kids, sorry we didn't see any crossbills, but you did see twenty-three other species of birds," said Ranger Sally when the group returned to the visitor's center." Does anyone have a favorite bird from the walk?"

"I liked the raven the best, because they're smart," said Gary.

"Yes, Gary, ravens are very smart birds. I really like them, too. Everyone thank Tilly and Artemis for coming with us today," said Sally.

"Thanks, Til ... Art ... y ... mis," said the chorus of children.

"Thank you, Ms. Sally, and thank you kids for being a great group," said Tilly.

"See you later, Gary," said Artemis to his new friend.

"Bye," said Gary, glancing up from his checklist briefly before immediately going back to scribbling away at it.

"Lunch?" asked Tilly as the two climbed into her car.

"Sure," said Artemis. The two sped back toward town.

They arrived at Joy's, a local diner on the edge of the city that was modeled on a classic 1950s theme with one twist—it was automated. The car pulled into the gravel parking lot in front of the flashing "Open" sign. There were mostly families sitting inside with their children, who were entertained by the server robots bringing food to the tables. The pair seated themselves in a booth by the window and looked over the menu. Artemis used the touch pad to order the biscuits and gravy and a root beer float.

"Counting calories, I see," said Tilly.

"What's it to you?" said Artemis jokingly, but feeling annoyed.

"I'm kidding, pal. What's the matter?"

"Nothing's the matter. Why make the comment, though?"

"I didn't mean anything by it. Sorry. What's bothering you?"

"Wow, you like to pry."

"I'm not prying. I didn't mean to upset you. Jeez. I was just teasing you."

Artemis realized that his reaction was a little intense. "If you have to know, I was a fat kid. When I was in middle school, kids picked on me all the time. I don't like kids and I don't like people making comments about what I'm eating. Good enough?" he said, unable to keep his emotions from bubbling up again.

"I'm really sorry, Artemis," said Tilly.

"Don't be sorry, just think before saying things to people you don't know anything about," he said, getting even more upset.

The two sat in silence for a few minutes, eating while trying not to look at each other. Artemis thawed a little and tried to smooth things over.

"I did have a good time today. That Gary kid was cool. He was really interested in the birds. I think he liked them even more than Ms. Sally," he said.

"It seemed that way," said Tilly quietly. She paused a moment and then continued, "I'm not trying to pry—really—but can I ask you about how things have been going at work?"

"It's okay. I guess I'm still kind of tired and obviously a little grumpy," he said.

"A lot grumpy," said Tilly.

"Agreed," said Artemis with a sigh. "So things are up and down, but I found this book ... it's from one of my college professors. I found it in his papers on my quantum."

"Can I take a look?"

"But you don't have any lenses, do you?"

"No. Sure don't. I'll use yours," she said, smiling.

"Wow, that's kind of intimate."

"What's wrong with that?"

"Nothing. I just never . . . okay, here you go," said Artemis, taking out his lenses one at a time and handing them to Tilly.

"Nothing's happening," said Tilly after she put the lenses in.

"Oh. I need to let Princess Di know. I'm going to have to talk into your eyes," said Artemis.

He leaned in toward Tilly's face. He could smell her hair and see every detail of her face: her speckled brown eyes, her sun freckles, and a crooked front tooth.

"Princess Di, I'm giving Tilly guest privileges. And open up *The Coding Samurai*," said Artemis.

"Here we go. Have you read this part yet?" she said as she began to read from it.

Cultural Refinement

"What are you writing, Father?" asked Tama, watching her father write calligraphy as she stood in the entrance to the tearoom.

"Matsuo Bashō—a great poet. I'm writing one of his haiku," said Mitsuhide, moving the brush over the paper.

"Will you read it to me?" she asked.

"Summer grasses,

All that remain

Of soldiers' dreams," he said.

"So beautiful," said Tama.

"Samurai are fierce warriors, hard and strong. But inside we must cultivate a place of softness and peace."

"Why?" she asked, moving closer to him.

"As samurai grow strong, they can become arrogant. Hardness must be balanced with softness. To do this, I study the great poets. Moving the calligraphy brush is like a sword in my hand. I find pleasure in the movements."

"You missed a stroke," said Tama, kneeling down beside her father and taking the brush in his hand to complete the character.

"So I did," said Mitsuhide.

Lao's commentary

The Coding Samurai are skilled professionals. They love technology and immerse themselves in it so they can know as much as they can about their craft and how to apply it to create wonderful things. But living life absorbed in technology can be a detriment to personal development. Being a one-dimensional person who only can relate to computers is one who is lost.

Be highly skilled, but also be an interesting person. Throughout your career, you'll meet many people from many backgrounds. Being able to connect with them is a must. Having a depth of character and culture will help your career, as much or more than just being a skilled craftsman.

As skills grow, a tendency toward conceit and arrogance oftentimes emerges. To temper this tendency, channel passion for craft into passion about humanity and then express it somehow. Once I realized I had become a highly sought programmer, I started walking around with an air of superiority. I couldn't see that I'd conflated my programming skills with the quality of my character. I'd become a jerk.

The jerk started fading after I became a Big Brother to a boy who was really into programming but was living in a troubled home. The time I spent with Dominick knocked me down a few pegs and made me realize there's so much more to life than my ego.

****

"That's exactly what you did today, samurai!" said Tilly enthusiastically as she handed him his lenses back.

"I guess so," he said. "As you were reading that, I realized something."

"What's that?"

"I'm a one-dimensional person."

"No you aren't," said Tilly.

"Yes, I am. I spend all my time on technology. I don't connect with people."

"Today you didn't spend all your time on tech," she said, reaching out for his hand. "You connected with Gary. And you connected with me."

Artemis felt Tilly's hand in his. It was soft. Her thumb gently rubbing the back of his hand made his stomach flip. Tears began to well up in his eyes.

"What is it?" she asked.

"I'm inside these fake worlds all the time, and most of the time—and this is the saddest part—the only thing that matters is how much pain I can tolerate," he said, looking around the diner self-consciously.

"Go on," she said, holding his hand more firmly.

"I feel like sometimes it's the only emotion I care about. Every other feeling I have is a reaction to my goal of being able to experience as much pain as possible."

"What emotion do you feel now?"

"Something more real."

Tilly held Artemis' hand and looked at him softly.

"Thanks—for getting me out," he said, taking a deep breath and straightening his posture.

"My pleasure. And I know it's not all about pain when you're in your quantum. You told me about making those cool worlds—I'd love to see them sometime."

Artemis nodded and then asked, "How about you? How are you? How's work?"

"Work is fine. Actually, work is good," said Tilly, looking down at the table. "But you were honest with me just now about what you were feeling, so I'll be honest with you."

"What's up?"

"I'm pretty sad now, too."

"Sorry. I didn't mean to be a downer. What's the matter?"

"No, it's not you. Those kids remind me of my little brother. He was eleven when he became very sick. It was an autoimmune disorder. He died. I miss him so much sometimes."

"I'm sorry, Tilly. How long ago was it?"

"Two years ago. He was such a cute little guy," she said,

starting to cry.

Artemis sat quiet for a few moments, letting Tilly cry, before asking, "What was his name?"

"William. Billy," she said, smiling at Artemis with tears in the corners of her eyes.

Tilly leaned back in her seat and wiped away the tears. Artemis wished he was still holding her hand.

"Well, I should get home. I have some things to do, but I really appreciate you coming out with me today."

"Of course! I had a great time. Maybe I'll take up bird-watching. There's still a couple hundred to check off my list," said Artemis.

"My pleasure."

"The weather's great and we're not too far away. I think I'll walk home from here," said Artemis.

"Are you sure?" said Tilly, sniffling a little.

"Positive. Let's talk soon," he said before the two hugged briefly and parted ways.

Artemis crossed the road and walked over to the bike path before following it back into the city. The outskirts of the city left a lot of room for aesthetics—nothing to see but scattered patches of tall grass along the gravel shoulder of the road. After walking for a few minutes, Artemis received a message from Professor Lao.

Artemis, I received your message about

the equations in the code you've been working with. What's this project's purpose? If you have other screenshots, please send them to me.

Hi Professor—the project is called 'Groundswell.' It's a product placement application for VR worlds. I attached the other screenshots I had.

As Artemis walked along the gravel trail leading back to the city center, his lenses unexpectedly began flashing red again like they had the other day. This time a high-pitched tone burst into his ears as well. Then he saw an ad scroll across his vision that read "On sale today: buy *Physics at the Event Horizon: Quantum Computing and the Holographic Universe*."

Artemis arrived home and downloaded the book from the Black Hole—a shopping site that really sucks you in. Dense at 554 pages, the book intimidated Artemis as he began reading the introduction.

"One of the biggest surprises that physicists have discovered in recent years is the similarity between the physics at the event horizons of black holes and the physics of quantum computing in certain states. Researchers at Carnegie Mellon University have found that the core information that stores physical laws can be altered in unusual ways during certain phenomena. One of these is the event horizons of black holes. The other is an error-checking process within quantum computers that is used to protect quantum information from degradation."

Artemis began reading the next paragraph in the book. He was feeling drowsy, and his head bobbed halfway through the first sentence. By the end of the second sentence, Artemis had fallen asleep.

CHAPTER EIGHT
Self-Expression

Monday, Artemis plopped into a seat next to Beyoncé just in time for his first meeting—the retro, a meeting for the team to recap and critique the most recent iteration of work. He reached into a large box of donuts and pulled out one dripping with chocolate.

"Good morning," Beyoncé said to him.

"Morning. Mmmm. Good," said Artemis with his mouth full of the gooey chocolate-covered sweet. "How was your weekend?"

"It was great. I groomed cats at the animal shelter. It was for this thing called Volunteer Marathon."

"I did that, too. Not cat grooming, but the volunteering thing, with my friend Tilly. We chaperoned some kids on a bird walk."

"Ooooh. Are you dating?"

"No, she's just a friend," said Artemis. *She's being a bit forward,* he thought. "She's actually the recruiter who helped me get this job. She's been showing me around the Mountain while I get used to it. Oh, she's sending me a message right now."

Artemis, I really had a great time with you yesterday, but I can't hang out with you anymore. Sorry.—Tilly

"What's the matter?" asked Beyoncé after Artemis' face soured.

"I don't know why, but my friend said we can't be friends anymore."

"All right, everyone. Let's get started with this iteration's retro," said Brad, getting the room's attention. "Let's put everyone in a good mood and start with everything that went well. Anyone can start."

"I guess I'll start," said Eric, one of the DOTs. "I was happy with the work that John did on the migration. It really made my tasks easier."

"John made migration go smoothly," said Brad, typing the words into the spreadsheet under "Things that went well."

"Likewise. I thought Eric did a solid job on the migration," said John. "He's giving me credit, but really it was the groundwork he did that made it go so smoothly."

"How about I just put 'John and Eric's teamwork made migration go smoothly'?" said Brad.

Eric and John smiled at each other and nodded in agreement.

"Okay, who's next?" asked Brad.

"I'll go," said Artemis. "I did a great job with refactoring the authentication module. I don't know how it got like that in the first place, but it was horrible. It would be so much better now, but I got pulled off the project, so it still probably looks like someone bald programmed it."

"Don't be too modest, Artemis," said Deepak as several people in the room chuckled. "I'll continue. The offshore team continues to outperform. They finished cleaning up the code that Artemis so clearly denounced."

"Offshore team is doing great," mumbled Brad, continuing his notes. "Alright, now to talk about where we can improve. Remember the guidelines: no blaming; bring solutions, not complaints."

"I guess I'll go," said John. "I had a task to integrate one of our partners with our API. The main challenge is that the programmers working for our partner don't appear to have a working knowledge of how the Internet works."

The room erupted in laughter.

"So what can we do to make these integrations go smoother?" asked Brad.

"We don't have any control over the competency of the employees working for our partners. The only thing we can do, short of writing their code for them, is to write more documentation or try to extend our API to make it even simpler to integrate. Other partners aren't having any issues integrating, though, so I don't know how much time and effort we want to spend here," said John.

"Write more documentation," said Brad, typing up John's suggestion in the solution column.

The meeting lasted another hour as the team continued to examine their recent work. When the meeting ended and Artemis stood up to leave, Brad stopped him.

"Artemis, can you hang back a second for a quick one-on-one?" he asked.

"Sure," said Artemis as he sat back down and nervously waited for the room to clear.

Brad shut the door after the last person exited and sat on the edge of the table. "Artemis, I usually do these one-on-ones every month, but I thought today would be a good time to sit down and talk with you. So, how about you start? How have things been going?"

"I think things are really going well. I feel like I'm doing really good work," said Artemis, forcing a smile.

"You have been doing really good work. You've surprised me with the level of some of your coding. You're beyond the other interns programming-wise."

"I don't know what to say. Thanks. I thought I must be messing up, since you took away my task."

"I want to talk about some other things."

"Oh, okay. Like what?" asked Artemis, fidgeting in his chair.

"I wonder if you are having some difficulties adjusting to the work environment," started Brad. "I wonder if—"

"I'm fine!" interrupted Artemis.

"I'll be blunt, Artemis. You have some growing up to do if you want to fit in better with the team."

Artemis lowered his head in shame. His shame turned to

anger—suddenly, he felt trapped in Lepton Mountain.

"Look, I know you're embarrassed about what happened at Jeff's house. I blame him for most of that. And the thing with the email that circulated never should have happened, period. I talked with Tony about that," said Brad.

Artemis' stomach knotted as he listened to Brad. Artemis was doing everything he could to move past that event, but it kept coming back to haunt him. He wondered if it was ever going to go away completely.

"It was big of you to take on the refactoring. I'd say most if not all of the team wanted nothing to do with that task," continued Brad. "When I saw what you did with it, I knew I was working with someone with talent. None of what I'm saying to you has anything to do with that."

"So what am I doing wrong? I know I messed up at Jeff's house. I'm trying my best to prove to the team that I'm not just some clown," said Artemis.

"You're trying too hard," said Brad. "You're trying so hard to prove yourself that it's working against you. Like today in the retro. During 'what went well,' did you notice that the others tried to mention things they appreciated about each other? Did you notice that you were the only one who gave yourself a compliment?"

"No, I didn't mean it that way. I just wanted the team to know that I was useful for something."

"I know, Artemis. I'm trying to help you. You can put the

stuff from Jeff's behind you. You don't have to prove yourself to anyone but yourself. I think, from what I know about you, that you believe in your abilities. Only you know if you are doing the best job you can. And that's what matters most—your own self-respect."

"I understand. I guess I seem like a real jerk to the team."

"Don't start beating yourself up. That's not the point of this conversation. Go out there and keep doing quality work, but start thinking more about being part of the team. People want to like you because you're a likable guy. Just give them the space to do that."

"All right, I will."

"Do you have any more questions for me?" asked Brad.

"Maybe. How long has Deepak been on the team?"

"He's been here almost since the beginning. Why do you ask?"

"He's the only person who I feel doesn't *really* like me. When he makes fun of me, I don't think he's joking."

"Deepak can be a bit of a strong personality, but he knows his stuff—he's exceptionally well trained and extremely passionate. He can be rough, but don't let him bother you. If you think he's really out of line, though, let me know."

"Thanks, Brad. I feel like a big weight's been lifted."

"You're welcome. Now get back to work," teased Brad.

Artemis smiled at Brad and left the room. Even though he felt slightly better after talking with Brad, he was still torn up inside. After his third attempt at trying to concentrate on coding, he stopped to visit the book that had been getting him through the rocky days at work.

"Log off of BSP network and connect with Princess Di."

"Hi, Artemis," said Princess Di.

"Hi, Di. How about reading some of *The Coding Samurai*?"

"Okay."

Self-expression

"Look at how beautiful I've made this bonsai, Father," said Tama as Mitsuhide arrived home on his horse for lunch.

"I can still see you in this bonsai," said Mitsuhide, pointing at a scar on the tree's bark. "There should be no trace of the artist in the bonsai. Only display your work when your touch can no longer be seen."

Tama looked at her father, disappointed. "It would make me happy to have your approval," she said.

"You honor your father, Tama. Don't be discouraged, but if you rely upon others to give you satisfaction in your work, you lose the power of self-respect. If you put your heart and soul into your work, it will be self-evident to those who matter."

"I understand," she said.

Lao's commentary

Self-expression is vital to the human spirit. However, at work, self-expression must be tempered. Refine how your personality and feelings are conveyed as well as the timing of when to convey them.

Regularly congratulating oneself in front of coworkers won't have the desired effect, which is to be appreciated. It's far better to point out the merits of others, which will create trust and rapport. Even if managers and coworkers don't give the praise one feels entitled to, don't try to elicit praise or brag about your accomplishments. Others have their own agendas and are mainly concerned with how your efforts make their jobs easier.

Accept compliments and criticism alike with grace. Being complimented for a job where you didn't try your hardest can have negative consequences. You might start believing that you don't need to try your hardest to get praise and, as a consequence, stop trying to do your best. Likewise, don't dwell on criticism, as it's just one person's perspective. Find any value you can in the feedback and move on.

The Coding Samurai lets his personality shine mostly through craftsmanship. This doesn't mean walking around stone-faced and unemotional, which would likely only alienate you from your peers and others. Show playfulness, ingenuity, smarts, and wit through your work. At the office, this is where your spirit will be most evident, not in chitchat and trips for coffee.

Don't forget that you must be appreciated for your long-term efforts and talents. Plenty of managers and organizations confuse the humility of The Coding Samurai with weakness. I once had a manager who always came to me with big problems before presenting "her ideas" to upper management. This attention felt really good for a while until I realized that I was getting the same cost-of-living raise as everyone else on the team and she was getting a 15 percent annual bonus. Careers might seem long, but wasting too much time in an ungrateful environment can wreck the trajectory of a promising career path.

****

Beyoncé stopped by and tapped Artemis' shoulder.

"Sorry to interrupt," she said.

"That's okay. Let me log off my home quantum," said Artemis.

"Wait. You have a quantum at home?"

"I do. It was kind of like payment from my college professor for a project. Best gift ever."

"Tell me about it! I got mine the same way. Not from a professor, but from a relative."

Artemis looked at Beyoncé curiously. "That's a generous relative. Those things aren't cheap."

"No kidding, but for them maybe it's not too much money. Let's just say that side of the family had some success in the music industry," she teased.

Artemis stopped and thought about who Beyoncé's wealthy relative might be before asking her, "So are you running Pathways or Gopher?"

"Gopher, of course! Pathways is great and all, don't get me wrong, but you just can't do what you can with Gopher World," she said.

"I agree completely," said Artemis, excited that he'd met someone with such compatible hardware.

"Do you dig?" asked Beyoncé.

"Of course I do. How about you?"

"You know it. I love making places for people to explore and seeing the worlds other people are digging," she said.

"Mine are more like laboratories than a social hangout. I think I told you I'm in F.O.A.L. Most of what I do is on their network."

"Here, I'll send you an invitation to my place. If you're on tonight and not doing anything with your F.O.A.L. buddies, swing by. I'd like to know what you think of my stuff."

"That'd be great."

"Alright, then. I expect to see you later!" said Beyoncé as she sauntered back to her pod.

****

Artemis was having dinner at home when he sent Tilly a message.

Hi Tilly. Whatever I did, I'm really sorry.

You didn't do anything, Artemis.

This doesn't make any sense. Why we can't be friends?

We can't. I'm your recruiter.

Who cares?

My boss. Sorry.

Artemis was trying to come up with a reply when he received a message from Beyoncé.

Hey, Artemis. I'm digging if you want to meet up. Here's the address: htp>us.wv.GeekAuChocolat.

"Htp" stood for Holographic Transfer Protocol. It was one of several protocols built into IB. As a result of the NSA spying in the early 2000s, countries had no desire to let the United States government monitor IB to the extent that it controlled IA. Each country managed their IB network centrally, so IB addresses began with the top-level country code.

Once inside Princess Di, Artemis entered the address Beyoncé gave him and waited for the wormhole to load. Artemis found himself at the gate of a Middle Eastern city. Colorful, intricate tilework decorated the walls of the gate. Every direction was blocked off except the path into the medina of the city. He smelled spices and felt hot air blowing against his neck. A narrow, brick road between the walls allowed passage. His steps on the stone blocks leading deeper into the city echoed loudly down the passage. As he walked past a water fountain set into an alcove, he realized that some of the steps weren't echoes— someone was behind him. He turned around but saw only blackness. Whatever was approaching was heavy. *Maybe there's more than one?* he thought.

He heard the clapping grow louder but still couldn't see anything. Whatever was making its way down the passage was incredibly close now. It sounded like it was right behind him. Artemis jumped to the side just as the furry head of a donkey emerged from the darkness and passed him while towing a cart. Sitting in the cart was an old man in a dark brown robe with distant eyes. He stared blankly at Artemis before disappearing into the passage.

Artemis laughed off the eerie welcoming that Beyoncé had programmed for her guests. He continued walking down the passage until he heard music playing from one of the homes leading off to the right. He followed this even narrower path until he came to a very large wooden door, painted red and decorated with a carving of the sun, moon, and stars. He knocked and the music quieted. When the door opened, Beyoncé stood in the entrance wearing a bright pink djellaba, a bejeweled crown on her braided hair, and gold slippers adorned with rubies and emeralds.

"Wow, you look amazing!" said Artemis.

"Why thank you," she said. "I'm glad you made it. Come inside. There's a few other people here."

Beyoncé led Artemis to a room dimly lit with candles. Colorful tapestries hung on the wall. Three people, who all looked to be a few years older than Artemis, sat on billowy cushions on the floor.

"Everyone, this is Artemis—one of the new guys in our group at work," said Beyoncé. "Artemis, this is the gang."

"Hey, everyone," said Artemis.

"That's Mei," said Beyoncé, pointing to the only other woman in the room. Mei was slender with short, thick, black hair that slightly covered her eyes. She quietly nodded to Artemis. "The big, redheaded guy is Bits," she said. "And last but not least is Lukas."

"You want some jerky?" asked Lukas.

"No thanks. Virtual jerky—not my thing," said Artemis.

"Suit yourself," said Lukas, munching on another piece.

"So what do you guys like to do?" asked Artemis.

"Whatever sort of degenerate things we come up with," said Lukas, flicking the long hair on top of his head back to reveal shaved sides and a small tattoo above his ear.

"Oh yeah? Like what?" asked Artemis.

Lukas and Bits smiled at each other. "Turn on 'belch-mode,'" said Bits.

"Turggn ogghff beuurf-murrde!" yelled Beyoncé, suddenly sounding like she had a serious digestive problem. The room filled with the smell of rotten eggs.

"He asked!" said Lukas, while Bits chuckled and Mei shook her head.

"That's something I never thought of doing," said Artemis.

"Bits loves playing with sounds," said Lukas. "He was born deaf as a white cat, but his haptic suit lets him hear in wormholes.

I have to give him most of the credit for belch mode."

"Thanks, man," said Bits, giving Lukas a high five.

"This is what I get for letting my friends be admins in my home world," said Beyoncé. "Fortunately, most of the time I'm impressed with their skills rather than disgusted."

"So, what are you all up to tonight?" asked Artemis.

"Nothing. We're bored," said Mei while sitting motionless on the cushion.

"We could go to my wormhole if you guys want to see it," said Artemis.

"But you just got here and you haven't even seen Poop Room," said Lukas.

"And he isn't going to!" yelled Beyoncé. "Why did I even bother making this great outfit if you guys are just going to gross out the guest?"

"Just a suggestion," said Lukas, while Bits laughed beside him.

"I've never had anyone visit my wormhole. It'd be cool to have some people over," said Artemis.

"You poor boy," said Lukas with a sly grin. "Never had anyone visit your wormhole. I can help you with that."

Artemis was uneasy around the new group of people he'd met, and he could feel a shell growing around him.

"I'm interested, Artemis. Are you guys coming or staying?" said Beyoncé.

"Sure, let's see what the kid has going on," said Bits.

"Can I have access to the navigation prompt?" asked Artemis.

"Here you go," said Beyoncé, handing the control over to Artemis.

Artemis put in the address to his wormhole and the group found themselves standing outside the biosphere.

"Mars. I could've guessed," said Mei.

"Why are my feet burning?" asked Bits.

"Yeah, mine are kinda hot too," said Lukas.

"I thought Mars was supposed to be cold. Jesus, my feet are on fire!" yelled Beyoncé.

Artemis thought for a second, then said, "Oh, I forgot the Level 15 burn programmed into the ground. I don't notice it anymore. I'll turn it off."

"How nice of you," yelled Lukas, hopping up and down.

"Turn it off, bro!" yelled Bits.

"Okay, it's off."

"Something is wrong with you," said Mei.

"Um, okay. Well, this is it. I've got a bunch of interesting things inside the biosphere, but let me take you into the main wormhole I'm working on," Artemis said, now feeling even more nervous about entertaining guests.

"Whoa, slow down. You can't just say you've got a bunch of interesting things inside and then skip right over them," said Bits.

"They are really interesting, but not nearly as interesting as where I'm taking you. If you guys ever come back, we can go inside the biosphere then," he said.

"Suit yourself," said Bits, picking up a rock and throwing it toward the mountains.

Artemis strolled over to the obelisk and touched it, bringing the group to the surface of Heidi. The last time he'd visited Heidi, he'd left time running at a rate of ten thousand years per hour. A dense forest had grown across the land. Because of all the changes, it took him a minute to orient himself while he explained to the group what he'd been simulating.

"So life here is based on methane?" asked Lukas.

"Yes—well, liquid methane," said Artemis.

"And what the hell is that giant glowing mountain thing?" said Bits, pointing at the harpstones, which had now caught everyone's attention.

"*That* is the first species to gain consciousness on Planet Heidi," said Artemis, smiling, full of pride at his work. "Actually, it's the second thing, but it evolved from the first thing."

"That's alive?" asked Beyoncé.

"It most certainly is," said Artemis. "It's doing something different than before, though. It wasn't changing colors like that the last time I was here, but that was about a quarter of a million years ago."

The group stood in awe.

"It's a little more sophisticated than the Poop Room, Luke," said Bits.

"Just a little," said Lukas. "I've got to upload this to Hologramville: hashtag-notthepooproom, hashtag-coolmountain, hashtag-skittles," he said.

"Skittles?" said Mei.

"Yeah, the rainbow of flavors. That things reminds me of a giant pile of glowy Skittles," said Lukas.

"Hmm. I guess so," said Mei.

"Hold on a second. Everyone be quiet for a minute," said Bits before yelling "Hel-lo!"

Everyone was quiet while trying to tune in to whatever it was Bits was picking up on.

"Did you see that?" Bits asked.

"See what?" asked Lukas.

"Hel-lo!" Bits yelled again.

"I saw it. It's flashing to the sound of our voices," said Artemis. "I'm Artemis. Nice to meet you," he yelled.

The mountain changed colors in sync with the pattern of Artemis' voice. After a brief pause, the mountain started flashing a new pattern of colors. It paused a few moments and then repeated the same flashes.

"Dude, the mountain is talking to us," said Bits. "You should record this, Artemis."

"Good idea," said Artemis, turning on the simulation capture. "We are your friends."

The mountain started flashing a new pattern. A series of four yellow flashes followed by three blue ones flashed across the harpstone's skin. Then the mountain turned red and stayed that color for a few moments before fading to a neutral color.

Immediately after that, Artemis found himself standing in the dark. It took him a moment to realize that he was no longer in the simulation. Princess Di had completely shut down.

What the hell is going on? he thought.

He received a message from Beyoncé.

What happened? We all got booted from your wormhole.

I don't know. My computer crashed.

Totally shut down. It's never happened

before.

Weird. I guess I'll see you at work tomorrow?

Yup. Thanks for hanging out.

My pleasure. I knew you'd be working on something really amazing. Thanks for sharing.

Thanks. I really liked your place, too,

and your friends.

Good night.

Artemis restarted Princess Di and waited until everything seemed to be working again. When he stepped out, Jef rubbed figure eights through his legs.

"You're right, little guy. Let's go out to the kitchen and have ourselves a snack."

CHAPTER NINE
Big Talkers

The following day, after morning stand-up, Artemis turned toward his workspace to see Deepak standing beside his desk. As Artemis approached, Deepak watched him closely.

"Good morning, Artemis," said Deepak. "Do you have a few minutes to get some coffee?"

"Right now?"

"Yes, if it's a good time."

"Let me check my email, see if anything is urgent, and then I can follow up with you."

"You don't need to do that. If anything was urgent, it would have come up in stand-up. Let's go."

Absent an adequate deflection, Artemis walked with Deepak upstairs to the Print-a-Bean in the BSP cafeteria. During the time the largest office printing company began acquiring huge amounts of market share in the coffee industry after the invention of printable coffee machines, they also began buying large shares of a huge retail coffee chain's stock as its price fell. Print-a-Bean was the end result.

"Order what you like. It's on me," said Deepak. "Treat yourself to some real beans if you like."

"That's okay. I don't mind getting my own," said Artemis.

"I insist," said Deepak, swiping his wearable across the scanner before Artemis could say anything more.

"Morning! Welcome to Print-a-Bean! My name is Tae, but my friends call me Kelly. We've been really busy this morning, so sorry if I was a little slow taking your order," said the robot to Artemis.

"It's okay. You weren't slow at all," said Artemis.

"I'd like to give you five percent off your order anyway, because you seem like a nice guy and that shirt is awesome!" she said. "So what can I get you?"

"Thanks. I'd like an Americano with the Costa Rican molecules," he said.

"Coming right up! And you, sir?" Tae asked Deepak.

"Decaf skim latte with Ethiopian arabica," said Deepak.

"Great selection. It'll be up in a jiffy. You gentleman have a great day," said Tae.

"Customer service is so much better now that we have help like her, don't you think?" asked Deepak.

"Well, I don't worry about getting regular when I order decaf, that's for certain."

"Excellent point, Artemis."

Artemis and Deepak sat down at one of the tables in the lounge. Deepak stirred his drink while Artemis sipped from his. Artemis tried to prepare himself mentally for the conversation with Deepak, steeling himself for whatever might come up.

"What do you think of BSP?" said Deepak, breaking the

silence with a simple question, absent any BSP air-punches.

"It's been great so far. I'm really glad to be here."

"Yes, we're innovating here in a way that will completely change the marketing landscape."

"I can totally see that."

"To do what we are doing here requires better-than-average people. Don't you agree?"

"Of course."

"What do you think it means to be better than average?" asked Deepak, still stirring his drink.

"Putting in extra effort. Giving each task your best effort," said Artemis.

"I'm sorry, but that answer strikes me as quite average. Most think they are better than average when in fact they are the definition of mediocrity—cookie-cutter people with cookie-cutter lives and cookie-cutter minds," said Deepak.

Artemis was overwhelmed by where the conversation was going. He wasn't ready for what felt like an assault and said, "If you're saying I'm just another average developer, that's fine, but I don't believe that."

"I wasn't saying that, but maybe you do feel that way, since you felt the need to defend yourself."

Overwhelmed by his emotions, Artemis wasn't able to articulate how he felt. He tried slowing his breath and relaxing his mind.

"Do you meditate?" asked Deepak. "It could help you."

"No. I don't really understand it."

"It's not a function of the intellect," explained Deepak. "I meditate as much as five hours a day sometimes. I have raised my consciousness to a level I never knew I could achieve. I can feel vibrations, energy, and even changes to the mood of rooms when I enter them. Look around at the tables. What do you see?"

"People enjoying their coffee. Talking with one another," said Artemis, searching for a way to escape this bizarre conversation with Deepak.

"Yes. They feel very light. I carried this lightness with me and have made it part of this place," said Deepak. "I have cleaned this room of negative energies and the people around me are benefitting from it."

"I see."

Deepak sat and gazed at Artemis for a few moments before continuing. "Why do you think you are here, Artemis?"

"You asked me here," said Artemis, squirming in his chair.

"I don't mean here for coffee, I mean in this life," said Deepak.

"I don't know. I haven't thought about it much."

"Like most," said Deepak with a look of equanimity. "I studied quantum physics and quantum computing at one of the best universities in India. I was surrounded by some of the most brilliant people in a country with almost two billion people. People used to say 'one in a million,' but now they have to say 'one in a billion.' When you are one in a billion, you have a responsibility. This responsibility isn't just to succeed by growing a large sum of wealth. Anyone can gather up a house full of gold and show it off to their friends and family—criminals do that. The responsibility is to parent the world."

"How's that?" asked Artemis, regretting asking it as soon as the question left his mouth.

"Parents have to make tough choices. Think about it like one of your computer programs."

"Like if I'm running out of spell bag slots and I see a clump of Fairy Ferns, which I need to make aid kits with, but I'm about to walk home from work and I know I'm going to find at least four or five spells I might be able to use, so I need to decide whether to use a bag slot on the Fairy Ferns or hold out?"

"I mean a program that you created."

"Oh, wow, I was way off."

"If you made a program that you really cared about, but it had bugs in it, what would you do?" said Deepak before finally taking a sip of his drink.

"I would debug it."

"And what if after debugging it you found more and more bugs?"

"I would try to fix them."

"And if you realized that there were too many bugs that couldn't be fixed and the program was never going to run the way you wanted it to, then what would you do?"

"I'd start over again."

"Yes," said Deepak with a serious look in his eyes. "What do you think of your old professor from college?"

"How do you know . . . I mean, do you mean Professor Lao?"

"Of course. We worked together."

"You did? He never mentioned it. I think he's a great man."

"Fascinating. Even with all the news stories about his methods, particularly those of his lab? I believe there was quite an uproar once about something he'd done."

"Yeah, there was, but people don't know anything about him. He was a great teacher."

"I'm sure. It's probably time to go back to work now."

"Yep. Good talking with you, Deepak," said Artemis, getting up as fast as he could.

"Oh, one other thing," said Deepak, stepping toward Artemis. "Apparently, there is a bug in the kernel of Gopher World. Did you know that when a certain cipher is sent to the holographic network adapter, the entire system will halt, leaving the user standing in total darkness?"

"No, I didn't know about that," said Artemis, feeling a tingle up his spine.

"Did you know your professor wrote that part of the kernel?" he said.

"No, I didn't know that either. I should get back to work," said Artemis. "Thanks for the coffee."

"You're welcome, Artemis. Don't be a stranger. Here is my

contact information," said Deepak, touching his wearable to Artemis' wrist.

"Got it," said Artemis before turning away from Deepak and walking through the lounge back to his workstation. *Bringing the machine to a grinding halt? Standing in the darkness? Did he know what happened to Princess Di last night? How? More importantly, was he trying to tell me it was the professor who brought her down?*

Back at his Mobipod, Artemis wrote Beyoncé.

Do you have a second?

What's up?

I just had an über-weird conversation with Deepak.

About what?

Not sure exactly. Hard to describe without sounding crazy myself—basically about how amazing he is and how he needs to parent the planet and delete crappy software.

Doesn't sound too crazy for Deepak.

Trust me, it was weird. But the craziest part came when I got up to leave. He said something that makes me wonder if my professor didn't have something to do with crashing Princess Di last night.

I think you're reading too much into it.

I know it seems far-fetched, but I'll tell you
more later. Will you be online tonight?

Look for me.

Big Talkers

Akechi Mitsuhide sent the servants from the kitchen into the dining hall
of Azuchi Castle where Oda Nobunaga entertained the shogun,
Tokugawa Ieyasu.

"Tonight the cook has prepared a special dish, made from fish I
selected this morning. You honor us so much, Tokugawa Ieyasu, that I
had the servants serve the meal on my family's ancestral plate ware,"
said Mitsuhide.

"Thank you, Mitsuhide. Please join us," said Ieyasu. "Your lord
and I were just discussing the Imperial Court."

"The Imperial Court—no, the Emperor himself—should fear the
Demon King, Oda Nobunaga," said Nobunaga, taking a deep drink
from his glass.

"Perhaps my lord has had too much to drink," said Mitsuhide,
stunned by his lord's words.

"Perhaps Akechi Mitsuhide would like to be the one sitting here,"
said Nobunaga.

"Of course not, Lord Oda," said Mitsuhide.

"But would the people call you Dairokuten Maou, Demon King
of the Six Heavens," said Nobunaga, standing up from his chair, "or
would they call you the Rotten Fishmonger of Jubei?"

As Oda Nobunaga finished speaking, he took the plate of fish from
in front of Mitsuhide and threw it out the castle window. Mitsuhide
wept inside at the sound of his family heirloom breaking on the bricks

below.

Lao's commentary

Being a big talker in the workplace will detract from one's accomplishments and stop people from associating with you. Big talkers are known for always thinking they know best and making sure everyone knows it. They criticize plans and ideas, seemingly never finding value in anything that doesn't come from them. If someone presents a solution to a problem, the big talker will give three reasons why it won't work. If someone else accomplishes something important, the big talker will say they have accomplished something greater.

Sadly, many big talkers haven't accomplished much. They excel not at creating but at tearing down. As a result of their insecurity, they believe that subtly attacking those with more influence will allow them to gain favor with enough people so that they may rise up. People who have contributed greatly and have been part of great successes understand that big talk doesn't accomplish anything, and so they avoid it.

In work environments, concerns over budgets, deadlines, and the decisions being made by the higher ranks breed talk among the workers trying to figure out their fate. This type of talk is normal and understandable. Also, sometimes when a team is trying to decide on a way to solve a problem and a debate emerges, one does have to speak from one's accomplishments and say, 'I solved this type of problem before and had great results with this method.' This may sound to some like big talk when in fact it's not.

One of the more embarrassing moments in my career came when I took part in disparaging a man who began coming to work late most days. His work grew sloppy and he asked out-of-the-ballpark questions in meetings. While getting coffee with a coworker, I felt the need to call him by his new nickname, Slothman. My coworker looked at me with anger and shared the fact that the man was her friend and was receiving chemotherapy for a brain tumor. The speech of the Coding Samurai is used to build up, enlighten, and accomplish team goals— not to tear down others and their ideas.

****

That evening, Beyoncé sent an invitation for Artemis to join her in her home world. Artemis walked the passageway to the red door and knocked. Beyoncé, dressed in another elaborate outfit, invited him in. Artemis immediately launched into the details of the conversation he'd had with Deepak at the cafeteria Print-a-Bean earlier in the day.

"He really said that he was responsible for the people in the Print-a-Bean being happy?" she asked.

"Yes, but as unnerving as it was to hear all of the kooky magic-meditation talk, the stuff he said about the bug that shuts down quantums weirded me out the most," said Artemis. "He said he worked with my professor, and that Professor Lao was the one who wrote the buggy code. It was like he was telling me that it was my professor who did something to my quantum last night."

"Why would Deepak know your machine shut down?"

"Maybe he meditated on it. Hell, I don't know!"

160

"Do you have the logs from your machine?"

"I haven't looked yet, but even if I do, I'm not sure there's anything I could do with them. Debugging quantum logs isn't the easiest thing in the world to do."

"No, but we both know someone who can. Get the logs while I call her."

"You're eager to help."

"What's that supposed to mean?" asked Beyoncé, crossing her arms.

"Just that I'm still new to this town and there's a lot I need to figure out."

"Just get the logs."

Artemis pulled up the console application for his quantum and started searching. He gathered up all of the system and access logs from the day before and sent them to Beyoncé. Artemis logged out of his console and saw Beyoncé in a chat session with Mei.

"I have a favor to ask you," said Beyoncé.

"Another favor, Bey? That's three this month already," said Mei.

"I didn't know you had a favor limit. Look, we really need your help. I'll talk with my aunt and see if she still has those shoes you said you liked when we were checking out her holographic feed," said Beyoncé.

"You're just going to ask your aunt for her shoes?" asked Mei.

"Yeah, she only wears them maybe two or three times, then they end up in her shoe room until my uncle makes her donate them to charity," said Beyoncé.

"Deal. What do you need me to do?" said Mei.

"We think someone might have done something last night to kick us out of the simulation. Artemis just sent me the logs. He thinks the attack happened through a bug in the kernel," said Beyoncé. "Can you find out what crashed his machine?"

"You're going to give me your aunt's shoes just for debugging a dump? This won't take long," said Mei before leaving the chat.

Beyoncé walked over to where Artemis was sitting and sat down next to him on the cushion. When she sat down, Artemis was able to smell her perfume, a sweet scent with hints of spice and musk. Her face was made up with bright purple lipstick; black mascara surrounded her eyes.

"I guess we have some time to kill while Mei looks into that," she said.

"Yeah, I guess so," he said, putting his hands under his thighs. He sat silently on the cushion staring at his feet.

"Aren't you going to say anything?" said Beyoncé, her eyebrows furrowed.

"Like what?" asked Artemis. "Umm, so do you have any pets?"

Beyoncé laughed. A chat request from Mei broke the uncomfortable moment.

"I'd say this was deliberate," said Mei without so much as a hello. "When a request with a particular header is sent, it will cause the machine to go down hard. It's so specific that it would happen with maybe one in a trillion requests. Whoever sent the request knew what it would do."

"You're brilliant, Mei," said Beyoncé.

"I'm looking forward to those shoes," she said before logging off.

"If it was your professor, why would he do it?" said Beyoncé.

"Maybe it was one of his lessons or something."

"What do you think he wants to teach you?"

"I don't know. But I'm going to try and find out."

"No, *we* are going to try and find out. LeBron, look up the goods on Deepak Gupta," said Beyoncé to her quantum.

"Damn, girl. Looking fine tonight. Oh, I see you got company. Another white boy? For real?" said LeBron.

"Just show me the results, LeBron."

"So here's what I found out." LeBron displayed the introductions of ten stories related to Deepak. They were all BSP press releases.

"This doesn't help," said Artemis. "Search for something more specific, like 'Deepak Gupta and Ambrosius Lao and military.'"

"That was going to be my next search. LeBron, search for what he just said."

"You got it, girl."

"Ahh, this looks better," she said. "LeBron, condense and summarize."

LeBron began reading. "Deepak was born in Calgary in 2003. His parents were both from India. His father was a politician but wanted his son to go into medicine, but Deepak really loved technology. This was from an interview he did in *Wired*. He was exceptionally talented at programming and attended MIT. That's when he started work on the kernel of Gopher World as part of a research project."

"What project?" asked Artemis.

"A DARPA project. They had been sponsoring a project for years to make robotic cheetahs. When the big breakthrough in quantum computing occurred, they sponsored research on an operating system to upgrade the cheetahs to run on quantum architectures," said LeBron.

"He left for college when he was sixteen. Quantum computing wasn't going to take off for three more years—it doesn't line up," said Artemis.

"Hold on, bro, and let me explain," said LeBron. "While he worked on the kernel of Gopher World, he also wrote more significant pieces of the operating system. Get this: he developed the code that binds neural sensors in the haptic suit to the operating system."

"Those are some of the most complex parts of the system," said Beyoncé.

"Before he got into technology, his dad wanted him to be a doctor, right? Deepak listened to his father's wishes for some time and already had a biology degree and two years of medical school when his father died. When that happened, he decided to give up medicine and follow his passion, quantum computing," LeBron said, keeping his voice low. "The cheetah robotics project was already almost three years into development. But the project still lacked one of the most significant pieces: the connection between the human brain and the operating system. With Deepak's medical training, he became a pivotal player in the project. He went to BSP after the private equity firm made Deepak's employment one of the terms of delivery of the next round of funding."

"So this guy is a super genius," said Artemis.

"Basically."

"And we're spying on him. Dumb, dumb, dumb," said Artemis ruefully. "What are we doing? We have to stop."

"Why?" asked Beyoncé. Artemis detected a bit of defiance in her tone.

"Because this guy is ridiculously smart. He's going to know we are up to something," said Artemis, putting his head in his hands and leaning against the table.

"We haven't done anything but casually search him. Maybe we're just huge fans. We know he has an interest in you. There's nothing weird about you looking up your mentor," explained Beyoncé. "We just need to be very, very careful now that we know the people we're up against."

"No. I'm done. We need to stop."

"No we don't. We need to keep going."

"This is too much for us. We're interns."

Beyoncé laughed at Artemis. "Hypocrite."

"Hypocrite?" he asked.

"I saw that book in your home world, *The Coding Samurai*—the one with the swords on it—and yet you're afraid of a little adventure."

"Maybe I'm a hypocrite, but you're reckless."

"It's not reckless! You might have grown up in the suburbs, but I grew up on the street. Ain't no egghead going to intimidate me," said Beyoncé, her nostrils flaring.

Artemis paused, then said, "No. This is too much for me right now. I have too much going on today and not enough energy to deal with something like this."

"What have you got going on that's more important than this?"

"I have a book I need to read," he said meekly.

"Egghead."

"And you didn't grow up on the streets."

"Maybe not *the* streets, but compared with you . . . anyway, you better stick close while we sort this out. By the way, I owe Mei a favor from doing you a favor, which means you owe me a favor," she said, crossing her arms and staring at him seriously.

"That seems fair. What do you want?" he asked, wondering

what he was getting himself into.

"Surprise me. And it better be good!"

Artemis left Beyoncé and warped back to his home world. He wanted to send Professor Lao a message to try to understand the situation more clearly, but he thought someone might be spying on him. He decided to log on to IA using his x86 and send the professor an email using PGP—the most secure messaging on IA. Artemis hadn't used PGP since one of his lessons with the professor in college, and he hoped he remembered how to use it correctly.

"Professor Lao, I met one of your old buddies, Deepak Gupta, today for coffee. He mentioned you used to work together. Thought I'd let you know. It was a little bit weird talking with him about you. I also wanted to see if I still had my PGP skills. If there's anything I should know, please write me back.— Artemis"

While still on his old computer, he made a new spreadsheet. In the first column he made a list of people and in the second column he assigned a color based upon how much he believed they could be trusted. Green meant trust, yellow expressed neutrality, and red signified distrust. A darker color indicated a stronger sentiment. He began listing people. Mom and Dad— dark green. Tilly—light green. Beyoncé—dark yellow. Deepak and Professor Lao—dark red.

CHAPTER TEN
Watch Commanders

A loud crack of thunder woke Artemis. The wind roared through the street below like a freight train. As usual, Artemis was running late; today he'd have to drive to avoid the typhoon-like weather outside.

After getting ready and petting Jef good-bye, Artemis took the elevator to the lobby of the building and sent a command for a car to come and pick him up. Once it arrived at the lobby entrance, he dashed to the car and jumped in.

During the short commute, each gust of wind pressed against the car so forcefully that he could feel it struggling to stay in a straight line. He turned on the news for the remainder of the five-minute commute to BSP.

"Tensions are erupting in the Middle East as Israel says a string of terrorist attacks were sponsored by neighboring states . . . Even after seven Global Climate Change Accords, the previous six months have broken all-time global heat records, as many countries still don't comply with the few remaining agreements . . . US government debt has hit an all-time high; the average citizen is now responsible for more than one million dollars in federal debt."

Artemis' car dropped him off at the building entrance. He

sprinted to the awning and walked inside. On his way to his desk, Brad stopped him.

"Hey, Artemis. I need to talk with you about something," he said.

"Sure. What's up?" *Do you have another pointless task for me to work on?*

"I'm leaving for a few days with some of the other leadership for an investor meeting. I have a meeting here this morning, and I'd like you to take notes for me. Can you handle it?"

"Sure," said Artemis, smiling at Brad. *That would be a yes.*

"John is in charge while Deepak and I are away. If you need anything, go to him or Brent."

"Got it. Have a great trip."

Artemis walked over to his workspace and logged in. As soon as he was online, Beyoncé sent him a message.

You're in late today.

Keeping close tabs on me? Power went

out.

You don't have an alarm on your wearable?

I don't wear it when I sleep. I don't like

things touching my skin at night.

So you sleep naked?

Ha ha

Did you hear? Brad and Deepak are going away for an investor meeting. This is good for us.

Meet me for coffee?

OMW

Artemis met Beyoncé in the lounge and sat at a table near the window to watch the storm. The wind buffeted the windows, shook the glass, and drove them to sit one table farther away.

"This is perfect. They're both going to be gone. We need to do a little snooping around and see what we can find out about what is going on," whispered Beyoncé.

"I don't know about that. I don't want to get in trouble. Brad's finally starting to trust me. He just asked me to take notes for him in one of his meetings," he said.

"Oh, we wouldn't want you to lose your note-taking privileges," said Beyoncé sternly. "Listen, we aren't going to get in trouble. We just have to be careful."

"Bravery isn't one of my strong suits," Artemis said. "I'll tell you what, see what you can find out and keep me informed."

"So you'd just have me do your dirty work? Grow a spine, Artemis," she said.

"Touché, but I'm viewing it strategically. Deepak won't suspect you like he would me. He obviously knows I worked with Professor Lao. I'll cover for you if anyone starts asking questions."

"Won't suspect me? Have you noticed anything about me that might lead someone to seeing me as suspicious?"

"No, like what?" asked a confused Artemis.

"Like I'm black?"

Artemis looked at Beyoncé, still puzzled.

"That favor you owe me keeps getting bigger," she said.

"Let's check back at lunch," said Artemis before getting up and making his way back toward the meeting room.

As Artemis walked by the interns' area, Wei Wei sat up in his Mobipod and looked around. Artemis heard a voice from behind him.

"Is something wrong, Wei Wei?" asked John.

"I'm writing a new algorithm, and while I've coded many performance gains, I've discovered an entirely new problem. Brad made you his delegate for issues that arise, so should I tell you about it?" said Wei Wei.

"What's the problem, Wei Wei?" asked John, who was now standing beside Artemis outside of Wei Wei's pod.

"I asked the business analysts for clarification, but they merely interrogated me for the information that I require from them. Clearly this exchange wasn't helpful," he said.

"What are you trying to find out?" asked John.

"When Groundswell is installed in a video game, advertisers are going to manage their products using the admin tool. Each product is lexically scoped to a category, like 'shoes.' As long as the VR world contains a shoe somewhere in the environment, the advertiser can display the product."

"I understand all that, Wei Wei. What's the question?"

"The advertiser gives the user incentives to try their product. Let's say one hundred credits. In this scenario, the user stops the simulation to try on shoes. They try on shoes and receive one hundred credits. Now, back in the simulation, if the person succumbs to death in the game and returns to the same coordinates, they can try on shoes again and receive one hundred more credits. I wrote a script that repeats this process over and over again. I have three billion credits. I can acquire a new car, but for some reason, I really want to buy ladies underwear," Wei Wei said. "I can't believe I just said that."

"Did you fall off the wagon or something, Wei Wei? For now, just fix the bug so that users only get credit once for the shoes. We can get more feedback the next time we do a demo," said John.

"Sounds delightful," said Wei Wei, going back into the Mobipod.

"Artemis, shouldn't you be working on something?" said John.

"I'm just on my way to a meeting that Brad asked me to attend and take notes for him," said Artemis.

"He didn't tell me anything about that," said John.

"He stopped me on my way in. I told him I would."

"Go back to your pod and keep working on your tasks."

"I'm pretty certain—" began Artemis.

"You're not to go to that meeting."

"All right," said Artemis, shaking his head and going back

to his pod. He then sent Beyoncé a message.

> Wow, John used to be so quiet and basically invisible. He just jumped all over me when I said I needed to go to a meeting Brad asked me to attend.
>
> *Tony said John was at his pod for fifteen minutes earlier just watching over his shoulder while he worked.*
>
> I can't believe I'm writing this, but I'm actually dreading Deepak being gone if this is who we're stuck with.

While following John's directive, Artemis read from *The Coding Samurai.*

Watch Commanders

"What's this?" asked Mitsuhide, bursting through the door of Oda Nobunaga's council chamber to see Nobunaga's page standing beside him.

"The note in your hands tells you what it is," said Nobunaga. His page, Mori Ranmaru, smiled widely.

"I'm no longer Watch Commander? Then who?" asked Mitsuhide.

"Mori Ranmaru," said Nobunaga, nodding toward his page.

"Your *wakashu*? He's still a boy," said Mitsuhide, dropping the paper in his hands.

"Not any longer. He can seek his own *wakashu* now. If only you'd had a son, perhaps he could have learned from Mori Ranmaru's sword. He learned much from me," said Nobunaga.

"The men will not follow him," said Mitsuhide. "He's not qualified."

"They will follow him because you will make certain they do," said Oda Nobunaga. "Now tell me the name of your watch commander."

Mitsuhide gritted his teeth and looked coldly at Mori Ranmaru. He turned his gaze toward Oda Nobunaga, softened his eyes, bowed, and said, "Mori Ranmaru."

Lao's commentary

The Coding Samurai listens to those around him, regardless of either person's status. Listening is one of the most important skills of leadership and should be practiced from the start of one's career. Only by listening to as many people as possible can you make the most accurate assessments.

Leaders who take on a mindset of always being right, who stop thinking and only dictate commands to those under them, will alienate themselves from those they are responsible for. When they aren't present they will be mocked and ridiculed and find they are no longer effective. They become dimwitted as they no longer believe that they need to research, analyze, and communicate. They believe in the divine right of their position and so foolishly turn off their brains. Arrogant and bullying behavior isn't leading, it's abusing power.

The Coding Samurai in a leadership role has a responsibility to manage the mood of the team. If the team needs encouragement, it should be given. If the team needs to be pressed, the leader must press them. If the team needs incentives, the leader should be creative in getting them to achieve their goals.

Leaders must also share responsibilities and delegate power. When team members are empowered, they take ownership and think more. In these scenarios, the leader trusts their team members and supports them, helping them with resources and political issues. This tactic of sharing power and responsibility will lead to the group being more effective and much stronger than a group who only takes orders.

I wasn't a born leader, but once I became a professor, I realized that there were rooms full of youth looking to me for guidance. I had to practice patience, compassion, and humility. I had a student who always seemed distracted and wore a stupid smile. Initially, I wrote this student off as a dimwit. It wasn't until I had this student again for a senior project that his genius became apparent to me—when his work had already been mentioned by a Nobel Laureate. Another professor had already gleaned the potential in this student and had taken him under his wing. From this I learned to restrain myself from looking down on others and to treat people with equanimity.

****

Artemis felt a tap on his shoulder. It was John.

"Enjoying your book?" said John, not waiting for a response. "I checked with Brad and he wants you to go to a meeting for him and take notes. He said you have the information. You should get going. You're late."

Artemis stood up and walked past John, all the while looking at him out of the corner of his eye. He made it to the meeting already in progress.

"Sorry I'm late," he said.

"You must be Artemis. I'm Sandy. Please take a seat," said the stocky woman with short hair at the head of the table.

"I'm just here to listen," he said.

"We're going over some new requirements and figuring out which teams are responsible for making changes," she said. "Mateo, you were saying that your team will need to make some I'll-go-get-'em changes."

"Excuse me. What kind of changes?" asked Mateo, a Hispanic man in his early thirties.

"I'll-go-get-'em changes. That's what you said, right?" asked Sandy.

"Sandy, we need to make some *algorithm* changes. We don't have anything that can handle those types of requests. We'll need to add them," said Mateo.

"So when can you have that ready?" asked Sandy.

"We don't have all the requirements, so I'm not really sure," said Mateo.

"Best guess based upon what you know: Is this a one-month thing, a two-day thing? Ballpark," she asked.

"Well, I want to make it clear that this is just a SWAG and not going on anything but the extremely vague requirements we have," said Mateo. "I'm not even certain I can give a ballpark figure, but I'd say we are looking at about three days' development. That is a very, very rough, practically useless estimate, though."

Artemis leaned over and whispered to the guy with a mustache sitting next to him, "What's a SWAG?"

"Stupid Wild-Ass Guess," whispered the guy in his ear.

Artemis was taken aback. He smiled at him and whispered, "Thanks."

"So Mateo's team will have their stuff ready in three days. Katie, once you have Mateo's changes, you're ready to go, right?" said Sandy as Mateo dropped his head and shook it slowly back and forth in utter disbelief.

"We'll still need to test it and have Mateo's team make any other changes that come out of that, but yes, we are basically ready," said Katie.

"Brady, tell your people to start reaching out to the advertisers and schedule a demo four days from now," said Sandy.

"Hold on, Sandy. We don't have all the requirements," said Mateo, clinching the edge of the table. "What we have are some very vague ideas from the business on what they want. We need real requirements."

"Just get started with what you have. I'll have someone from product management meet with you later today and answer more of your questions," she said. "That's it for now, everyone. Thanks."

It was hard for Artemis to believe that this was a typical

corporate meeting. *Surely there aren't very many meetings like this one,* he thought.

He wanted to recharge, so he walked to the Refresh Room. Four pods lined the room with a light above each one indicating whether it was occupied. He sat in the only available pod and turned it on, then strapped his forearms into the machine so it could perform cryotherapy. A chill came over him as the machine induced his body's natural response to low temperatures. Soft music played while his capillaries opened, allowing rich, oxygenated blood to course through him. When the timer bonged, the machine gently warmed him to a slightly more comfortable temperature. He felt much better.

As Artemis left the Refresh Room, his lenses flashed red again. Another curious message scrolled in front of his face.

"Pretty Good Day for Privacy," it read.

Pretty good day for privacy. Pretty good privacy. Pretty good privacy! PGP!

At his pod, Artemis remoted in to his computer at home. He opened up his PGP application and saw a new message in his inbox.

"Artemis, I need to tell you something that you might not be happy with. Before I was at the university, Deepak and I indeed worked together on a project. We were both researchers and were brought together to run some experiments. I had some concerns about him at the time, but many scientists are a bit odd and I didn't think much of it. I mean, look at me. I need you to try to

178

find more of the code in Groundswell that is similar to what you've sent me. I've attached some search patterns that may help you find those pieces of code. Finally, have you finished reading the book *Physics at the Event Horizon: Quantum Computing and the Holographic Universe*?—Professor Lao"

Holy shit monkeys! What in the hell?

"Professor, why didn't you tell me that you worked with Deepak? You've been sending me other messages through my lenses? You need to tell me what's going on. Should I be concerned?—Artemis"

"Yes," read an immediate response from Professor Lao.

Artemis panicked and ran to the roof patio. Beyoncé was waiting outside the entrance of the cafeteria.

"How's it going?" she said.

"Terrible," he said.

"What happened?" she asked as the two made their way into the line.

"You aren't going to believe what just happened," said Artemis, making his way over to the print-your-own-pasta bar.

"Same here. But if you have stuff to share, keep it to yourself. Too many people," she said quietly, nodding her head around. "Tell me about the meeting."

"Do I look like I'm about to have a heart attack? Because I feel like I'm about to have a heart attack."

"Calm down, Artemis. People are looking at you. Now isn't the time."

"Okay. I'll pretend my life isn't crazy for a minute. I don't know if people aren't listening, or they don't understand each other, or people are just incompetent, but the meeting just went in circles," he said, pushing the buttons on the machine to make an Alfredo sauce lasagna. "The meeting could have lasted three minutes, but there was one person who couldn't understand what everyone else grasped, but she was actually the one running it. She just ignored what everyone was saying and dictated how things would happen."

"And this is what Brad deals with most of the day?" asked Beyoncé while making her selections.

"I assume so, yes."

"So tell me about your revelations," said Beyoncé, lowering her voice as they sat down in a quiet corner of the patio.

"It's true. My professor at school worked with Deepak on some project. He admitted it," said Artemis. "I asked him if I needed to worry and he said yes."

"I don't know what to say," she said, crossing her arms. "You're in a tight spot, ain't ya?"

"Thanks for the comment, but I'm aware of the situation," said Artemis.

"I don't think you are. Can you trust him?"

"No. I mean, I really want to, but I don't really know. But he gave me some search patterns to try and find more of the weird code," said Artemis.

"That doesn't mean anything. What if he gave you search

patterns to look in the wrong place? Keep that guy at arm's length," she said.

"So what did you find out?" asked Artemis.

"You know the room that's locked, but there are always people in there with white lab coats?" she said.

"Where they do the A/B testing?"

"That one. Well, I got in there and found some things."

"How'd you get in there?"

"Let me just tell you what I found."

"Okay."

"I found these files with a bunch of interns listed in them. Except the files don't use anyone's name. They just call them 'Intern Ten, Intern Twenty-Six.' That's some weird shit."

"Yes, that's weird."

"But then I read some more, and it started talking about how they were monitoring these interns and watching for certain things."

"Like what?"

"Like what kind of foods they were eating. What kind of clothes they wore."

"So marketing stuff? Makes sense, it's a marketing company."

"No, Artemis, this was some real fucked-up kinda thing. It said things like, 'After fifteen treatments, Intern Nine stopped eating pizza altogether.'"

"No one stops eating pizza altogether."

"I know. And then it started saying things like, 'After one hundred treatments, Intern Eight was sent to work with the offshore team, Intern Nineteen was sent to work with the offshore team, Intern Twelve was sent to work with the offshore team.'"

"Why are they sending the interns to work with the offshore team?"

"I don't know, but they've sent a whole lot of interns—interns who've lost the taste for pizza—to go and work where they eat a whole lot of curry."

"This is insane, Bey," said Artemis.

"Keep your voice down!" said Beyoncé. "It's not all I found."

"Like this isn't enough! This is insane! What else could you have found?"

"In the report about the interns who stopped eating pizza, it said, 'Once Intern Twenty-Six played Beastville for two months, his pain tolerance increased to Level 24.'"

"Beastville," said Artemis. "I'm beta testing that game!"

"I know," said Beyoncé, almost starting to cry. "You're Intern Twenty-Six."

CHAPTER ELEVEN
Education

"What do you mean, I'm Intern Twenty-Six?" asked Artemis.

"Intern Twenty-Six from Minnesota. It's you," she said.

"So Beastville, it's not a game, it's . . ."

"A BSP experiment."

Artemis ripped out his FourthForce lenses.

"I'm sorry, Artemis. There was no good way to tell you."

"Maybe you were looking at it wrong."

"It was your photo in the file."

"What else did you find?"

"Not a lot of details. By the time I found the dossier on you, I heard some people coming."

"But there were other files."

"Twenty-Six, Artemis. Intern Twenty-Six. Yeah, there were a lot more files."

"Do you know who told me about the game?"

"Your professor."

"He said he thought I would like it. And he was right. I'm addicted to it. It also explains why he picked me to work on his project when there were so many better students. I'm not someone with potential. I'm just a suitable test subject."

Artemis stood up from the table, ran over to the composting

container, and vomited. Employees at the surrounding tables stared at Artemis as he retched into the garbage. Beyoncé made her way over to Artemis and put her hand on his back.

"Don't ya'll have something better to do?" she shouted at a nearby table of people staring at Artemis.

****

After abruptly leaving work, Artemis tossed a holographic cat toy to Jef, who arched his back and then pounced at the toy before scurrying across the floor. With Jef occupied, Artemis opened up the printed copy of *Physics at the Event Horizon: Quantum Computing and the Holographic Universe* he just had delivered and started to read.

The first chapter revisited the math of the holographic universe. Physicists had discovered that during certain events, fundamental information at the core of the earth's universe acted in unusual ways. During the error-checking process in quantum computers, scientists could coerce quantum particles to attest they were of one type, when in fact they were of another type. Essentially, they could get the particles to lie about their actual values. Initially, scientists considered this to be of no real consequence, simply a quantum particle parlor trick they found clever.

However, in chapter four, Artemis discovered something that absolutely stunned him. After researchers and engineers developed the peripherals and haptics that would allow a human to tightly couple to a quantum computer, they tested their gear on animals. Using haptic suits designed for mice, scientists were able to create a pipeline between the mice's neurological systems and the quantum computer. With this setup, the mice were able to navigate virtual worlds with thought alone. If the quantum computer sent a negative message, the mice would think about trying to go in a different direction.

One researcher's mouse-maze experiment used the quantum particle parlor trick to coerce false memories. When a mouse found a piece of cheese in the maze, it received a reward in the form of a positive memory sent to its neurological system. By altering the information during the error-checking process, however, the next time the mouse navigated the maze, it recalled the memory negatively and would run the other way.

Other researchers pointed out that in mice it was quite simple to manipulate the way they recalled experiences. In more complex beings it might prove more difficult. However, the researchers imagined some dreadful scenarios. For example, someone who enjoyed sea fishing might go into a virtual world and board a fishing boat that would sail far out into the ocean. While onboard he might engage in rewarding battles over the aquatic beasts. However, the programmer of this world could taint the code using the newly discovered method so that whenever the person left the virtual world and recalled his experience, he would have an intense fear of fish, sailing, or even the ocean itself. The researchers described how if this programming were done in an elaborate, subtle way, the participant might even form entirely new outlooks on life. While the research was never able to confirm these theories, it emphasized the importance of more research in the area. The researchers' names were Deepak Gupta and Ambrosius Lao.

Artemis ran to his old computer to email the professor.

"Professor, I just finished chapter four. Why did you tell me about the book? Why are you sending me messages? Tell me the truth. I know about the interns."

Why did I do that? Should I go to the police? What the hell is going on? I need to figure this out. Let's go back to the beginning. I first started using quantum computers with Professor Lao. That was just about one year ago. Other than Princess Di, the only other quantum I've been in is my work machine at BSP. Did Deepak tamper with my memories using either one of those? Since Deepak creeps me the hell out and I want nothing to do with him, I think I can assume he hasn't messed with my head. Otherwise, I'd actually want to be his little buddy. Maybe. Is Deepak a bad guy too, or is he really trying to help me?

He wanted to talk things through with someone, but who could he trust? Anyone from work could be affected by Groundswell, including Beyoncé. Right now there was one person he thought most likely not to have had their mind polluted by Deepak or Professor Lao.

Tilly, are you free?

I'm chatting with a friend.

Look I really need to talk with you about something. Can you meet me?

How important? We aren't supposed to be talking and it's getting late.

SUPER IMPORTANT.

All right. Where do you want to meet?

How about the park where we did the bird walk.

A city park after dark . . . that's kind of creepy. How about the diner in your building? But you can't mention it to anyone where you work.

Okay, I'm going down there now.

I'll be there soon.

Artemis took the elevator down to the lobby of his building and walked to Uptown Diner next door. A favorite hangout of young urban professionals, it was packed.

"Wherever you're comfortable, sugar," said the woman behind the counter. She was in her thirties, with dirty blonde hair pulled up under a bandana. She peered over her black, horn-rimmed glasses and said, "There's a booth open in back. I'll be with you in a minute."

Artemis walked past the gumball machine to the booth in the corner that looked out onto Lovelace Street. He scanned the room robotically as if in a dream. He gripped the edge of the table with his hand, trying to convince himself that the hard surface was real. He read the cardboard insert of inspiring sayings on the table to try and settle his mind.

"Do you like those?" said the waitress, standing beside the booth.

"I like one of them," said Artemis. "Some of them don't make much sense to me."

"Which one do you like?" she asked.

"'A positive attitude may not solve all your problems, but it will annoy enough people to make it worth the effort,'" said Artemis, reading the card.

"That's my favorite one, too," she said. "So what would you like?"

"How about decaf coffee?" he said.

"Coming right up," she said. The bell rang above the entrance door. The waitress turned and said, "I'll be right with you."

"I'm actually with him," said Tilly, walking toward the booth.

"Can I get you something while I'm here?" the waitress asked.

"Just water, please," said Tilly.

The waitress left the two alone at the booth. Tilly was

wearing sweatpants and a T-shirt, and her hair was pulled back in a ponytail. She looked concerned.

"Artemis, what's the matter? You sounded really freaked out," she said.

"I am freaked out," he said.

"Did something else happen at work?" she asked.

"Yes, but it's not really simple to explain," he said. "I feel like what's happening can't be real."

"Slow down. Start from the beginning," said Tilly.

"How much do you use quantum computers?" he asked, while scanning the room for anyone watching.

"I don't," she said. "My company is cheap as hell and I'm not into the whole augmented reality thing."

"Great," said Artemis, cutting her off.

"Why's it great?" asked Tilly.

"Try to hear me out," he said. "Wait a second. You had on my lenses on Volunteer Marathon Day."

"For like two minutes. I came out in the middle of the night to talk with you. Now spill it," she said, more irritated than Artemis had ever seen her.

"BSP is doing experiments on people. They've put mind-altering code into the software. They've been experimenting on me. My college professor, who I thought was my mentor, is actually the one who set me up and sent me here. I think I'm going crazy. I don't know if anything about my life is real. I'm so scared that before I came down here I even thought about jumping off the roof of my apartment building."

Tilly studied his face for a moment, then said, "As soon as you and I started becoming friends, my boss told me that I needed to cut off contact with you. That doesn't happen in normal situations."

"So you believe me?"

"I'm not calling the mental health crisis line right now, but tell me more."

"At college, my professor singled me out—asked me to be his assistant. I believed he was mentoring me, but he was really just part of whatever is going on with BSP. They gave me this game to play that used quantum physics to make me learn to love pain. It's so sick—I actually started craving pain and trying to tolerate more and more of it. They've been doing experiments on some of the interns—including me."

"That is sick. But you chose to come to BSP, didn't you?" Tilly asked.

"I don't know. Did I? I used the quantum computer that my professor supposedly gave me as a gift to do research on BSP when I was back home. Who knows how that messed with my head? Here's what I don't get. My professor asked me to read a book, a very difficult book on quantum computing, the holographic universe—" he said.

"The stuff scientists say means that we aren't really real, that we are just like information in a big computer?" Tilly interjected.

"Basically."

"I don't believe any of that stuff."

"Don't believe it, but it's the very math and science in that book that gave us quantum computing and the technology that we're all using today," said Artemis, staring at her, tapping his foot and shaking the table.

"Whatever. Just tell me why you're confused."

"The book explained how during development of the haptic suits for these computers, it was Professor Lao and a guy, Deepak, from work, who found a way to hack the information relayed to the wearer."

"And what's that mean?" Tilly asked.

"It means you could brainwash people. Imagine using a quantum computer to watch a movie that had a scene about eating donuts. The donuts smell good and they look good," said Artemis. "But by hacking the information, even though your brain registers the experience positively, when you recall the memory, it lies about what you saw. The next time you see a donut, you might vomit."

"That's crazy," she said.

"Yes, and Deepak, the other researcher who was studying hacking memories, is the guy I work with at BSP. He bought me coffee one day and told me how it was my professor who probably did something to my computer."

"This is too much!"

"Jesus Christ, Tilly, if it's all too much for you, don't you think it's too much for me, too?" said Artemis. "That's why I needed to talk to someone who doesn't work for BSP or know the professor. I know this sounds nuts, but I don't know who else to talk with right now. Please, believe me. It feels like a dream that I'm not waking up from."

"It's hard for me to believe you. But I don't think you're crazy," said Tilly. "It's just hard for me to understand. I haven't studied any of these things," she said.

"The project at BSP, Groundswell, will be launched soon and millions of people—eventually billions—will be using it," said Artemis.

"How soon?" she asked.

"Next week. The launch is being timed with a huge price cut in a consumer-grade quantum computer. The idea is to sell these quantum computers with Groundswell pre-installed and create a marketing revolution. And just like the ones they used to experiment on me, you only have to wear the lenses to have the software twist up your mind."

"Are you sure?"

"I found some code that I think is going to do exactly that. But the only person I know who can decipher it is my professor. But I feel paranoid about everything and everyone. I don't feel calm enough to think clearly," he said.

Artemis' wearable buzzed. It was Beyoncé.

It's getting late. You coming online?

Not likely. We'll talk in person

tomorrow after stand-up.

Okay. You sure you don't just want to dig to my wormhole and tell me now?

Not at home.

Where are you?

Having coffee with a friend.

Okay. Talk tomorrow.

"Sorry. It was my friend from work, at least the person I think is my friend," said Artemis.

"What's his name?" asked Tilly.

"She's a her. Beyoncé."

"Like the pop diva?"

"Uh-huh. How can I tell if I can trust her?"

"Let me think," Tilly said, redoing her ponytail. "Why don't you arrange for the three of us to meet somewhere? It's my job to size people up, and I'm pretty good at it. We'll all have a chat. How's that sound?"

"Let's do it," said Artemis, momentarily excited before becoming wary again. "Can you be my friend again?"

"Artemis. I haven't stopped being your friend," she said, looking directly at him.

"I need you to know that our friendship is all I'm going on right now. So thank you," he said, reaching out to put his hand on hers. "Don't contact me at work. Here's a private key to send messages to my wearable."

"I've never sent anything with a private key."

"It's easy," said Artemis, signaling for the waitress to come over. "If you get a message from me, just enter that code and you'll be able to read it," he said as the waitress arrived at their table.

"How are you two doing?" she asked.

"We're ready for the bill," said Artemis.

"It's $8.96 NAD. Using your wearable?" she asked.

"Yes," said Artemis, holding out his wrist to swipe it.

"You're all set. Have a good night," she said.

"You too," said Artemis before the waitress walked back to the counter. "Moments like these always seem to take place in diners," Artemis said to Tilly.

"According to your hypothesis, it must be something in the holographic universe's programming," she said.

"But something doesn't quite line up."

"What's that?"

"The pink neon sign isn't flickering like it would be if we were characters in a story."

"Hmm. I guess you're right."

****

"Di, read *The Coding Samurai*," said Artemis, feeling safe enough without wearing the lenses or the haptic suit to have Di read to him. He lay on his bed to try and fight off his thoughts long enough to sleep.

Education

"What are you reading, Father?" asked Tama upon entering the tearoom to find her father with a book in his hands.

"The history of Japan," he said.

"Why are you reading it?" she asked, twirling in her dress.

"A samurai should be more than a coarse brigand," said Mitsuhide, setting down the book. "During times of peace, a samurai must increase his knowledge and understanding of the world."

"So now is a time of peace?" asked Tama.

"Yes, but I fear the days remaining are few. If I learned anything from this book, it's that war is always just around the corner."

Lao's commentary

The Coding Samurai walks a path of continuing education. After you attain a degree or certificate, the journey has just begun. The Way of the Computer Warrior *is to continue educating yourself through research, projects, and reading outside of work.*

Continuing education sometimes consists of skimming or reading books and blogs. Blogs are largely opinionated, typically concentrate on smaller problems, and don't require the editorial vetting of comprehensive works. Books, unfortunately, almost become irrelevant as quickly as they are published in the fast-paced world of technology. While some blogs and books are rich in useful knowledge, working projects are a much richer source of education for the Coding Samurai.

Grow a foundation of general knowledge in whatever area you've chosen to work. Continue to practice the basics of programming and revisit early concepts occasionally. Many young Coding Samurai want to go straight to high-level frameworks before mastering the languages those frameworks are written in. This is like spending time practicing a spin kick without knowing how to throw a punch.

The Coding Samurai can further stand out from the pack not just by keeping up with the trends of technology, which many times are more fickle than trends in pop music and fashion, but by specializing in one or two areas that few pay attention to. This might mean learning the ins and outs of a particular encryption specification, or studying software accessibility guidelines. To relate this to the samurai: Think of continuing education as training in weapons. Samurai practice the basics of sword work forever. However, once a solid foundation with the sword has been acquired, the samurai can learn other less common weapons and tactics, such as the crossbow and attacking from a horse.

Nevertheless, this type of specialized training should never be pursued at the expense of fundamentals. I once had an interview with an engineering company that used a specialized programming framework. I studied that API framework for weeks because I really wanted the job. When I interviewed, they hardly asked me anything about it but asked me a lot of questions about fundamentals. I hadn't reviewed the basics for a while and couldn't articulate solid answers. I didn't get the job.

CHAPTER TWELVE
Military Science

When Artemis woke up the next morning, he felt too afraid to go to work. Still in his pajamas, he sat down on the floor beside his bed to gather his thoughts. *I wonder what Deepak would be doing in my situation—probably hanging upside down in some crisp white linen outfit and trying to levitate cutlery or something.* He thought about his parents back in Minnesota, took the plastic ball from his nightstand, and turned it on. Beams of light projected the illusion of his miniaturized parents holding each other in his living room.

What I wouldn't do to just be back home having one of Mom's breakfasts.

Artemis stood up to get ready for work. After showering, he grabbed his sling pack from the closet. Tucked in the corner were his old combat boots that he hadn't worn since high school. He put the boots on and left for work.

At BSP, a determined Artemis passed Brent and pumped his fist in the air as he chanted, "BSP!"

"BSP, young man," said Brent, also punching the air and smiling at Artemis' enthusiasm.

Artemis made his way to the morning stand-up meeting. Everyone but Brad and Deepak, who were still away, gathered in the task board area where maintenance workers had installed new panels. He arrived in the middle of a heated argument between John and Suzi, another DOT on the team.

"But look, if we upgrade the containers, we can also upgrade the product display viewport to Mimi 3.7," said John.

"Mimi 3.7?" asked Suzi.

"Yes. It's a significant upgrade," said John.

"What's wrong with 3.6?" asked Suzi.

"It doesn't have beveled framing, ultra-zoom, and a bunch of other things that are in 3.7," said John.

"And why do we need all of that now?" she asked.

"We don't have time to debate this all day. The guys on *Qubits'* forum are raving about it. *Daily Brogrammer* says it's awesome," said John.

"Ever hear of hype, John?" she said.

"I'm in charge while Brad and Deepak are away. I'm putting a task on the board to upgrade it. I'll do it myself," he said.

"I've seen this type of situation many times; I don't feel we've done our due diligence," said Suzi.

"Fair enough. Let's move on," said John, brushing off Suzi's comment.

Without Brad in stand-up to keep everyone focused, what was supposed to be a brief meeting drifted into the weeds. Artemis sat and listened as people gave long explanations about how they were solving particular problems. While three people engaged in a discussion around a new API end point, Artemis noticed Beyoncé staring at him. She looked concerned. When stand-up ended, she was waiting for him outside the meeting room.

"Sorry I missed you last night," she said.

"Me too. Things are crazy right now," he said.

"Deepak and Brad are going to be back soon. We need a plan for the day," she said.

Artemis wanted to pretend that it would just be a normal workday, but he told himself to let go of that wish. He'd have to keep pushing on toward the truth, even as the people he'd brought closer to him had unknown agendas of their own.

"I have a plan," said Artemis. "One of us will try and find anything that might point toward what exactly Groundswell is doing. The other one will try to access Deepak's calendar so we can see who he meets with, what the meetings are about, or anything that might give us a clue as to what's really going on."

"I like it. You look at the code and I'll get Deepak's calendar," said Beyoncé.

"I'm thinking the other way around," said Artemis, wanting to avoid getting inside any of the quantums today.

"I did all the digging yesterday. It's your turn."

"I have a migraine," said Artemis. "I don't want to have those damned lenses in my eyes."

"Fine, I'll do it."

"Brent would have access to everyone's calendar, wouldn't he?" asked Artemis.

"I'm fairly certain."

"Okay, I'll talk with Brent. What about the code?"

"There's only three million lines. Finding exactly what we're searching for shouldn't be a problem," said Beyoncé sarcastically.

"Ninety percent of the code is auto-generated. Ignore that stuff. That should narrow it down quite a bit," said Artemis.

"When do we regroup?"

"I'll send you a message this afternoon."

"Be careful."

"You, too."

Artemis thought about his spreadsheet of trust. He began to wonder if he should color the cell for Beyoncé light green, but he decided to keep it yellow.

Artemis walked out to the lobby where Brent sat. He was chewing on something while fixated on his computer screen.

"Hi, Brent. Sorry to interrupt."

Brent jumped a bit in his chair. "Oh, my! You scared me, young man! I didn't even hear you."

"Sorry. I meant to tell you on my way in that you look really nice today," said Artemis.

"Thank you."

"Your shirt really brings out the blue in your eyes."

"Oh, stop it."

"Anyway, you must be busy as always keeping everything going around here," Artemis said.

"Yes, typical day. I'm trying to figure out how I'm going to get five managers in an hour-long meeting together. Their schedules are booked out for a month and they need to meet by the fifteenth. It's just impossible, but this is what I do every day."

"I don't know how you do it, Brent."

"I've learned a few tricks over the years. Is there something I can help you with or did you just come out to chat?"

"Both," said Artemis. "I have a few questions for Deepak, but for some reason I can't pull up his contact information on BSP Net."

"I can get that for you. You're Artemis . . ."

"Pound. Artemis Pound."

"Here it is. I'll send it to you."

"Actually, can I just swipe my wearable?"

"I'm sorry, that's against protocol."

"I'm really hoping to stay off my quantum until this migraine goes away. I need to get a hold of him urgently."

"I suppose just this once," said Brent.

"Could I please have his calendar, too? He wants me to start thinking about my career track and said I should study his calendar to get an idea of what being a lead is like."

"Look at you, already getting noticed by the big dogs."

"A little too soon if you ask me," Artemis said, swiping his wearable. "Thanks, Brent. Have a good day."

"You, too, Artemis. I hope your headache gets better soon," he said, going back to whatever he was working on.

Artemis walked into the work area to find Wei Wei and Tony standing outside Tony's Mobipod. Tony squatted down with his feet pointing away from each other. He moved his head sideways from shoulder to shoulder while pressing out his hands to each side following the rhythm of his head movements.

"What are you guys doing?" asked Artemis.

"Working," said Tony.

"Doesn't look like it," said Artemis.

"I guess not. This is really fun though. Wei Wei, you try it," said Tony, who started chanting, "*O rey chhori, O rey chhori.*"

Wei Wei squatted down and mimicked Tony's dance moves. Artemis stood and watched while the two of them made their eyes wide and danced in sync with each other as if they'd been practicing together for weeks.

"You guys are something," said Artemis, trying to stay cool but feeling a panic attack welling up inside him. He remembered the spirit of combat and took a deep breath. *Relaxed and adaptable. Centered and focused.* He sat down in his Mobipod to pretend he was working while he examined Deepak's calendar.

Deepak met with Jeff once a week for a meeting called "progress update." He had weekly meetings with some of the other lead developers and architects. He also had daily stand-up with the entire team. Occasionally he would meet with one of the leads from the offshore team immediately after their weekly planning meeting. Artemis took note of the dates and times of those meetings for the past few months, as well as the next scheduled meeting. He was sure there must be clues in the conversations Deepak had with the offshore team's lead developer. Artemis was about to close the calendar when he noticed a monthly recurring meeting called 'The Old Man.'

The old man. Who could that be?

Artemis closed Deepak's calendar and then opened up his work email on his wearable to discover what appeared to be a mini-crisis unfolding. The first email from John said, "Upgrade to Mimi 3.7 complete! You're welcome!"

About fifteen minutes later, several other emails arrived from various team members replying to John's email.

"When I run the app now, if I need to display more than one product in the viewport, I get error 485, 'no available viewport,'" said one of the many emails complaining of issues following John's gloating report regarding the upgrade.

"John, this upgrade appears to have broken the build in several of our subprojects. Please fix," said an email from another team member.

"John, I know the blogosphere says how great the upgrade is and how easy it is to perform, but these people don't understand our domain. We don't have the luxury of skipping over all of the details. Please back out your change," wrote Suzi.

"*Ouch*," thought Artemis. "*She warned him.*"

Artemis, still refusing to wear his lenses, spoke into them while they floated in their lens container.

"Print out a copy of *The Coding Samurai*."

Military Science

"If I'm to support you, I need to know what Oda Nobunaga has taught you," said Mitsuhide to Mori Ranmaru in the war room of Azuchi Castle.

"You needn't worry, Akechi Mitsuhide. I'm well trained in both army and combat principles," said Mori Ranmaru, smiling.

"How many battles have you fought in?" asked Mitsuhide, standing up and pressing both his hands on the table.

"I've fought," said Ranmaru, pushing a stack of papers toward Mitsuhide.

"One battle? Two battles? Training and warfare are not equivalent. We'll all be better served if you tempered your haughtiness."

"I know things even the mighty Akechi Mitsuhide doesn't know. Do you think Oda Nobunaga only taught me to ride a horse and fire arrows? Do you fear that I have superior knowledge, Mitsuhide? Why do you think I'm now Watch Commander?"

"This knowledge you speak of. Has it been tested or is it only in your mind?"

"Get out of my sight, Akechi Mitsuhide."

Lao's commentary

One can only speak confidently from experience. To make bold claims based upon what has been read about in books and blog posts is foolhardy. Learning patterns and practices is only the first step. You have to have experience to better know how to apply the technologies and practices you're espousing.

You must also thoroughly understand a system to understand the consequences of changing it. It takes years to know a large system well. It's impossible to ever truly master a large enterprise system, as it's constantly in flux. Many architects find themselves in positions where it's the lead developers under them who know the system mechanics. Having no hands-on experience, this type of architect can only prescribe academic solutions to problems. Don't end up in this situation. Stay close to the code by continuing to program the system if you ascend to the rank of architect.

Finding a mentor and talking with the strongest developers in the organization is another way to keep a foothold. Learning from those with experience leads to success; leaning on hype and opinions leads to stumbling. Find those who've walked The Way of the Computer Warrior *within the organization and ask them about the systems they're familiar with. Each organization's systems and processes are unique, just as each samurai clan had particular methods of military science.*

A junior programmer on my team at a large bank bought into the hype surrounding a new file format. He changed a bunch of our processes to use it, thinking he was advancing the system. He didn't understand that the new file format was too bloated for our requirements. He came into a meeting boasting of his accomplishment only to leave with his tail between his legs when we told him that the overnight jobs all failed because of his changes. He spent the night in the office reverting all his code and fixing the failed jobs.

****

Artemis sent an encrypted message to Beyoncé to tell her of

his success obtaining Deepak's calendar.

I got the calendar. How are things on your
end?

> *Good. I zipped up a package with code*
> *that matches the search patterns and the*
> *other changes we're looking for. What's*
> *next?*

Let's meet at my place tonight. 7PM.

> *I'll be there.*

Artemis then sent Tilly a message.

I need you to come to my place at 6:45
tonight. Can you make it?

> *Sure. Will she be there?*

Yes.

****

At 6:43, Artemis' intercom notified him that he had a visitor.
He checked the monitor and saw Tilly standing in the lobby.

"I'll buzz you up," he said.

She arrived at his door wearing what he suspected was her
work outfit, a business-casual pantsuit. The styles from the early
2000s had recently become fashionable again.

"I'm glad you made it," he said.

"How are you doing?" Tilly asked.

"Fine, for what it's worth. We made some progress today."

"We?"

"Beyoncé and I. She searched for source code while I got a copy of Deepak's calendar."

"Do you trust her now?"

"I kept my distance and didn't use my quantum, just be to be safe," said Artemis right as his intercom buzzed again. "It's her. And the gang."

"The gang?" asked Tilly.

"She brought her friends with her," said Artemis, pressing the button to let them in.

"Were you expecting them?" she asked.

"No," he said before opening the door. "Hey, everyone. I wasn't expecting the whole crew, but welcome," he said.

Beyoncé's smile at Artemis turned to consternation when she noticed Tilly sitting on Artemis' couch. Mei, Lukas, and Bits followed her inside.

"I don't think we've met," said Beyoncé to Tilly.

"Hi, I'm Tilly," she said, reaching out to shake Beyoncé's hand.

"Beyoncé," she said, taking Tilly's hand. "These are my friends, Mei, Lukas, and Bits."

"Nice to meet you all," said Tilly.

Bits began moving his hands in a series of gestures and

patterns.

"Are you signing?" asked Tilly.

"He said, 'I don't think your place is big enough for six people, but good thing Mei is child-sized,'" said Lukas.

"Bits is deaf?" asked Artemis.

"I told you that the night we met, but he was in holographic form and didn't need to sign," said Lukas.

Artemis stood silent, a little stunned.

"Bits and I met in college at the disability center where I worked. Been friends ever since," said Lukas.

"Unfortunately we brought you, you big ogre. Maybe you should sit in the hallway," said Mei.

"Have you shared everything that's going on with everyone?" Artemis asked Beyoncé.

"Yeah, so what?" asked Beyoncé defensively. "What about her? Does she know?" she continued, pointing at Tilly.

"She knows. I had to talk with her because she's never used a haptic suit before. She's the person I could talk to who had the highest probability of not having an infected brain," said Artemis.

"But maybe mine is? Is that what you're suggesting?" said Beyoncé.

"Maybe, but look—"

"So you trust her, but not me?" Beyoncé said, raising her voice.

"I don't distrust you," he said.

"But you don't trust me. You just don't distrust me," said

Beyoncé, getting angrier. "Come on, you guys; let's go."

"That was a quick visit," said Lukas. "We didn't even get to the cocktails."

"Hold on!" yelled Tilly. "There's something wrong and we're the ones who can do something about it. I'm not here to interfere. Artemis is right. If this Deepak guy and Artemis' professor have made something that is messing with people's heads, you guys need me. You guys practically live in those lenses and suits, and I've never been in one. Please, stay and talk this through."

"She's right," said Artemis. "Today at work, Tony and Wei Wei started dancing and chanting outside their pods. They didn't even seem to know why. We have to assume any of you could also be influenced."

"Okay, maybe I got a bit emotional," said Beyoncé, putting her hand to her chest.

"Lukas, how about making those cocktails you mentioned. Do you mind? Everything's over there," said Artemis, pointing to the cabinet in the kitchen.

"The boys at the club voted me 'Mr. Stiff Drink' on more than one occasion," said Lukas, walking over to the kitchen and rummaging through the cupboards.

Mei and Bits squeezed onto the couch next to Tilly. Artemis pulled in two barstools from under the kitchen counter and gave one to Beyoncé. He squatted down in the center of the room and projected his wearable screen onto the wall.

"Here's what we know," said Artemis. "I'm guessing you've heard most of what's going on from Beyoncé. At BSP, I learned that Deepak has a daily meeting with the offshore team, but once a week he has an extra fifteen minutes scheduled with the lead, Raj. I'm guessing those meetings have some valuable information," he continued. "But he also meets once a month with someone. The meeting just says 'The Old Man.'"

"The Old Man? What did you say your professor's name is?" asked Mei.

"Professor Lao," said Artemis.

"Then you might be interested to know *lao* means *old* in Chinese. Professor Lao. The Old Man," said Mei.

"You're brilliant, Mei," said Artemis.

"What application are they using for the meetings? Mei can probably dig her way into it," signed Bits.

"I've got a different idea. Dial the old bastard up right now. We don't have time to play any more games. Let's do this now," said Beyoncé.

Artemis' stomach flopped. The thought of confronting his mentor terrified him, but he didn't know what else to do.

"Okay, Bey. Let's do it," he said.

Artemis took off his boots and sat down on his futon before dialing the professor.

"Hello, Artemis," said the voice on the other end through the speakerphone system.

"Hello, Professor."

"How are you doing?"

"I'm okay, but obviously things are a bit more dramatic here than what I was expecting."

"Apparently," said the professor. "Where are you now?"

"I'm at home."

"Good. That's good," said the professor.

He sounds distracted, thought Artemis. "Professor Lao, I know you're a liar."

There was a long pause before the professor spoke. "Yes, Artemis, I'm a liar," he said deliberately. "Please understand, this is complicated for me."

"How?" asked Artemis.

"The project that Deepak and I worked on—he left for the private sector where he felt like he'd have more autonomy. I, of course, stayed on at the university," said Professor Lao. He paused again, then said quietly, "I'm still working on that project."

"But what about the project you and I did? We were always working on that. How did you have time to work on something else, too?"

"I wasn't, Artemis. The project you and I were working on is the same project."

"That doesn't make any sense. We worked on an anti-bullying platform for social networking—not a military innovation."

"The experiments Deepak conducted with the haptic suits

were indeed to test forms of what can be simply described as mind control," said the professor before taking yet another long pause. "Are you certain you want to know all of this?"

"I'm all ears," said Artemis, feeling a wave of emotions well up inside.

"Remember that IA was built by the military, by DARPA specifically. Once social media emerged in the early 2000s, the military and intelligence organizations had a very intense interest in it, particularly the most dominant platforms. Social media became the avenue to control the views of the people," explained the professor. "Content providers pushed specific agendas, but arguments were more compelling when group influencers posted links to content or when they posted their own personal views. DARPA began studying how information passed through social networks. They wanted to figure out ways to interrupt or guide messages to benefit the aims of the military and intelligence agencies by targeting these group influencers. Deepak's work took it to another level."

"Yeah—the level that includes experimenting on college kids."

"Deepak left the project, not because he thought it was unethical to mess with people's minds but because he felt hamstrung by bureaucracy and red tape. We had arrived at a point in the project where the implications of using the power of the technology we'd created were so shocking that no one wanted to sign off on the next level of human trials, including me."

"The next level? So you were already using humans for experiments?" asked Artemis.

"Yes, of course. The military had hundreds of haptic suits that leveraged Deepak's technology and was using them on soldiers during so-called training exercises in simulated war zones. Soldiers were put through stressful scenarios: accepting a gift from a small child that might be a bomb, sweeping a building for hostiles, and so on," said Professor Lao. He paused for a moment, then continued, "During these scenarios, the haptic suit had the ability to deliver physical pain to the soldiers' nervous systems in order to create actual fear responses. When the soldiers left the simulation, they were taken to a room and asked to recall specific moments when they experienced a great deal of pain and fear. Those in the control group who didn't receive the quantum affectation experienced a normal amount of cortisol and epinephrine. However, those in the other group had significantly reduced levels of both stress hormones. And not only that; some of these soldiers released dopamine when recalling the extremely painful experiences."

"Whoa. So that's what they were doing to me—trying to make me a soldier?" asked Artemis.

"Something like that. With Beastville, they wanted to see if they could take someone meek—for lack of a better word—and elicit the same type of response as the soldiers. They needed a control group to compare against those who gravitate naturally toward militarism and warfare."

"What about all of the other work we were doing for the university?" asked Artemis.

"We were also working on a more subtle part of the project—a social networking platform to try and cure humanity of extremist views. We weren't directly altering people's minds on a quantum level, but we were doing everything else. You're very familiar with the law that Congress passed—the Digital Social Network Compliance Act. The military helped shape the law. We received money to create a product that would leverage all of the DARPA research on influencing social media to shape the mind of the country in ways suitable for national security," said Professor Lao.

"What about free speech, though? I can say whatever I want on social media," said Artemis.

"Oh, my boy, times have changes. Before you were born, people could still create social media accounts without using a government-issued ID card. Soon after that, the Supreme Court said anonymous speech is not protected free speech. Tier-one free speech is only available to corporations, and tier-two free speech is open to citizens, but not anonymously. Anyone could make a fake account on the Internet and say any racist, homophobic, hateful thing they wanted without putting their name on it," said the professor.

"I'd heard that, but I can't imagine what that would've been like."

"No, because everything is so different now. So yes, you

have free speech, but your name, address, biometrics, social security number—your complete identity is associated with everything you share on social networking. Everyone is much more self-censoring than in the past. Many emotions, thoughts, ideas, and perceptions never see the light of day now that nothing is anonymous," said the professor.

"So not being anonymous cleaned up a lot of the trash. What else did our project need to do?" asked Artemis.

"If anyone says something undesirable to the government censors, the software platform influences the network to create the desired outcome, which is for citizens to think in a non-extremist way in the interest of national security. You can still write anything you want, but the network will come down like a gloved fist. Someone who posts unwanted views won't receive a criminal punishment, but he will receive social pressure applied in a subtle manner until he changes them, or at least until he doesn't post them any longer. Words of contrition from someone who has said something undesirable will trigger controls in the system to let that person back into the fold," said the professor.

"So it's not really free speech at all. The social price is too high for anyone to dare speak a certain way about sensitive topics being controlled by the platform," said Artemis.

"Exactly."

"It sounds un-American to me."

"Welcome to the new America."

"So what does this have to do with BSP?"

215

"My lab was getting funding not only from the government project but through a grant from BSP. When Deepak contacted me about the very generous infusion of cash I was getting, I overlooked some of the details."

"Go on."

"When I gave you that game to play, I was told it was just a marketing app. I was never told that it had the technology used on the soldiers and that it was going to be used on you the way it was."

"You *what*? Tell me you didn't just tell me that it was you who sent me into Deepak's twisted arms."

"I'm sorry, but I did. I didn't think he would go this far."

All of Artemis' fears and confusion about who might have played with his memories flooded his entire being at the professor's confession. His heart raced as the full realization of how he'd been moved around by others had placed him in this dangerous position.

"You've been lying to me since the day we met—first tricking me into working with you on the project by telling me it was to help protect against bullies. I guess you sized me up perfectly. And then you let me believe that I actually had a choice to make about which job to take. You didn't have any time after graduation to give me advice because you'd already set it up behind the scenes. What else have you done?"

"You are in a dangerous situation, Artemis, and we—"

"Yeah, one that you put me in!" shouted Artemis.

"I hope you can forgive me, because we need to work together now."

"Work together? I never want to talk with you again."

"You don't have a choice," Professor Lao said sharply. "You don't know what the code is going to do. You are a lost little puppy, confused and alone. I'm the only person who can get you through this. If you don't work with me, Groundswell will be launched, and you won't be able to help yourself, your friends, or anyone else."

"Good-bye, Professor."

"Goddamn it, Artemis, I'm trying to help you!" yelled Professor Lao just as Artemis hung up the phone.

CHAPTER THIRTEEN
Laziness

"Never in my life would I have imagined myself in this sort of situation," said Lukas.

"I thought *our* conversations were odd," added Bits.

"Artemis, I know that had to have been incredibly hard to hear, but I think your professor is right," said Beyoncé.

"I thought you were on my side!" shouted Artemis.

"She is, Artemis—we all are. But listen to her," said Tilly. "If Professor Lao is telling the truth, he can help us—he can help you."

Artemis tried to see a way out of the situation that didn't require relying upon anyone over the age of thirty. "I don't know what to do," he said.

"Call him back and see how he can help," said Beyoncé.

"We're not going anywhere, Artemis," said Mei.

"All right. I'll call him," said Artemis, tapping his wearable to make the call.

"Hello?" said Professor Lao.

"My friends convinced me to hear you out," Artemis said.

"I want to help you, Artemis."

"How am I supposed to believe that?"

"The day of your graduation, Deepak paid me a visit."

"So that *was* him I saw you talking to after the ceremony. I remember now!"

"Yes, that was him. He told me that I needed to continue to monitor you, and that he was giving me the quantum to give to you. He said my lab was taken care of for the next twenty years, all the way beyond my retirement. But then something happened that I didn't expect."

"What?"

"You found my old book."

"*The Coding Samurai?*"

"Yes. I recorded what you did with Princess Di the first night and rediscovered it with you. I read through it and it reminded me of the person I used to be, the man who had character and discipline. I saw my old self staring back at me with a disappointment greater than anything I could have ever imagined. I was up all night—a mess of feeling sorry for myself. But then I started feeling sorry for you and what I had done. I decided that night I needed to help you, but I also had to be careful. I needed to try to stay under Deepak's radar, which isn't easy. I couldn't just tell you. There's so much money behind the work at the university and BSP that they would do who knows what to both you and me had I reacted so directly. I wasn't trying to do anything but get you out of the mess I put you in."

"What about my quantum shutting down?"

"What about it?"

"Did you do it?" asked Artemis.

"Yes. I noticed some unusual traffic in your quantum, as if someone might have been trying to hack in."

"Wait. Someone was trying to hack into Princess Di?" repeated Artemis.

"Professor Lao, what about the interns being sent to the offshore team?" said Beyoncé.

"I've never been privy to that information. I'm not an insider, just an old sellout that BSP found useful," said the professor.

"So what now?" asked Bits.

"Deepak has relationships with many important people backing the project in both private industry and the government. In every way, he has leverage that I don't. We have to be very careful. We are on our own with this. If we try to bring charges against him or BSP now, he has plenty of time to create space between him and whatever he is doing and make us look like fools," said Professor Lao.

"I'm going undercover," said Artemis.

"To do what?" said Beyoncé, crossing her arms.

"Deepak wants me to think he's on my side. I'm going to play along, get close to him and try to find out what's going on," said Artemis.

"It's probably also the best way to get in over your head," said Tilly, her upper lip twitching.

"Glad to see you grew a spine, but I have to agree," said Beyoncé, looking at Tilly.

"Maybe, but I'm going to take that chance. That means I'm going to need you guys even more. If I start acting weird, I need you to find a way to pull me out," said Artemis.

"We've got your back," said Lukas while handing out cocktails.

"Thanks, Lukas. Beyoncé, I need you to search for more code so we can it send it to Professor Lao and have him take a look at it," said Artemis.

"Okay, but I don't like this. I don't think you need to go into the enemy camp. Let Mei see what she can do," she said.

"It has to be done this way. There's too much risk that Deepak will catch Mei digging," said Artemis. "Is everyone on board?"

Everyone consented to Artemis' plan, even Beyoncé, though she did so begrudgingly.

"So what do I do now?" asked Beyoncé.

"Just keep a close eye on me and try to stay off your quantum," he said.

"Get back with me as soon as you have more code," said Professor Lao.

"We will. But I still haven't forgiven you, Professor. The only reason I'm talking with you is because we need you," said Artemis, ending the call.

The group sat for some time in the apartment, nervously joking around and playing with Jef. After several drinks, Mei tossed Jef the holographic ball. He chased after it and crashed into Beyoncé's drink sitting on the floor.

"We've probably had enough," said Mei.

"We're with you one hundred percent, Artemis," said Lukas in response to something Bits signed. Bits then turned to Tilly and signed something else.

"Slow down, big guy. You two just met," said Lukas in response to whatever Bits had signed to Tilly.

Tilly sat motionless with an uncomfortable expression on her face.

"All right, let's get going," said Beyoncé flatly as she gazed off into the distance.

Beyoncé and the gang walked to the door, and Artemis took Beyoncé's arm from behind. She turned around to face him. He smiled and said, "BSP," punching the air.

She laughed, did the same, and then left.

"So what do you think?" Artemis asked Tilly.

"I think you've got some good friends," she said.

"I think so, too. I'm still really scared."

"Me, too."

"I don't want you to go. Will you stay here tonight?" asked Artemis, taking Tilly's hand.

"Okay," she said, taking off her shoes.

"You don't know how happy I am that I can see you again," said Artemis, moving close to Tilly on the couch.

"Me, too. I thought about you every day."

"All I could think about was talking with you at the end of

the day to find out how you were doing, or getting to see you and maybe doing this," said Artemis, leaning in to kiss Tilly.

"That would have been nice. I thought the same thing."

"Really?"

"Almost. Maybe also doing this," she said, leading him into the bedroom.

****

Artemis woke up the next morning with Tilly lying next to him. Her eyes were closed and he thought she resembled an angel. He kissed Tilly on the forehead, rolled off the bed onto the floor, and did forty-five push-ups. The most he'd ever done was thirty-eight.

"What time is it?" asked Tilly.

"Seven thirty."

"It's so early."

"I have a big day. I'm going to have to go."

"What are you going to do?"

"I need to make Deepak feel like I'm completely on his side."

"How are you going to do that?"

"I have a couple ideas."

"Stay close," said Tilly, reaching across the bed to take his hand.

"I will," he said, looking at her lying on his bed half covered in his X-Men sheets.

He went to his old computer and logged in.

"What are you doing?" asked Tilly, sitting up in his bed.

"Updating my spreadsheet."

"What's it for?"

"Who I can trust and who I can't. I'm changing Beyoncé from yellow to light green and Professor Lao from dark red to light red."

"Am I on that list?" said Tilly, giving him a serious look.

"Um, yes?" said Artemis sheepishly. "But you're green. You've always been green. And I'm making you dark green. Same color as my parents."

"Good," she said, throwing a pillow at him.

His wearable alerted him that he had a shipment arriving in three minutes. He dressed, then took the elevator to the lobby of Crockford Apartments, walked past the decorative waterfall, and strode out the back door to the drone delivery pad. As he walked outside, the drone was returning to the air. Artemis picked up the package from the landing pad, put it in his backpack, and began walking. Gusts of strong wind pushed at his back as he walked the half-mile stretch to the BSP building.

"Good morning, Brent," Artemis said, entering the lobby.

"Good morning, Artemis."

When Artemis entered the DOT work area, he saw Brad talking with Jeff—the leadership had returned. Artemis stared at his Mobipod. He hadn't logged in for two days now. He knew that if Deepak looked at his activity, he'd start questioning what Artemis was doing. He decided to set a timer and log off after fifteen minutes. He started searching through the source code for check-ins by Raj, the lead for the offshore team. When the alarm sounded, he felt like he'd found enough of what he needed. Artemis walked to the meeting area and waited for everyone to arrive.

"Good morning, everyone," said Brad as the last of the team members filed into the room. "We had a successful meeting with the investors. We're in good shape to launch. I'll spare you the details, but it was a very positive meeting."

"Before you left, we'd decided we didn't have the manpower to finish the remaining features by the launch date. What changed?" asked John.

"Deepak was able to persuade them to fund us to expand the offshore team. We also cut a few features back for the first release," said Brad.

"What features? We were already down to the minimum viable product," said John.

"Just a few pieces here and there that we can circle back around to next release. I don't want to get mired in the details right now," said Brad.

John retired his questioning but still looked displeased.

Everyone took turns going around the room reporting on progress. When the meeting concluded, Artemis waved to get Deepak's attention.

"Deepak, do you have a few minutes?" asked Artemis.

"Today I'm very busy. Is it important?"

"I think so."

"Just a few minutes."

Artemis had pulled up some of the source code he'd looked up earlier in the morning.

"So what can I help you with, Artemis?" asked Deepak.

"The past few days I've been going through the codebase trying to learn more. I kept coming across some poorly thought-out designs and amateur implementations," said Artemis.

"Every codebase has bad code. Where are you going with this?" asked Deepak.

"The code I keep seeing seems to always be written by the same person. I just wonder if there isn't a training opportunity here," said Artemis, showing Deepak the source code by projecting it onto the wall with his wearable.

"Raj? He's very busy, but a lot of this has laziness written all over it," said Deepak. "Thank you for bringing this to me."

"I also wanted to let you know that I thought more about the talk we had before you left. I know I need to grow if I'm ever going to be the best. I hope I can learn more from you—when you have time, of course," said Artemis. "And I have a welcome-home gift for you."

Artemis reached into his backpack and pulled out the package he'd had delivered. Deepak took the package from Artemis and opened it on the table. He reached through the stuffing and pulled out a chessboard. The artist had carved the chess pieces from marble. The red pieces were inspired by Hindu gods and goddesses. The white pieces had been shaped into British troops.

"It's a classic from when they used real boards and pieces."

"I know," said Deepak, his smirk melting into a smile. "I will have time soon. Keep up the good work."

"Thanks," said Artemis, turning off the display of his wearable and leaving the room.

Artemis said a silent "thank you" to *The Coding Samurai*'s chapter on laziness, which had inspired his plan.

Laziness

"Where is the watch commander? Where is Mori Ranmaru?" Mitsuhide asked a samurai at his base in Tanba Province.

"He is in his tent," said the samurai.

Mitsuhide hurried his pace to Mori Ranmaru's tent. He ripped open the tent's flap to see Ranmaru with his pants down behind one of the pages on his bed.

"What are you doing?" asked Mitsuhide in a rage as Ranmaru leaped to his feet while pulling up his pants. "So these are the things that Nobunaga has taught you? While the men prepare the camp, digging latrines and constructing defenses, you waste your time in here with this boy?"

"That's what I have you for, Mitsuhide, to make certain things are being done correctly," said Ranmaru.

"Get out! Get out!" yelled Mitsuhide, slapping Ranmaru across the head repeatedly. "Go back to Azuchi Castle to your lord. I don't need a worthless, lazy whelp like you in my camp."

"This is not your camp, Mitsuhide," yelled Ranmaru, grabbing his *wakashū* and running toward his horse. "Come, boy. We're leaving this place."

Lao's commentary

Laziness is quite common in the workplace, mainly because the consequences typically aren't severe—if they exist at all. People overpromise and under-deliver and those who are affected tend to merely lower their expectations. Unless you're truly overworked, which is a reality sometimes, the Coding Samurai does everything he can to not skip essential duties. If there's time to catch up on the news or read other articles of interest, there's more than enough time to not hurry through tasks.

Writing code is like writing a poem: only after multiple revisions will it be complete. A coder who consistently believes his first attempt at solving a problem is good enough isn't walking The Way of the Computer Warrior. *Iterating and refactoring code into an elegant solution demonstrates craftsmanship. Many of the differences between the work of a junior-level programmer and a senior-level programmer have nothing to do with the cleverness of the code and everything to do with the degree of thoroughness. Experience teaches that this level of completeness requires much more effort than initially conceived. Programmers who are content to fritter away their time don't value themselves. Realize that craftsmanship is a reflection of who you are and your legacy. If you work in an environment that doesn't value craftsmanship, it might be time to leave.*

I worked on a contract once for a newspaper during a time of struggle for the industry. I worked next to a full-time employee who spent almost all day on a video game forum. During status meetings he always said with a shifty look in his eyes that his work was blocked. Sometime later, he asked for a reference from me. There is no way in hell I would recommend a lazy coder like him to even watch paint dry.

****

Artemis didn't feel good about throwing Raj—someone he'd never met and knew nothing about—under the bus, but he needed a way to get closer to Deepak. He walked down the hall to the Refresh Room so he could call Tilly in private. He opened the door and walked in on Wei Wei and some of the people in lab coats working on one of the units. One of the men glared at him and waved at him to leave the room. "Sorry," whispered Artemis, closing the door behind him.

He crept to the roof patio, but there were still too many people around. He turned the corner of the food printing station and bumped into Beyoncé.

"Bey, what's up?" said Artemis in a whisper.

"Not here. Let's go outside," she said, pulling him by the arm and leading him toward the elevators.

Outside, the drones were buzzing so loudly that Artemis thought he might as well be standing under a train.

"I tricked Suzi into running some of the searches. I've got some code to get to the professor," she said.

"That's great news. I had a meeting with Deepak. I think I've successfully made him believe that I'm totally under his spell."

"What now?"

"We need to get the code to Lao and figure out how to throw a wrench into Groundswell."

Beyoncé just stared blankly at Artemis for a moment before saying, "We're gonna need a big fucking wrench."

CHAPTER FOURTEEN
Verbal Expression

Artemis arrived at work the following morning not giving a damn that he was late for another meeting. He walked into the lobby and said hi to Brent.

"BSP?" asked Brent while doing the air pumps.

"Not today, Brent," said Artemis, continuing into the rec area.

Artemis sat down and read for a few minutes to help calm himself.

Verbal Expression

"Daughter, it's time for you to leave here. It's time for you to marry," said Mitsuhide to Tama.

"Why is it time?" she asked as the two stood in the garden gazebo outside their home.

"It's not safe here any longer. I've secured a partnership with Hosokawa Tadaoki. You must marry him to ensure our house continues."

"The Prince of Tango?"

"Yes. His house is strong. He will come here tomorrow to take you to his castle."

"But I want to stay here with you, Father," said Tama, taking her father's arm in her hand.

"If you don't go with him, I fear none of us will live. Tama, it's your duty to do this," he said. "Will you go to him?"

"Of course, Father. I will do as you wish."

Lao's commentary

While some in IT may be cynical, sarcastic, morose, and even despondent, the Coding Samurai aims to accept tasks with grace and genuine interest. Don't adopt an attitude of being burdened with the work you are given. If this way of thinking becomes a habit, your career will become a heavy load that slowly drags you deeper into an unsatisfied view of life. Even if you are planning on quitting a job, don't let your attitude drift toward the negative as you will only be training your mindset to be poor at the start of your next job.

Sometimes work is work—not at all glamorous or fun. This situation isn't one to mourn. Having a professional IT job at any level, while sometimes monotonous or boring, usually pays well and doesn't require too much personal hardship other than occasional long hours. It's not possible or reasonable to convey gratitude and enthusiasm at every task, but at least be grateful on the inside.

Showing gratitude isn't slavish devotion to our employers; it's a way to honor ourselves. We don't want to train our minds to think in a toxic manner. We appreciate the good fortune of not being in a severe situation like homelessness or not being able to work at all because of a medical condition.

Nevertheless, sometimes a work request can truly be too much. If a task is unreasonable, be clear in explaining your concerns in a way that doesn't come across as complaining. Break down the reasons why the request is unreasonable and ways it can be changed to make it more realistic. If you're typically enthusiastic about work, when you do raise an issue, the manager will likely find it a much more reasonable complaint.

My first professional job interview pitted me against a few high-powered coders from elite colleges. We were going to write GPS software for military satellites. My excitement pervaded all of my answers. When I got the call from my new manager, he explained it was my enthusiasm that put me into the number-one slot. If you think all candidates for that type of opportunity show excitement, you're wrong. Many go in cocky, unengaged, or halfhearted.

****

He walked over to the morning stand-up right when the meeting was ending.

"Hello, Artemis," said Deepak.

"What did I miss?"

"A very important announcement," said Deepak.

"Oh yeah? What?" asked Artemis.

"It was pointed out recently that there are some problems with the leadership of the offshore team. We've decided to send someone to help," said Deepak.

"Who?" asked Artemis.

"You."

"Me?"

"Yes. You'll be working with Raj until launch."

"Why?"

"It's your reward for being so diligent," said Deepak with a subtle tone of irony. "A perfect training opportunity."

Artemis wanted to run screaming from BSP. *Hell no, I'm not going* is what he wanted to say. Then he remembered what he'd just read and said instead, "What an opportunity!"

"I was hoping you'd be pleased," said Deepak.

"This is great news. But let's say I don't want to go."

"When you started, you signed an addendum. If you willfully violate any direct and reasonable request that impedes the launch of Groundswell, you will owe BSP a whole lot of money. And I'll kill your cat." Deepak laughed. "Just kidding. Not kidding."

"When am I supposed to go?"

"Tomorrow—to Chennai. Brent is sending you your ticket information. I believe he already gave you my contact information and calendar, so you'll have that if you get into a pinch."

"Okay, then. Well, I should be going," said Artemis, turning away from Deepak and trying to look casual as he walked to his Mobipod.

"Hold on, Artemis," said Deepak.

Artemis turned around. Two large men wearing white lab coats were standing next to Deepak.

"I think this news has you a little stressed. Why not spend a few minutes in the Refresh Room?" he asked.

"No, that's okay. I'm feeling great," said Artemis.

"I insist. These gentlemen will make certain you are taken care of," said Deepak.

The men approached Artemis and began leading him toward the Refresh Room. Artemis quickly texted Beyoncé:

Hey, urgent problem. Deepak is sending me
to the offshore team.

What!?

He's sending me to India tomorrow, where
I'll likely be turned into a coding zombie.
And he has two guys in lab coats taking me
to the Refresh Room to *relax* me.

That is the baldest thing he could do.

Are you going to go?

WTF do you mean am I going to go?! I just
said two guards are taking me to the Refresh
Room.

"Sir, we need you to stop texting and get refreshed now," said one of the men.

"I don't want to get refreshed," Artemis said to the man.

"Sir, you have to get refreshed now. Now please sit down," said one of the men, pushing Artemis toward the chair. The other man fiddled with a couple of vials next to Artemis.

Something came over Artemis and he kicked out his foot, tripping the man holding the vials. The man stumbled forward and dropped them, scattering the tiny vials across the floor.

"What are those?" asked Artemis.

"Just a relaxant. Sit down, sir."

Artemis sat in the chair and watched the man slide a vial into a compartment on the side of the refresh chair. The other man watched over Artemis. The first man closed the door on the compartment and started the refresh program. Artemis felt the cool fluid enter his bloodstream. It was different from the last time. His head became cloudy—certainly not refreshed.

"Something's not right!" shouted Artemis.

"Everything's okay now," said the man.

Artemis had heard the same thing from the vet when his family had had to put down the family dog. The two men left Artemis in the chair and left the room. Artemis walked over to one of the chairs and reached around on the floor for one of the vials he'd seen roll underneath. His fingertips made contact with it and he clasped his hand around it, then jumped up and ran out of the room. The two men were nowhere in sight.

As he left the Refresh Room, Artemis had an overwhelming memory of taking a survey in college. He was sitting in Professor Lao's office after class one day and clicking through a survey. The survey asked questions like: "How many friends do you have?" "Do you spend a lot of time alone?" "Are you a nervous person?" He saw a cloudy image of himself as a student handing the datapad back to Professor Lao and Lao thanking him.

What's going on?

Artemis collapsed on the floor. He sent a message to Beyoncé.

"Come and get me. I'm outside the Refresh Room."

Beyoncé found Artemis lying on the floor. She crouched down and hugged him.

"Dial the professor and forward the call to me," she said.

Artemis did as she asked. He leaned against her for support as she led him down the hallway to the elevators.

"It's Beyoncé," Artemis heard her say. "Deepak did something to him and left him in the hallway. Arrogant piece of shit isn't even trying to hide anything anymore."

Artemis remembered something from his first day of work. When he was leaving, a man called out to him. It was Deepak. The memory was clear. Deepak had emerged from the shadows and stood confidently under the light, perfectly centered on the BSP logo on the shimmering white tile floor. "It looks like it's time for you to go," he'd said.

"He says he's remembering things," Artemis heard Beyoncé say. "I don't know. I've only been with him for five minutes and for four of them I've been talking with you."

"Bey, tell the professor to go fuck himself."

"He said to go fuck yourself," said Beyoncé into her implant. Artemis laughed.

"I'm going to get you home," Beyoncé said to Artemis.

****

Beyoncé laid Artemis down on his bed and started an encrypted HoloMeet. Professor Lao beamed into Artemis' studio apartment at the foot of his bed.

"Reflux," said the professor.

"Hello to you, too," said Beyoncé.

"It's what they've done to him," he said.

"Professor, would you mind telling me why I keep recalling things that haven't happened to me?" asked Artemis.

"They *have* happened. They reversed the quantum treatments."

"I remember the survey, asshole."

"Oh, yes. The candidate screening."

"God I hate you."

"Reflux will have also removed the pain tolerance you built up through playing the game," said the professor.

"Wait, what?" asked Artemis.

"Encoded within all of the quantum treatments is the information from the original memory and experience. There's a tag on all altered information. The Reflux drug affects neurotransmitters so that a tagged memory is unwound to the original state the next time it's recalled. So you are actually you again."

"The pathetic coward from the survey."

"Exactly. Artemis-the-experiment is dead. Which one would you rather be?"

"Neither," he said, standing up from the bed.

"You need to rest," said Beyoncé.

"What am I supposed to do about India?"

"Not now. We need to work on stopping Groundswell," said Professor Lao.

"Well thank you very much, Professor," said Artemis. "I kind of disagree."

"We'll get to your trip. I need you to do some things to your quantum first," said Lao.

"What things?"

"Apply these patches to lock out the BSP hooks they had into your quantum. That will also route our communication through my private network."

Artemis applied the patches to Gopher World while Beyoncé contacted the rest of the group.

"Alright, Artemis, we need a safe place to convene. Go to your home world and the rest of us will meet there," said the professor.

Artemis stepped into the quantum he'd been avoiding for the past few days. He shuddered as he recalled how many times in the past he'd put on the haptic suit and then had sought out tormenting experiences.

"Princess Di, load my home world," he said.

"Okay."

"Hot coals! Hot coals!" shouted Artemis, reacting to the Level 15 pain he was experiencing. "Di, turn off the hot rocks forchrissakes!"

The rest of the gang beamed in to the biosphere.

"India, huh?" said Bits.

"Yeah, but I guess you all don't have to, you know, help me with that right now," said Artemis.

"We will, Artemis, but first we need to go through all of this," said the professor, who was standing just outside the biosphere next to Mei, Lukas, Bits, and Beyoncé.

"Fine. Let's go to Planet Heidi."

"The singing mountains of Skittles?" asked Bits.

"The harpstones. Follow me," said Artemis, leading the group to the obelisk and taking them to the surface of Heidi.

It was the middle of the day when the group arrived. Many new life-forms, mainly plant life, stirred on the surface. Bizarre, twisting trees created a dense forest. Among the trees were thick-leafed plants shaped like vases. The leaves were patterned with swirls of color.

"You know, I have to say, it really does have a much better aesthetic than the Poop Room," said Bits.

"Agreed," said Lukas.

"Let's get closer to it," said Mei, pointing toward a mountainous harpstone. "We can talk on the way."

"I'm going to miss this in India," said Artemis.

"It must be hard for you, thinking about missing your computer," said Beyoncé sarcastically.

"Which is why I need you to take control of her. I'm giving

you super-user access to her while I'm gone," said Artemis.

"Are you sure?" she asked. "I know how much you love her. You aren't worried I'm jealous of her and will reprogram her to talk like a nasty old man?"

"No, I'm not."

"We can network Princess Di with everyone's quantums and give us way more power," she said.

"Why haven't we already done this?" asked Lukas.

"Because you guys would just use it to create a maze of bodily fluids and gore," said Mei.

"Probably," said Bits. "Which is even more of a reason why we should have done it."

"Seriously, you guys are a lost cause," said Mei.

"Hold up," said Artemis, almost slipping as they walked down the muddy slope toward the harpstone mountain.

"What do you see?" asked Beyoncé.

"Is that . . . Tilly?" asked Artemis.

"Where?" asked Lukas.

"Standing at the bottom beside that rock where it flattens out," said Artemis, pointing into the distance.

The group rushed to get to the bottom of the muddy path. If it was Tilly, Artemis thought something looked different about her.

"What are you doing here?" he asked as they approached the figure.

"I need to talk with you," replied Tilly.

"But who helped you get in here?" asked Artemis.

Tilly laughed. "No one helped me. But I have to tell you something really weird."

"How weird?"

"Probably the strangest thing you will ever hear in your life."

"What's going on?" he asked nervously.

"I'm the F.O.A.L. liaison for this planet," said Tilly.

"You're in F.O.A.L?" stammered Artemis. "I have completely lost it."

"This must be incredibly confusing for you," she said.

"I don't know who anyone is anymore," said Artemis.

"I'm still me."

"You knew I was in F.O.A.L. Why would you keep this secret?"

"F.O.A.L. is much bigger than you think," she said.

"How much bigger?" asked Artemis.

"Using our network of F.O.A.L. liaisons, such as myself, we protect life in almost twenty-five thousand quantum universes."

"So you're in F.O.A.L.? That isn't that bizarre. What are you doing in Lepton Mountain working as a recruiter then?" asked Artemis.

"Keeping an eye on the creation of life here on Earth, the epicenter of which is Lepton Mountain. Being a recruiter was a convenient job to stay in the know with all of the local happenings," she said. "And I'm still getting to the strange part. Follow me to the harpstones."

242

With everything Artemis had been experiencing recently, he was learning to let go of knowing what was real. He followed Tilly toward the glowing chunks of creatures until the group arrived at the base of the harpstones. Even in bright sunlight, the colors of the mountain glowed.

"I want to touch it," said Bits, walking toward it.

Bits stood in front of the mass and reached out his hand. When he touched it, part of the mound started liquefying where his hand had rested on it and began to drip down its surface. The group stood silently, watching as more of the mountain pooled on the ground before them. It began bubbling, growing, and forming odd shapes. A blistered arm emerged from the puddle of harpstones. Another arm emerged from the pool until finally a humanoid shape stood before them. The body flashed the same colors as the harpstone mountain.

"What the hell," said Artemis.

"*What the hell,*" said the humanoid shape.

"Whoa, what the hell!" repeated Bits, jumping backward in fright. The harpstone humanoid mimicked him.

The voice of the humanoid had many odd overtones to it: slight echoes, odd frequencies, detailed harmonies. Artemis raised his hand up to the creature. The glowing, humanoid shape mirrored him.

"My name is Artemis," he said.

"*My name is Artemis,*" said the shape in its eerie voice while flashing different colors.

The group erupted in a cacophony of exclamations at the interaction happening before them. The harpstone mimicked the voices and sounds of all of them like an odd, alien record.

"This is why I'm here, Artemis. When you joined F.O.A.L., you weren't joining an online community of nerds, you were joining an organization that began in another universe, that has the ability to cross quantum boundaries to spread compassion and prevent unnecessary harm and destruction to life-sustaining environments," said Tilly. "In fact, I haven't always been Tilly, or human for that matter."

"So Tilly, you're trying to tell us you're what, an alien?" asked Beyoncé, giving an incredulous look to everyone else in the group.

"My name in my world is Tilleena. This is what I look like there," she said, projecting an image from her wrist.

A muscular humanoid image appeared, covered with soft, blue fur. She wore short, green cargo shorts and a black vest that covered her chest. Her head had an equine shape to it, though she was clearly a cute variety of the species.

"So wait—when you stayed the night," said Artemis, "and we . . . are you saying that I . . ."

"Don't think about it like that," said Tilly.

"I fucked a pony," he said, pacing in circles.

"Damn. And I thought you were scared to do it with a black girl," said Beyoncé.

"We've heard the weird part now, right?" asked Bits.

"Artemis! I need you to catch your breath. We have to coordinate, not just how to keep you from being sent to Chennai but how to stop BSP and Deepak from launching Groundswell. It's my responsibility and yours as a F.O.A.L. cadet."

"Why did you stop being my friend? I needed you so much," said Artemis, crossing his arms.

"Someone from BSP did actually call my boss and tell him I needed to back off. I felt like I could do more from a distance at that point. I needed to keep my cover. Maybe I didn't—but that was my instinct," she said, reaching out to touch his forearm.

"I don't understand even what you are," he said, leading her down one of the paths away from the biosphere.

"I'm me. I'm the person you've been spending time with."

"How did you get here—on Earth?"

"F.O.A.L.'s detection grid alerts them when life-sustaining quantum universes come into existence. We received an alert because of technological activity on Earth. I was sent to build a F.O.A.L. organization to monitor what was going on."

"And they just beamed you here like in Star Trek?"

"No. But it's much more sophisticated quantum technology than how you visit the harpstones. There's still a barrier between your world and the world of the harpstones—only information can pass. But I'm truly here in your world on Earth."

"What happens to you on your planet when you come here?" he asked her as they passed underneath a massive stone arch.

"I'm a mini–black hole in a containment chamber."

"You're a black hole?"

"Just a little one."

"How long has it been since you were home?"

"Twenty-four Earth years."

"Your entire life?"

"We're inserted in a fetus, the moment before consciousness arises. The information of my being was firewalled off in the encoding of the life-form until a certain maturity—when my memories and identity began leaking through."

"That sounds terrifying."

"It's tough for a ten-year-old when she starts to realize she's an alien."

"How do you get back home?"

"When I die on Earth, I'll return to my containment chamber and the mini–black hole will be restored into Tilleena."

"And you do all this for F.O.A.L.?"

"Not for them but for life. It's what I would hope a higher life-form would do for me."

"What makes you a higher life-form than humans?"

"We developed a technology where by putting thoughts down using symbols, we cause quantum worlds to appear."

"So you write them into existence?"

"Basically. Humans created software that requires millions of lines of symbols to create virtual worlds and they believe themselves to be incredibly advanced. We're able to create worlds much more efficiently. We can create worlds with only around eighty thousand symbols."

"You write worlds as if writing a book?" asked Artemis as several burning-out stars shot through the sky above them like green and blue fireworks.

"Our letters are more like vibrations. We wrote Earth's universe in sixty-four thousand vibrations."

"You wrote Earth?"

"Well, my species, Astrohipparion, wrote it. It was the sixteen thousand three hundred and eighty-fourth book we wrote."

"So if you wrote Earth's universe, why do you have to come here as Tilly? Why not just change the ending to protect us from Groundswell?"

"We aren't omnipotent. The cosmos doesn't work that way. We can begin worlds, but we can't toy with them at will. There's no reverse switch. Only forward. Once a world begins, it's autonomous. The only way we can operate within it is to become a denizen of that world in the way I described."

"Are you the first one to arrive on Earth?"

"Once we saw how brutal humans were becoming, we sent others of our kind to try to guide them."

"When?"

"Several times, but it didn't help."

"What happened?"

"The worst outcome was when one of us was crucified. Afterward, everything he had tried to teach humans was twisted and perverted. It was a total disaster. That's when F.O.A.L. adopted a code of noninterference."

"So, wait. My lover is . . ." he said, trying to sort out his epiphany.

"Is . . ."

"Pony Jesus?"

"Please stop calling me a pony."

"Sorry. I'm being a jerk."

"Yes, you are," she said, stopping and turning back toward the biosphere, which had grown small on the horizon.

"So maybe I'm still just being a jerk, but how do you know you aren't just a crazy person?"

"We can transmit information signals. Others from my planet sent me the photo of myself that I showed you."

"What other kinds of information?"

"Many kinds. Once we used a burning bush to try and teach early civilization the basics."

"There's so much I want to understand."

"I know. And I want to tell you, but we can't spend any more time now. We need to focus on our objective," she said, leading Artemis back toward the group. "Now it's time to do something. Are you ready to fulfill your F.O.A.L. oath?"

"Sure, why not," said Artemis.

"Your friends need to be sworn in before I can share anything else."

Tilly surveyed the group before asking them, "Is there

anyone here who is unwilling to swear an oath to the causes of F.O.A.L.?"

"I'd need to hear it first," said Beyoncé.

"Do you swear that, to the best of your ability, you will acknowledge the precariousness and preciousness of life-forms in this quantum landscape and others, that you will only interfere in the natural order of things when absolutely necessary, and that, regardless of your ability and power to create and destroy life, you will be a friend of all life?" asked Tilly.

"Mosquitos too? Hell no," said Beyoncé.

"Yes, mosquitos too," said Tilly. "I need everyone to take the oath."

"Pushy little pony, ain't ya?" said Beyoncé.

Tilly glared at her and then repeated her request.

"Okay, we'll take it," said Beyoncé.

Tilly led the group through the oath as they repeated after her.

"Except mosquitos," muttered Beyoncé at the end.

"Artemis, F.O.A.L. maintains a lab far from here. I'm putting things in motion with other F.O.A.L. members to help you get there," said Tilly.

"How is he going to keep in touch with us?" asked Beyoncé.

"Food recipes," said Mei.

"Food recipes?" asked Artemis.

"Steganography. We communicate with each other as if we're in a food club, sharing food recipes that we enjoy printing.

The molecular structures will contain the messages we want to send," said Mei.

"W-w-what?" said Lukas.

"We all need to install an app called Food Chain. It contains a database of every printable recipe and the breakdown of the molecules required to print it," she said.

"It's pretty tough to write a letter with food molecules," said Artemis.

"That's where the next app comes in—Food Coma. Type in your real message and it will create a recipe that can be sent to the other person. They enter the recipe and the passphrase into Food Coma and the real message is displayed," said Mei.

"Hairy. What's our passphrase?" asked Beyoncé.

"Let's use 3.14159265358979323846," said Mei.

"The first how many places of pi?" asked Artemis.

"The first twenty," said Mei.

"The first twenty? That's it?" asked Lukas sarcastically.

"What's the problem? I can recite pi to two thousand places. I thought I was making it easy on you," said Mei.

"Let's get started on a plan to deal with Groundswell," said Tilly. "Artemis, you need to rest so you have your wits about you when the time comes to escape. The rest of us will meet first thing in the morning."

"What about Jef?" asked Artemis.

"I'll take care of him," said Tilly.

"I still have so many questions for you," said Artemis.

"Later," she said, gently touching his arm.

"You guys have control of Princess Di now. Stay. Or come and go as you please. Just don't turn Heidi into Planet Poop," said Artemis.

"No way, man. This is beyond epic. We'll take care of her for you," said Lukas. "Plus, we swore an oath."

"Be careful," said Beyoncé.

"I will. Take care of yourself," said Artemis before pulling Tilly off to the side.

"What's up?" Tilly asked.

"So the stuff that happened with us . . . was that real?"

"Did it feel real to you?"

"The realest thing I've ever experienced."

"We're going to get through this," she said before kissing him good-bye.

When Artemis left the quantum, he noticed a message on his wearable from his parents.

"Hey, Son. We miss you. Your mother and I hope you're getting settled. We'd love to come and visit next week," wrote his dad.

My parents! This is happening so fast.

Artemis called his dad immediately. "Dad. I would love to see you, but I have some news. The company's getting ready to launch a new product next week, and they need me to go to India to help the remote team finish their work. I'm leaving first thing in the morning for Chennai!"

"Slow down, Son. Chennai? That's in India?" asked his dad.

"Yes, Dad, it's in India."

"My gosh, Artemis. You've not been there very long. I guess you've made a good impression."

"I guess so. I love you and Mom very much and really miss you, but now isn't a good time. We'll make plans as soon as I get back," said Artemis.

"How long are you going to be there?"

"The product launches in a couple days, so hopefully not beyond that."

"After that, you really should make some time for us to come down."

"Okay," said Artemis, adding defensively, "I'm really busy with work right now, though."

"I know, Artemis," said his dad with some irritation in his voice. Then he sighed. "Don't tell your mom I said this, but she had a few tests come back."

"Tests? What's wrong? Is Mom sick?" asked Artemis.

"We still don't know exactly what's wrong, but I thought you should know. She's fine right now. I don't want you to worry."

"How am I supposed to not worry? If you didn't want me to worry, you shouldn't have told me."

"I only told you so you'd make some time for us when you get back. Be careful. Let us know if you need anything."

"I have to go and get ready."

"Have a safe trip. Here, say hi to your mother."

"Artemis, what's going on?" asked his mom.

"I'm going to India for a few days to finish up a project. How are you?"

"India? What are you going to do with Jef?"

"Uh, well, it's just for a few days. My friend is going to watch him."

"You be careful. We're here if you need us."

"I love you very much."

"We love you, too. Artemis. Let us know when you get there," said his mom.

"I will. Bye, Mom," he said before ending the call.

"I wish you were coming with me, Jef. I don't want to go alone," said Artemis, petting the furry kitten sitting on his stomach. Artemis closed his eyes and tried to sleep as Jef kneaded his claws into his belly. Artemis knew he wouldn't be able to sleep anyway, so he didn't bother trying to make him stop.

CHAPTER FIFTEEN
Keeping Death in Mind at All Times

At five thirty the following morning, Artemis woke up to a knock at the door. He looked at the security monitor and saw a man and a woman standing outside. He opened the door.

"Good morning," said the woman. "We're here to take you to the hyperloop."

"Wait here. I'll be back in a minute," said Artemis.

"I'll come with you," said the woman.

"That's all right. I can manage on my own."

"I'm certain you can. I'll follow regardless."

He grabbed his portable and sling pack and left with the BSP thugs to catch the train to the Cape May Hyperloop Port. They reached Lepton Mountain Station, the recently built line that connected the commercial center at Lepton Mountain to the underwater hyperloop port in Cape May, New Jersey, for transit to Europe. The three of them followed signs to the platform hall. The brick walkways were slick from a slight rain that had fallen. The concourse held the ticket counters, coffee stands, an ice-cream shop, and a few restaurants. At the far end were the doors to the elevated platforms.

"Now boarding the train to the Cape May Hyperloop Port at Platform One," said an announcement over the intercom.

Artemis walked with his guards to the platform, where a sleek-nosed maglev train waited. The trip from Lepton Mountain station to the hyperloop would take about forty-five minutes. He stepped onto the train and tried to find a seat among the mostly professional crowd. He sank into a cushioned seat and turned on the news while waiting for the train to depart.

"China's desperate attempts to find drinking water has neighboring countries on edge. It's estimated that only one-tenth of the water in the country can now be safely treated for drinking. Many parts of China still aren't connected to imported water systems, meaning tens of millions of citizens are forced to drink contaminated water. The average lifespan of Chinese citizens has continued to drop while lifespans in developed countries in Europe and the United States continue to slowly rise. Neighbors fear military force will be used to coerce them to divert portions of their clean water to China's massive engineering project, called the Great Pipe. Its purpose: pump as much clean, imported water through the country as possible," said the newscaster.

A sounding bell announced the doors were closing. A few last-minute arrivals hurried through before they closed.

"Passengers, please take your seats. The train is departing for nonstop service to the Cape May Hyperloop Port," said the voice on the intercom.

The train began its gradual acceleration to 350 miles per hour as Artemis watched the lights outside flash faster past the window. When the train reached maximum speed, Artemis turned from the window and noticed the thugs staring off blankly at who knows what. He typed a message into Food Coma and entered the first twenty places of pi. It displayed a list of weird ingredients: cardamom, tofu, egg whites, and corn. The app prompted him to give the recipe a name. He called it "Indian Breakfast Snack." Once decoded, the message would read, "On the train. Miss you guys already."

A few moments later, a recipe appeared in Food Coma called "Pecan Icing." It read, "I miss you, too. Safe journey.—Tilly"

Artemis closed the app and took out the printed copy of *The Coding Samurai* that he'd brought for his journey.

Seems appropriate, he thought, reacting to the chapter title.

Keeping Death in Mind at All Times

"Men, Oda Nobunaga rests at the Honnō temple. Let's give him a procession. We ride to Kyoto," said Mitsuhide, sitting upon his horse outside of Castle Sakamoto.

Mitsuhide's army fell into formation and began the journey along Lake Biwa toward the city. An hour had passed when the army neared Honnō-ji. As Mitsuhide and his troops crossed the bridge over the Kamo River, the gate of Honno-ji could be seen situated on a nearby hill.

"The enemy awaits at Honno-ji!" yelled Mitsuhide, whipping his horse from a canter to a gallop. His troops followed him to the gate of the temple.

"Master Oda, a sentry has spotted Akechi Mitsuhide and his army charging through the gate," said Mori Ranmaru, running into his lord's chamber.

"What? We are completely undefended. How many?" said Nobunaga.

"His entire army," said Ranmaru. "They've already killed the bodyguards."

"Then it's time," said Nobunaga.

"For what?" said Ranmaru.

"Since you were under my guidance, I taught you to keep death in mind at all times."

"You did."

"Death has arrived. Ran, don't let them come in. Set fire to the temple. Akechi will not have my head."

Lao's commentary

When walking The Way of the Computer Warrior, *we don't have to face death daily as part of our duties (unless perhaps we are working in a war zone). However, keeping death in mind still has its place in our lives. Death cannot be thought of only as our mortal ending, but also as the endings to periods in our life. Life happens in cycles; by paying attention to them, the Coding Samurai will be prepared when they arrive.*

For contract professionals, death can be thought of as the end of a contract. Keep that ending in mind, knowing that today could be the day the client terminates the contract. While those in full-time positions will likely not change employers at the same pace as contractors, change will come, either because of a layoff or because it's time to move on. Never let marketable skills deteriorate by no longer keeping up with trends or engaging in continuing education.

Doing work with no market value that's only useful for the client or employer is not keeping death in mind. By taking it for granted that an employer will always take care of your career, or by believing that it's okay to take a contract in the short term doing work with no market value, you can end up in the sobering position of realizing your skills aren't competitive. It's a gut-punch to realize that the recent months or years of your career have only been useful to an employer who no longer has work for you.

I keep actual death in mind each day of my life. The Way of the Computer Warrior *is a way with purpose, not an aimless wandering through the woods. I continually ask myself, "What do I want to accomplish before I die? Am I doing the most I can to honor myself and my dreams? Does my work reflect who I want to be in life? If I died today, did I live my life fully?"*

****

If I don't make it back, at least I died trying, thought Artemis before tucking the papers back into his pocket.

As the sound of the train's engine changed from a high-pitched hum to a growling, low-frequency rumble, Artemis saw the hyperloop port appear in the window. After the train stopped, Artemis gathered his things and stepped off. He immediately smelled the salty ocean air and heard waves crashing on the shore. The hyperloop port stood before him. It occupied a much smaller space than a traditional airport and housed thousands of shuttles, most of which were en route underneath the Atlantic

Ocean. The main terminal, a ten-story glass enclosure, housed a food court as well as a long ticket counter. The guards handed Artemis his ticket as they made their way directly to the security line. Security was a short tunnel about ten feet long. By the time he exited the tunnel, Artemis and his gear had been scanned and analyzed for threats.

"Get in line. Someone will meet you when you exit the hyperloop in France," said the woman guard.

He entered the line for the loading zone—the main platform for the Trans-Atlantic Hyperloop. When he arrived at the platform, a number displayed on a screen indicating which of the lanes to enter. One hundred tubes were bound together in a 10×10 square. An elevator took Artemis to the fifth floor. When the gate opened, he walked to the sixth lane, where another small line formed.

"Please hold on to any small bags you'd like in the main cabin and leave the remainder with me to store in the aft of the shuttle," said the smiling attendant.

"I just have my carry-ons," Artemis said to her.

Several shuttles were queued behind the one ready for departure. Approximately every five minutes, the lanes would shoot an individual shuttle containing ten people into the hyperloop and across the Atlantic to the port in Europe at La Rochelle, France. Once inside his shuttle, Artemis sat in a comfortable reclining seat and watched a welcome-and-safety message.

"Welcome aboard the Trans-Atlantic Hyperloop. Soon you will undertake an amazing trip across the Atlantic. The hundreds of miles of steel tubes rest comfortably underneath the water to reduce the effects of above-ground weather and human interference. Your trip will be completely safe and problem free. However, in the unlikely event a problem would occur, your shuttle will come to a complete stop until an engineer can address the problem. If your shuttle comes to a stop, don't panic. A hyperloop representative will contact you through the holographic display and keep you company for as long as you require. Now sit back, relax, and enjoy your journey," the woman said.

Artemis set up his portable and soon heard the alert that his shuttle was next in line. He felt a gradually increasing force while the shuttle reached incredible speeds on its way to Europe. Then the initial pressure subsided. At cruising speed, the shuttle moved as if it was sliding across butter.

With the euphoria of the hyperloop launch fading, Artemis began thinking that he was too young to think about death—until recent events. His comfort came from knowing he had the support of his friends and family. *Is that enough? What do I actually want? What am I doing all of this for?* Wealth, fame, a family, a legacy—all of these entered his mind, but he still didn't know what he wanted most. For now, he decided he only wanted to drink some orange juice and sleep.

Artemis woke up to the sound of the bell alerting him that he was arriving in La Rochelle. He organized his belongings and put his shoes back on. The shuttle slowed to a stop and the door opened with a hiss. An attendant greeted him on the platform.

"Thanks for traveling the Trans-Atlantic Hyperloop. Enjoy your stay wherever you are going and safe travels!" she said.

"Thanks. The exit is this way?" Artemis asked.

"Yes, follow the lighted path across the platform," she said.

Artemis started walking along the platform when he received an alert from Food Coma.

"Make sure to file a police report in Budapest.—Tilly," it said. He had no idea what it meant.

At the end of the platform, a man in a jumpsuit approached him.

"Hey there, Artemis. I'm here to ride along with you," he said, putting his arm firmly around Artemis' neck.

"Wonderful," said Artemis.

The next leg of the journey would take him from La Rochelle to Baghdad via the train with one switch in Budapest. His train was scheduled to leave in thirty-five minutes for the three-and-a-half-hour train ride to Budapest. He left the terminal and caught the shuttle to the high-speed rail station. Similar to the one in Lepton Mountain, this network of trains was funded under the same World Bank project.

Artemis felt exhausted. He dragged himself to the train leaving for Budapest. He found a quiet corner where he hoped he could sleep. He put on his sunglasses, stowed his gear in the bin above the seat, and covered himself with a blanket as his guard took the seat across from him. As soon as he nodded off, he was awakened by a tap on his shoulder.

"Is anyone sitting here?" asked a female voice.

Artemis shook off the blanket and raised his head to see a woman a bit older than him leaning over him.

"No, not that I know of," he said.

"Do you mind if I share the cabin with you?" she asked.

"No, it's fine," he said.

The fashionably dressed woman was traveling very light. Other than a purse, she only had a small shoulder bag. When she reached up to put her bag in the bin, the sleeves on her blouse slid down to reveal several tattoos, including one of a baby horse. He couldn't see clearly what the others depicted.

"That's better," she said, settling into the seat next to Artemis and across from his guard. "Busy day. All the other cabins were full, but this looks like a good one. I'm Jaqueline. What's your name?"

"Artemis," he said, reaching out his hand to be polite but wanting only to go to sleep.

"Was that your first time riding the hyperloop? I'm assuming you just came from there," she said, shaking his hand.

"Yes, my first time," he said.

"What did you think?" she asked.

"Smooth and fast. Way more comfortable than flying or taking the train," he said.

"I agree, but isn't it incredibly lonely?" she asked.

"I'm so tired that I slept most of the trip," he said.

"My friend is tired," interrupted the sportive-looking thug.

"You're better off for it. I can't ever let go of the fact that I'm basically all alone, except for the nine people packed in behind me, people that I can't even see, in a tube a hundred meters under the ocean. If something happened, I'd die alone. It'd be like dying in space. At least on an airplane or a train, there's a couple hundred other people with you. If there's a horrible accident, at least you see the faces of others on your way out, as horrified and shrieking as those faces may be," she said.

"I'll certainly have a new perspective on my return," said Artemis.

"Sorry, I guess I needed to get it out and you're the first person I've talked with since getting out of that tube," she said.

"I'm just exhausted, so I'm not much of a listener right now," he said.

"That's okay. When I'm inside that thing, I wonder who would take care of my dog if something would happen. I wonder who would miss me, who would be glad I was gone. It just gets me into a really morbid state of mind," she said.

"Take a hint, lady," said the BSP escort.

"I'm sorry. I don't mean to bother you," she said.

"I'm just very tired and will probably just sleep through the ride," he said as the bell signaled their departure.

"Oh, we're leaving now," she said. "I know I just keep

prattling on. I think that's it, though. It's the water. I must have a deep subconscious fear of drowning. I don't feel this way on planes or trains or in my car. It's got to be the underwater part of it that gets me in such a tizzy."

"Tizzy" was the last word that Artemis heard before falling asleep. While he slept, he had a dream that he was back in high school and part of a talent show. He and a dozen or so of his classmates were to perform in a dance contest. He was home in his bedroom practicing all of the moves. In the dream he had amazing talent and could dance in a way he never could in real life. As he danced, his parents kept coming up to his room and dropping off different Indian dishes. They brought paratha and mint chutney, then samosas and lamb rogan josh. After every song they brought more delicious dishes to his room. As he danced he reached his hands into the plates to sample the delicacies.

Then, in his dream, an automated car brought him to the school auditorium. The parking lot was packed full of vehicles. He was serene about performing the dance routine that he'd perfected. The auditorium erupted with applause as he entered.

"And now, we present Artemis Pound and the Dancing Dauphins," said the announcer.

Artemis leapt into the air from halfway down the aisle before landing gracefully on the stage, where he was met by the rest of the dance troupe. The music and light show commenced as Artemis moonwalked across the stage. One of the dancers came up to Artemis and tore off his shirt. Unaffected, Artemis continued dancing. One by one, the other dancers slid up to him and tore off his clothes until he stood naked before the audience. The music ground to a halt and the audience sat in stunned silence as the lights turned on and only Artemis remained on stage. Artemis woke up from his dream to an attendant shaking his shoulder.

Groggy and confused, Artemis took a few moments to fully wake up and prepare to leave the train. His guard and Jaqueline were both gone and he didn't see any of her things either. He stood up and opened up the bin above him to get his bag. It was empty. He panicked as he opened up all of the bins only to find each one empty. His sling pack was also missing, along with his portable computer. He stepped into the aisle and saw that he was one of the remaining few on the train.

"Someone stole my stuff!" he said to an attendant.

"No speak English," said the attendant, who appeared startled by Artemis' declaration.

Artemis remembered the last message from Tilly. He ran off the train to find help. Once on the platform, he glanced in both directions. To the left, a holographic display featured a friendly woman casually walking in circles under a massive sign that read "Mega Globe." Recognizing it as one of the company's ubiquitous sponsored directory services, Artemis jogged over to it.

"Hello. English," said Artemis.

"My name isn't English. It's Paulina. Ha ha. That's a joke," said the display.

"Not a funny one at that."

"In order to serve you better, please tell me: How can I be funnier? Was my joke insensitive, too subtle, sophomoric, or something else?"

"I just need help."

"I'm sorry but that isn't one of the options. Would you like me to repeat them?"

"No, I just want information."

"I heard you say information. What kind of information?"

"Airport directory."

"I'm sorry. The directory is temporarily out of service. Would you like to hear the weather brought to you by Mega Globe?"

"I think you mean Mega Suck. Forget it."

"I don't understand 'Mega Suck.'"

Seeing a sign for the ticket office, Artemis made his way past the line of people glaring at him to report his situation.

"English? Do you speak English? My things have been stolen. I need to file a police report," he said to the ticket agent.

"The police office is down the hallway," said the woman in the kiosk.

Artemis ran down the hallway toward the police station. He stopped quickly when he realized something else was missing: his wearable. He patted all of his pockets. The only thing he had left on him was *The Coding Samurai* book in his pocket and the hundred-dollar bill he received on graduation from his aunt and uncle that he'd been using as a bookmark. He realized it was the first time he hadn't had any piece of technology attached to him since he could remember. He felt more naked than he had in his dream.

CHAPTER SIXTEEN
Frugality

"That's the best description I can give you," said Artemis to the policeman taking down his report at Keleti train station. He was surprised and relieved at how well the policeman spoke English.

"The tattoos on her arms—are you certain you can't give me any more detail?" asked the policeman.

"There were some letters, people's faces, and other things I couldn't make out. That's the most honest description I can give. Oh, and a little horse," said Artemis.

"Like this one?" asked the policeman wryly, displaying a small horse tattoo under his collar.

"Yep. Just like . . ." Artemis began saying until having the stark realization that F.O.A.L. was indeed much bigger than he could have imagined. ". . . that," he finally muttered.

"We've printed you a temporary ID, Mr. Biggle, should you need to prove your identity—only valid here in Hungary. We appreciate your cooperation. If something comes up, we'll be in touch."

He handed Artemis an identification card that said his name was Tom Biggle from Lepton Mountain.

"Are you sure this is my ID?" asked Artemis, leaning in toward the counter and whispering intensely.

"Yes, *Tom*. It certainly is, *Tom*," whispered the policeman.

Artemis nodded while putting the card in his pocket.

"I think you should get a coffee," said the policeman.

"Um, okay. Where should I go?" asked Artemis, scratching his head.

"Leave the terminal and walk along Kerepesi. At this time of day, there's just one coffee shop open. You look like you need a pick-me-up," said the policeman.

"Thank you," said Artemis.

He left the terminal and walked to Kerepesi, keeping his head down and glancing around to see if anyone was following. Across from an old statue of a man, he saw a City Change and several other banks near a coffee shop called Mozaik Café. He started to go inside but decided he'd walk around the block first to see if it had a rear entrance. He turned the corner and walked down a filthy alley. At the end of the block by some dumpsters, he waited a moment to see if anyone else entered the passageway. Satisfied that he was alone, he searched out the back door to the café. There were a few other people inside when Artemis entered the tiny establishment. Its white walls and fluorescent lighting brightened the five or six small tables and wooden chairs.

"*Jó reggelt. Segíthetek?*" asked a young woman behind the counter. Artemis didn't understand her and wished he had his wearable to translate.

"Do you speak English?" asked Artemis.

"A little," she said, pinching her fingers together and then pushing her hair away from her eyes.

"Coffee, please," said Artemis.

"Real bean okay?" she asked.

"I'd love real bean," he said.

She set the cup of coffee on the counter. "Seventeen hundred, please," she said.

"Oh. I'm sorry, I was robbed on the train," he said.

"Robbed? There are some bad people. I'm sorry they take your things. Don't tell anyone, but you take this," she said, pushing the coffee toward him.

"I'm Tom. Tom Biggle. Should I stay here?" he asked, probing to see if, like the policeman, she was in on what was happening.

"Yes," she said. "My name is Teca. Have seat over there. I have something for you. Just a minute."

"Thank you, Teca," he said.

Artemis found a table by the window with a view of the clock on the wall and sat down with his coffee. He scanned the sidewalk and the road outside for anyone suspicious who might be looking for him. Everything seemed normal. He felt the small book in his side pocket and pulled it out to read.

Frugality

"Tama, your father has killed Oda Nobunaga. You must leave here," said her husband, Hosokawa Tadaoki.

"Killed Oda Nobunaga? Where will I go?" asked Tama.

"To the hamlet of Midono," said Tadaoki.

"But that's several days' trek through the mountains."

"Yes, but you will be well hidden there. Those loyal to Oda Nobunaga will be searching for you," said Tadaoki. "Take this money. It must last you until you reach the Hosokawa mansion," he continued, handing her a stack of coins.

"But this will barely buy enough rice for three days. It's not enough."

"You'll have to make it last. There is no more money now. Toyotomi Hidetsugu forced me to pay him my debt. I'll send more as soon as I can. The mansion is well supplied for now," he said.

Tama took the money and her pack, covered her head with a hooded robe, and began walking the road into the mountains.

Lao's commentary

The Coding Samurai is also wise to practice being frugal and modest. Particularly in the case of contractors, having a savings to cover three to six months of expenses is a vital necessity. In many markets, there's a lot of work for contractors but not necessarily a lot of good work. You don't want to have to take undesirable work because of a lack of savings. Taking work out of desperation can take your career backward instead of forward. The loss of future earnings compounds over time because of a lack of frugality.

Overspending on things to try and impress others and demonstrate status when one can't truly afford it can not only result in alienating yourself from peers, but it can also create financial hardship. It's far better to splurge on tools or training that can help grow skills. These types of investments help keep you engaged with your career.

On the flip side, people laughed at samurai who were skinflints. I worked with a developer who would never eat lunch with us away from the office. He preferred to pack a peanut butter and jelly sandwich every day just to save money. Buying coworkers coffee and going out to lunch with one's peers from time to time is necessary to make friends and connections. Doing this freely without expectation of reward can go a long way toward growing goodwill and a good reputation. Don't be frugal to the point of not enjoying life and being seen as stingy.

****

"Come back here," said Teca, waving to Artemis and leading him behind the counter and into the back office. "Here," she said, handing him a datapad.

Artemis took it, and she left to attend the counter. He was glad to not be walking the earth as a savage, without any tech at his disposal. Still, he was surprised that he had actually started to like the freedom of being disconnected. He checked the datapad and saw a message from Tilly.

"Go to the City Change; it's the bank next door. I've wired you some money. Then come back to the coffee shop," it read.

The bell on the door jingled. Artemis peered through the small office's door to see if someone had entered the shop, but it was just a group of customers leaving. Teca came back into the office with a fresh cup of coffee.

"Are you with F.O.A.L.?" he asked.

"Who? No. My friend tell me you will be here and to give you message. Are you in trouble?"

"Sort of."

"How?" she asked.

"It sounds crazy, but someone is trying to put some really bad software into a product that's about to launch," said Artemis quietly.

"And?"

"And my friends and I are going to stop him."

"What product?"

"The new quantum computers loaded with Groundswell."

"I have one of those ordered. It's coming next week!"

Artemis walked to the front door, scanned the growing crowd on the sidewalk, and then ran out of the office. He reached the City Change next door, walked in as casually as he could, and waited in line. The line was short, but it moved slowly. Too slowly for Artemis' comfort. He looked around furtively to make sure nobody was watching him. Finally, the teller, a thin bald man, waved him over to the counter. Artemis looked over the man's appearance and concluded that time, not fashion, had determined his baldness.

"*Jó reggelt.*"

"Good morning, sir. Do you speak English?" asked Artemis. The man shook his head no and then scooted in his chair to scan the room. He yelled something to one of his coworkers. The coworker yelled something back to him, and the man looked at

Artemis with a disappointed face while shaking his head again.

"ID?" managed the teller.

Artemis nervously handed over his false identification card. The teller examined it closely, alternating his gaze between the ID and Artemis.

"I'm waiting on a wire," said Artemis. "A wire?"

"Biggle," said the teller in a thick accent. "Wire."

The teller walked over to a burly, well-dressed man Artemis assumed was a supervisor. Not for the first time in the past few days, Artemis felt the hairs on his neck stand on end. His mind raced. *What if the fake ID hadn't worked? What if somehow Deepak, or whoever was working with him, had managed to place operatives in the bank?* He started to perspire as he tried to notice where the exits were located.

The bald teller and the burly man in the suit looked over at Artemis, then walked slowly back to the counter. Artemis was about to run when the teller reached into the drawer and removed some bills. He pointed to each stack, trying to find out from Artemis which type of bills he wanted. Artemis exhaled slowly and wiped his brow. He pointed at the smaller denomination and smiled. The man smiled back and began counting out forints for Artemis, before handing him 357,255.23 forints in cash and coin. Artemis took his receipt, thanked the man, and left City Change. He forced himself to walk back to the coffee shop. It wouldn't do to draw attention to himself by running out of a bank. As he approached the coffee shop, he looked cautiously through the window. Teca was still at the counter and the same customers were still inside. He decided to walk inside.

"This is for all of the help," said Artemis, sliding 1,000 forints across the counter to Teca.

"Not necessary, but I do have a message for you. Just down the street, to the right, is the Black Hole electronics warehouse. Find Elias."

"Thanks, Teca. You're an angel," he said, leaving the forints anyway.

As he walked down the street, he thought every pair of eyes was staring at him. A giant storefront stood out among much smaller shops in the urban area. A constant flow of automated, single-person shuttles lined up to pick up and drop off passengers. As he approached the electronics store, Artemis noticed a middle-aged man and woman lingering outside the store. They appeared to be window-shopping, but Artemis got a bad vibe from them. He caught them looking over their shoulders to glance his way. He tried not to look at them as he entered the store. Once inside, Artemis was immediately greeted by a salesman.

"*Üdvözöljük! Segíthetek?*"

"I'm sorry. I don't understand. Do you speak English?" asked Artemis in response.

"Hello! You don't appear to have our app installed on your wearable," said the salesman in impeccable English. He glanced at Artemis' arms. "Oh, that's because you aren't wearing one."

Salespeople were typically suspicious of anyone not wearing a wearable or implant. Being young and wearing urban clothes, yet without a wearable, indicated that Artemis might be trouble. Some people didn't wear them out of principle, but their numbers were few.

"I'm looking for Elias," said Artemis, staring at the salesperson.

"You found him. Tom Biggle? Let's get you over to our wearable and implant department," he said, extending his hand.

Artemis noticed a small horse tattoo on Elias' wrist as they shook hands. He glanced back at the front window. The middle-aged couple had entered the store and stood looking at a display by the front counter.

Artemis and Elias made their way down the brightly lit aisles, past office furniture and the boxy, blue kiosk that sold cables and connectors. They arrived at the wearable and implant section. Glass racks showcased all of the latest devices.

"So, what color shield for your implant?" asked Elias.

"I don't do implants. Show me your wearables," said Artemis.

"Are you sure? We have a fantastic implant installation service. In and out in fifteen minutes or less," he said. "And we have an implant here made just for you."

"I see. Let's look at that one then."

"That's the spirit," said Elias. "Come this way."

Artemis walked along with Elias to the implant installation

area and waited while the installer finished up with the current customer. The installer waved Artemis over to sit down.

"Don't be nervous. I do twenty of these a day," said the young woman with nearly white hair and many piercings.

"If it's more than Level 10 pain, I'm going to cry like a baby."

Artemis shuddered, thinking that just a day ago he would have laughed off Level 25 pain.

"You won't feel a thing; this antiseptic has a local anesthetic. I'm going to use this tool to slide this part of the implant under the skin. If it freaks you out, look away," she said.

Artemis watched her slide in the implant. Two small filaments poked out of his skin.

"Now I need to connect the magnets," she said.

There was a bit of pressure when she used the tool to install the thin magnets in his forearm. She took the interface out of the implant's box and applied it to his skin, lining up the magnets in the user interface with the ones in his arm. The interface molded to his skin and covered the thick part of the forearm close to his elbow.

"All done. Turn it on and your DNA footprint will let you sync to your implant, as long as you haven't mutated," she joked.

"I don't think I have, but I don't really know anymore what I am," said Artemis wryly. "It's syncing now. I see my messages," he said, noticing a message from Professor Lao. "Where do I pay?"

"Just swipe. It's 304,567.34 forints," she said.

I hope Mr. Biggle has some loot.

He swiped his new implant to complete the transaction, then hurried down the aisle leading out of the store. The middle-aged couple was nowhere in sight. He found a street bench by a statue being used as a pigeon roost and sat down to read the professor's message.

CHAPTER SEVENTEEN
Exactions

Artemis looked up from his implant and checked the pedestrian traffic. No sign of the couple or anyone else who looked suspicious. He stared across the street, still conflicted between feelings of betrayal and affection for the professor.

"Call this number when you receive this message," it read.

Artemis tapped the number.

"Where are you?" asked Professor Lao.

"Just outside the Black Hole warehouse in Budapest. Where are you?"

"I'm in Lepton."

"What about Tilly?"

"This F.O.A.L tech she's sharing—unbelievable."

"What's going on with this implant? It says I'm Tom Biggle, but it's supposed to be synced with my DNA."

"Synced with DNA and epigenetic markers which can be turned on and off. After the woman on the train eliminated your guard and sent your things on to India, she also gave you an injection which altered your epigenetic markers to match Tom Biggle, a fake identity based upon your basic genetic profile."

"What about Deepak?"

"We have no reason to think he doesn't believe you're still

in his control."

"No, I mean, what else do you know about Deepak and what he was doing to me?"

"Sadly, you were nothing to him. No more than a hamster in his lab."

"Why hasn't anyone stopped him?"

"Deepak is what I call an extorting minister. Everything he does is to position himself and create confusion," said Professor Lao.

"And if something doesn't go his way, he is a master at shifting blame and attention elsewhere. I already read that chapter," said Artemis.

Exactions

"Hosokawa Tadaoki has refused your call to aid," said Mitsuhide's messenger, returning from the Tango Province to the army camp along the river by Shōryūji Castle.

"Then he has played me for a fool," said Mitsuhide. "With only ten thousand men, we are no match for Nobunaga's avenger, Hideyoshi."

"Should I send another message, General Akechi?" said the messenger.

"It's no use. Hosokawa never intended to live up to his side of the bargain. It would have been better had he just stolen his dowry."

"What do you mean?"

"A thieving minister takes money here and there, but the damage stops there. An extorting minister is far more destructive. He bends the ear of his lord only toward him. Once he has gained his trust, his web of lies brings his lord to ruin. I trusted a liar."

"What do we do now?"

"We march south. We will take our position using the river to flank us. Make certain this note reaches my daughter. You must send it secretly," said Mitsuhide as he used his brush to write kanji on a piece of calligraphy paper.

"As you wish," said the messenger.

"And give this one to my page. If I should fall in battle, he is to make certain the note also reaches her. Again, no one must know," said Mitsuhide.

Lao's commentary

When a manager or lead role is an extortionist, first he will seek to undermine the existing way by criticizing it and spreading whispers through the organization. Once he's convinced enough people to do things his way, he will have wrested control away from others. Now if things turn out poorly, he can blame everyone around him, saying they didn't do things properly because of others' lack of experience or misunderstandings.

These type of people in IT are far more costly to the organization than those who take two-hour lunches or boxes of pens. Why? The extorting employee knows how to manage relationships upwardly. He tells those above him what they want to hear while sacrificing those under him when convenient. Unfortunately, it's in the nature of the extorting employee to seek more power and influence. As a result, many times this person will be promoted over those who have more character, more experience, more skill, and more genuine concern for the company or organization.

At the NGO I worked at, a newly promoted architect redesigned the enterprise system. Poor thought comprised this new design. Many people closer to the actual code and with a deeper knowledge of the systems advised against it. The architect isolated us and ensured we weren't invited to meetings and discussions. With his design, the new system failed in so many ways that the organization lost $3 million in contracts over the following three months. The architect blamed the developers who implemented the system, proclaiming that we were incompetent and didn't adhere to his design. He proclaimed that it was developer incompetence that caused the problems and that this proved why he didn't include us in discussions to begin with. Everyone under the architect agreed that the fault of failure was the architect's design, but the organization remained at the mercy of the person who used his position in a self-serving way.

****

"You know, Professor, I know what I need to do."

"What's that?"

"Go home," said Artemis.

"Home? Back to Lepton you mean?" asked Professor Lao.

"No, I mean Minnesota home. I mean ice-fishing, hot-dish, lutefisk home. I mean somewhere where there aren't conspiracies and pony people and military projects and all of . . . *this*. That's what I mean," said Artemis, showing a depth of anger that Professor Lao had never seen.

"You can't go now. And if you stop now and let Deepak do this, you'll never be able to go back," said the professor.

"Before I left, I got a call from my dad. Mom is sick. That's my responsibility, not something I can't really do a damn thing about. I'm an intern," said Artemis.

"Yes, Artemis, you're an intern. But you are part of something bigger now. And I know this isn't what you want to hear, but even if you go home, what will you do for your mother? You aren't a doctor. You can't heal your mom. You *can* stop Groundswell," said the professor.

"I'm just so scared."

"I know. And I've been a craven fool," replied Professor Lao. "But we need you."

"I still don't know if I trust you."

"You have to decide."

Artemis found it difficult to imagine that all of the wonderful experiences he had in college with the professor were faulty memories. Regardless, he knew that even if the professor was still lying to him, he had to take a chance.

"Where do I go?" asked Artemis.

"Reykjavík. The F.O.A.L. lab is there—fully equipped with everything you need. Tilly and all of us will connect with you tomorrow. Do you have enough money to get there?" asked the professor.

"I do. But I've been saving for a DIY Brew machine, not for spy expenses," said Artemis, feeling another yearning to just be a college student again.

"When this is over, drinks are on me. Now get to Reykjavík as quickly as you can. When you're on the island, let me know and I'll tell you where to go next," said the professor.

"I'll try to catch the next train to Paris and fly from there."

"I'll be waiting for your message," said the professor before ending the call.

Artemis walked back to the Keleti train station and bought a one-way ticket to Paris. In spite of Professor Lao's assurances, he kept waiting for someone to spot him and try to apprehend him. The next train was scheduled to leave in twenty-five minutes. He grabbed a quick lunch from a kiosk before boarding the train. Once in his seat, he tapped his implant and said, "Search one-way flights from CDG to KEV leaving this evening." His implant returned a list of options, all of them expensive. *So much for the DIY Brew,* he thought while booking a flight that would have him arriving in Iceland at 11:10 p.m.

At the Charles de Gaulle Airport, he thought he spotted the middle-aged couple from the electronics store in Budapest, but he couldn't be sure. He headed to the plane and hoped for the best.

****

The flight attendant made a pass through the aisle one last time as the plane made its final approach to the Keflavík Airport.

Through the fog, Artemis could see ocean, rock, and a strip of lights on the runway. The plane touched down with a screech.

"Call the professor," said Artemis.

"Hello," said the professor.

"I just landed; I'm still on the plane."

"Tonight you are going to stay on a farm just outside of Reykjavík. In the morning, they'll take you to the lab, and we can get started. When you enter the reception area, someone will have a sign for you. Go with them. And don't communicate with anyone else, not even the other interns. We can't afford to signal your whereabouts to Deepak," said Professor Lao.

"Got it. I'll talk with you tomorrow," said Artemis.

Artemis walked down the jet bridge and into the Keflavík Airport. He made his way from the gate to reception. Through the faces in the crowd, he saw the couple from outside the Black Hole in Budapest. They were talking to an airport security official. Artemis panicked. Surely they were working for Deepak. It made sense. Rather than apprehend him, they must have followed him to find out who he was meeting. Artemis ducked his head and started to turn the other way when he picked out a slightly older man with red hair and a red beard holding a sign that read "Mr. Biggle." He would have to walk past the couple to get to his ride. He took small steps toward the man with the sign, his legs almost giving out with each step. He kept his focus on the couple. What difference did it make if he made eye contact with them? They obviously knew who he was and where he was going.

Artemis walked up to the man with the sign and said, "I'm being followed by that couple. We have to lose them."

The man laughed. "The Einarssons? Not likely."

"You know them?"

"Of course I know them. Iceland is like a small town. Mr. Einarsson is a fisherman who lives not far from me. He and his wife were just vacationing in Budapest."

"So you're sure they aren't spies?"

The man laughed louder.

"Yes. I'm Viggó. Welcome to Iceland," he said with a deep, rumbling voice.

"Are you taking me to the farm?" asked Artemis.

"I am."

"How far away is the farm?"

"Thirty minutes."

Viggó led Artemis to the car and told it to navigate to the farm. The car exited the airport and entered the highway along the black, rocky coast. Artemis had never been anywhere so desolate. Nothing but water to the left and nothing but black rock to the right. No buildings, no animals, not even any trees. Artemis stared out the car's rear window and saw only darkness. The absence of headlights let him relax.

"It's quiet here," said Artemis.

"Yes," said Viggó.

"Have you lived here all your life?"

"I have."

"Do you have any brothers or sisters?"

"I do."

In the distance, Artemis saw a few lights flickering along the coast. As futile as it might be engaging Viggó in conversation, he would ask him one more question. "Is that a town up ahead?" asked Artemis.

"Vogar."

"What's in Vogar?" asked Artemis, already kicking himself.

"Nothing."

Artemis furrowed his brow as he thought about spending thirty more minutes in the car with a companion who only gave one- and two-word answers. "It's been a hell of a day. Do you mind if we stop for a drink in the city?" asked Artemis.

"Mind?" said Viggó, laughing. "No Viggóson minds stopping at the pub!"

"Your name is Viggó Viggóson?" asked Artemis.

"Indeed. One of Iceland's finest names!" he said.

"Okay, Viggó Viggóson. Take me to the pub!" said Artemis.

The car exited the highway onto the tight, narrow streets of Reykjavík. They traveled past Hallgrímskirkja, lit up to reveal the proud bronze soldier atop the pedestal in front of the iconic church.

"My sister was married there," said Viggó.

Apparently, Viggó only needs the thought of drinking to start opening up.

"What's your sister's name?" asked Artemis.

"Björk," said Viggó reverting back to one-word answers.

"Bjork Viggóson. Pretty name."

"No. Not Viggóson. Viggósdóttur," said Viggó, amused at Artemis' denseness. "I'm Viggó's son. Bjork is Viggó's daughter. She is Bjork Viggósdóttur," said Viggó, teaching Artemis a lesson in Icelandic culture.

"Ahh," said Artemis.

"Hey, car, park on Bankstrasse," said Viggó.

The car made a right, found the next spot, and pulled up to the curb. The streets were full of drunken revelers. Most of the people were in their twenties, but many of them were clearly younger, even in their mid-teens. They were dancing and singing in the street.

"All right, Artemis, let's drink!" shouted Viggó as he grabbed Artemis' shoulder and squeezed.

Artemis exited the car and circled around to meet Viggó in the street, where he was already drinking from a bottle given to him by one of the guys dancing near them. Someone smashed a bottle on the sidewalk, which inspired several others to do the same.

Artemis followed his new friend as he danced and sang with other partiers in the street. Nothing but pubs and restaurants lined this part of Bankstrasse. There also didn't appear to be anyone over twenty-five.

"This place!" said Viggó, pulling Artemis by the arm.

"What's so special about this place?"

"All of the most beautiful women of Iceland drink here," said Viggó.

"Are you serious?" asked Artemis, imaging a bar full of pretty, smiling Icelandic women. "Okay. Let's go," said Artemis.

"Oh, you are going to be so happy."

The two entered Lebowski Bar on the corner of Laugavegur and Klappaarstigur.

"Perfect timing," said Viggó.

"How's that?" asked Artemis.

"Happy hour," he said, entering the movie-themed pub.

"At midnight?"

"It's always happy hour."

Artemis followed Viggó inside and couldn't believe his eyes. Along with a few bearded men, young Icelandic women filled the place. Viggó turned to him and smiled.

"See, I told you," said Viggó.

"Yes, you did," said Artemis, stunned.

"Hey, buddy, get my friend and I a couple pints and some Nihilist wings," said Viggó to the man behind the bar, who looked like he could be Viggó's brother.

Viggó turned to a young woman behind the bar. "Björk, I want you to meet my friend Artemis," he said.

"Is this your sister?" asked Artemis.

"My sister? No, this is my friend Björk," he said.

"Oh, I thought it might be your sister. They have the same

name," said Artemis.

"This is Iceland. Half of the women here are called Björk. This is Björk, she is Björk," said Viggó, pointing to a girl across the room. "The other bartender is Björk."

"I see. Björk the bartender, would you pour me a pint, please? Actually, make it two," said Artemis.

"Two! Spoken like a Viggóson. Make it two for me as well!" said Viggó, giving Artemis a bear hug.

"So I was told not to ask about your business here in Iceland, but what do you do?" asked Viggó.

"I'm a programmer," said Artemis.

"All right, a smart guy," said Viggó.

"How about you?" asked Artemis.

"I'm a fisherman," he said, pounding the pint of ale.

"What's the biggest fish you've ever caught?" asked Artemis, chugging from his glass.

"Easy question. A Greenland shark. Over ten meters."

"You're joking. That's over thirty feet long. Where did you catch it? How did you catch it?"

"Where I caught it is not down in any map; true places never are. Me and four crew took my ship, the *Uxi*, into the dark, stormy night, when fishing for shark is best. We left the port at Bolungarvík into the Denmark Strait. After many hours tossed upon the waves of the Greenland Sea, I spotted the giant," said Viggó.

"I can only imagine the sight of a behemoth like that,

surfacing in the crest of a giant storm wave," said Artemis.

"I saw it on sonar," said Viggó, pounding another glass. "I yelled for my captain's mate to circle the boat around so I could drop a line with bait. The beast wasn't hungry, but we Icelandic fishermen have a secret that the sharks can't resist."

"What did you do?"

"It's a secret. We caught hold of the beast and our tiny ship dropped into the water. One of my men fell overboard."

"My god."

"Two of my crew dove in to rescue him while me and the first mate struggled to reel the monster in. We fought her for three hours, until the sun began to rise. When we finally pulled her in and gutted her, we found out why she wasn't hungry."

"Why?"

"Her belly was full of a polar bear carcass."

"You're lying," said Artemis.

"Ask anyone in town," said Viggó, peering over the top of his glass. "They'll tell you I'm not."

"What happened to the crewman?"

"He drowned."

One of the women with shimmering black hair, a pale, round face, and glowing blue eyes walked up to Artemis at the bar.

"Hallo," she said. "I'm Björk."

"I could have guessed. Artemis," he said, extending his hand to her.

"This is the guy I told you about," said Viggó.

"He's the spy who helped you wrestle Big Bertha?" she asked.

Viggó winked at Artemis as he said, "The very one."

"Bartender, a pint for the lady," said Artemis before turning his attention back to Björk. "So what do you like to do here in Reykjavík?"

"Triathlons, art exposés. But my passion is philosophy," she said.

"Sounds very well rounded," said Artemis. "What do you study?"

"My latest paper argues for a reconciliation of monism and the appearance of plurality in the universe," said Björk, drinking half of her ale with one trip to her mouth.

"I think I'm in love," said Artemis.

"What?" she said.

"Nothing. Do you cover the nature of the universe as a two-dimensional holographic projection of information as it relates to monism?" he said.

"Enough philosophy. I've been drinking for an hour. Kiss me," she said before slamming the rest of her ale.

"Here? Now?" asked Artemis.

She leaned in and pressed her mouth against Artemis' lips. He started to kiss her back before realizing she was taking a slightly different approach. She flattened her tongue and pressed it against his, letting it rest there a moment. After the pause, she slowly moved her tongue up and down against his, keeping it flat and wide against his. Artemis had just experienced both the weirdest and the sexiest kiss of his life.

From the corner of his eye, Artemis saw Viggó smiling at him. He closed his eyes, smelled Björk's perfume, and felt her soft sweater against his hands. She pulled slowly away from him.

"My place is nearby. Should we go?" she said.

The amount of testosterone in Artemis' brain meant that there was only a one percent chance he would turn her down. He imagined the next several hours in her apartment, the two of them alone, doing god knows what. Then he thought about Tilly. He pulled himself out of the brain chemical–induced funnel.

"I can't believe I'm saying this, but no," he said.

The heat between them evaporated. Artemis took a step back as disappointment and irritation washed over Björk's face. He glanced over at a stunned Viggó, whose knuckles were white from gripping the handle of his ale.

"My friend is confused. Hold on a second," said Viggó, taking Artemis by the arm and dragging him to the other side of the bar.

"What's the matter with you, pal? That's the hottest, most desired Björk in all of Iceland. She is the Björk of all Björks— the über Björk. Do you understand what you are doing? There's not a man in Iceland who wouldn't use his girlfriend for shark bait to spend one night with her," said Viggó with a fury that left spittle on Artemis' face.

"I believe you, but I can't. I have to go now," said Artemis, pushing Viggó's arm away from him and walking back toward the other side of the bar.

"Björk, any other day, I would be walking out of here with you, but I have to leave. I know I'm probably making the biggest mistake of my life, but I still can't go with you. Good-bye," he said, leaning in and kissing her on the cheek before walking out of Lebowski Bar with Viggó trailing him.

Viggó caught up to Artemis by the car, where a group of youngsters were smashing bottles.

"I have to go. I'm only going to get a few hours' sleep as it is," said Artemis.

"Whatever you say, Artemis. You're my guest." Inside the car, Viggó said, "Hey, car, take us home," then rested his head against the window.

After leaving the city, the car wound its way through several roundabouts, going deeper and deeper into the country. After ten minutes or so, the car pulled down a dirt road to an old farmhouse. When the car stopped, Viggó was snoring.

Artemis shook him hard. "Viggó! Wake up!"

"I'm awake," he said. "Let's go. I'll take you to your room."

Artemis followed Viggó across the yard to the small guesthouse. A soft wind blew, and Artemis thought he could still smell a bit of the ocean. It was completely quiet out in the country. He finally felt safe.

"Viggó. I drank too much. I'm really hungry. Can I bother you for some food?" asked Artemis.

"I'll bring you something. Make yourself comfortable," said Viggó.

Artemis took off his shoes and sat on the bed. It was tiny but comfortable enough in his drunken state. Other than the bed, the guesthouse had a small bathroom, a bookshelf, and a chair. He looked at the books—they were all written in Icelandic and appeared to be very old.

"Here you go. Some water and a snack. You might not like it, but we love it here. It's the best I can do right now—too drunk," said Viggó.

"What is it?" asked Artemis, picking up a piece of the white meat from the tray.

"A bit o' Big Bertha. *Hákarl.* Really delicious," he said.

Artemis put the piece of Greenland shark in his mouth and immediately regretted it. *How can this possibly be meat?* he wondered. The texture was chewy and firm, but the taste was something like fish meat soaked in motor oil that someone had urinated in. After swallowing it, his stomach immediately turned over. He stood up from the bed, ran outside, grabbed a fence post, and vomited.

"Here," said Viggó, handing Artemis a glass of water.

"Can you make sure I'm up in a few hours?" asked Artemis.

"Yes. We'll have a great Icelandic breakfast. It will be much better for you than Bertha," said Viggó.

Once Artemis was certain that his stomach was settled enough, he staggered back inside to drink more water. Lumbering across the room, he lay down on the bed and watched the ceiling spin until he fell asleep.

CHAPTER EIGHTEEN
Principles of Warriors

"Hey, champ. Breakfast," said Viggó, setting down on the bed a tray holding juice and eggs.

"Thanks. What time is it?" said Artemis, covering his eyes.

"Ten thirty. Eat," said Viggó.

"Ten thirty? I was supposed to be there at ten! Dammit, I got too drunk."

"It's not the end of the world."

"It might be. We have to go," said Artemis, who suddenly felt his stomach turn. He ran into the bathroom and vomited.

"All that fussing has made you sick. You're going to have to eat," said Viggó before walking out the door.

Artemis took small bites of the eggs until they were gone. He found a bottle of ibuprofen on the counter and took a few. He turned on the hot water in the shower and stood in it for several minutes while trying to block out his thoughts.

Is this the best I can do?

When he heard a knock at the door, he quickly dried off and threw on his clothes.

"Let's go," said Viggó.

Artemis left with Viggó, and the car drove them to the laboratory on the northern outskirts of Reykjavík. The building blended in with other commercial offices. The car parked in the lot and Viggó escorted Artemis inside. The workspace was similar to BSP, only with a Nordic decor. A woman much older than Artemis walked over to greet them.

"Hello. I'm Hella Helgisdóttur, a friend of F.O.A.L. Thank you, Viggó, for bringing our guest," said Hella.

"You're welcome. I'll be off now," Viggó said before turning away and leaving the office.

"I'm Artemis," he said.

"Welcome. I'll take you to the conference room," said Hella.

Artemis followed Hella into a conference room, where a holographic welcome message played.

"Welcome to HoloMeet. Your meeting hasn't started yet. Your meeting will start when the chairperson arrives. If you are the chairperson, please enter or speak your code now. Welcome to HoloMeet," the voice repeated.

"Can I get you something to drink? Coffee, tea, water?" asked Hella.

"Tea, please," said Artemis, taking a seat.

The welcome screen flickered and in the center of the room sat Professor Lao's holographic projection. Before Artemis had a chance to say anything, Tilly, Beyoncé, Bits, Lukas, and Mei flashed into the meeting.

"Artemis!" shouted Tilly.

"Good to see you aren't being force-fed naan, pal," said Bits.

"Good morning, everyone. Thank you for being here," said

Professor Lao.

"I'm thrilled to see you all," said Artemis.

"Let's get started," said the professor. "This is my final analysis of the Groundswell code. Most of the time the system will behave innocuously. Occasionally, though, when users interact with the system, the code will affect the user's neurological system."

"How?" asked Artemis.

"Beyoncé was able to get one of the DOTs to run the Groundswell tests, previously something Deepak had only been doing with the interns sent to the offshore team," said Professor Lao.

"What happened?" asked Artemis.

"The guy who ran the Groundswell tests loves pizza—I should say he *loved* pizza," said Professor Lao.

"Loved?" asked Mei.

"In the tests, Groundswell simulated a pizza parlor where the tester had a rich sensory experience, with the molecular printer puffing the scents of the pizza into the haptic suit while he feasted on 3D-printed bites. He shoved bite after bite down his throat. After the subject left the Groundswell test, Beyoncé offered him a real slice of pizza," said Professor Lao.

"What happened?" asked Artemis.

"He tried to hit me," Beyoncé said.

"There's more. We've learned that Deepak has taken his technology to another level. His code not only coerces the original pieces of information to lie during the recall process; it can link those memories to other information in the subject's memory banks," said the professor.

"I don't get it," said Artemis.

"After he tried to punch me in the face, he started yelling for pakoras," said Beyoncé. "He was seriously pissed about the slice of pizza and the only thing that would calm him down was a pakora," said Beyoncé.

"I'm sure you can see how a system like this, used by billions of people, could alter humanity in horrible ways," said the professor.

"Planet Deepak," said Bits.

"Thanks, but no thanks," said Lukas.

"I should note, the test seemed to be operating with an exceptionally strong signal. The subject's reaction was violent because he received the equivalent of a thousand exposures of the signal in one sitting. This isn't normally how it would run. The program is insidious in that it alters consciousness over perhaps months or years. Someone like the tester who loved pizza will learn to gradually lose their appetite for it while simultaneously finding himself craving pakoras. Since this will ordinarily happen slowly, there wouldn't be a grotesque reaction," said the professor.

"What do you mean, 'grotesque reaction'?" asked Tilly.

"Think about it like someone who slowly puts on weight over a year or two. The subject and those around them daily might not notice. Only when presented with a picture from before the weight gain would the stark contrast be apparent," said the professor. "In other words, everyone in the world would become someone else at a snail's pace and no one might notice."

"We have to stop it. But what do we do?" asked Artemis.

"We need to organize ourselves with army and combat principles if we're going to stand a chance," said the professor.

A chessboard appeared in the HoloMeet. On one side was BSP, with a depiction of Deepak, Jeff, the Groundswell system, and the BSP building. On the other side were Artemis and his friends.

"I wanna be a knight," said Bits.

"Sorry, that role's taken. You can be my *wakashū*, though," said Lukas.

"Knock it off," said Mei.

"Beyoncé, you are our intelligence liaison. We need you to get inside BSP, install a back door to the network, and gather as much information as you can," said the professor as the hologram showed her penetrating the BSP building. "Tilly, you are our diplomat. I'm going to prepare some things for you and send you to speak with Jeff. We can only have this meeting once everything else is in place," said Professor Lao.

"Wait a second. Shouldn't Tilly be our cavalry?" asked Bits.

Tilly glared at Bits, and Artemis covered his eyes with his hands.

"Artemis, you're the watch commander. The rest of you are

our infantry. If diplomacy fails, we'll need to be prepared to stop the code in Groundswell from getting out. Artemis, Tilly arranged to have a quantum set up for you in the lab there. Lukas, Bits, and Mei, I understand you already have a quantum network set up," said the professor.

"That's right," said Lukas.

"We're going to link it to the network Artemis is on and give it a few upgrades. Beyoncé, Tilly, and Artemis report to me. The rest of you report to Artemis. If something happens and I can't be reached, Artemis is in charge," said the professor. "Does everyone understand their role? Any questions?"

"Yeah: exactly what the hell are we going to do to bring this guy down?" asked Bits.

"Deepak has hidden the quantum core of Groundswell within a wormhole. We must enter Deepak's lair, navigate his guardians and traps, and destroy it," said the professor.

"How do we do that?" asked Artemis.

"Tilly has provided us with some F.O.A.L. technology that I've been able to use to upgrade some of the peripherals I've been developing in the lab. Once you get to the core, someone will need to make contact with it while wearing the upgraded haptic suit. This should destroy the core," said the professor.

"That's it?" asked Artemis.

"Yes, that's it, but it won't be easy. Deepak will have made certain that it will be nearly impossible for anyone but him to reach the core. Expect the worst. We won't be able to communicate with anyone in the wormhole, but we on the outside will be doing everything we can to keep the attack up on BSP while you navigate Deepak's gauntlet."

"I'm ready. Where's my suit?" asked Bits.

"Some of the materials were quite difficult to find. There was actually only one place where I could have the quantum core-destroying suit assembled," said the professor. "That's the F.O.A.L. lab in Reykjavík."

"There's only one suit?" asked Artemis.

"There only one core-destroying suit," said the professor. "But Tilly's wealth of information provided us with a few more tricks that I was able to build into some suits here to support the mission."

"We need a name," said Mei. "We need a name for our army."

"How about the Poop Pirates?" asked Lukas.

"I'm not even going to legitimize that name with a response," said Beyoncé.

"The Coding Samurai," said Artemis.

"It's better than the Poop Pirates, I have to admit. Maybe not a lot better, but better," said Bits.

"Can we move on?" asked Professor Lao.

"Please," said Tilly.

"We've covered our army principles: the make-up of the group, our objectives, our roles, and . . . ahem . . . our name," said Professor Lao. "We have a lot more to prepare and little time to do it. Take fifteen minutes and then meet back here."

The meeting ended and Artemis sat alone, wondering if he'd ever see the real people on the other side of the holograms again. He started writing Tilly a message: "Hey, good seeing you." He deleted it and wrote another one: "Hey, been a long time." He groaned, deleted it, and sat at the table with his face in his palms. He felt disconnected, alone, and confused about his feelings for Tilly. Then his implant vibrated. It was her.

Hey, Artemis. I wish that was the real you sitting at the table next to me.

I agree. I was just writing you. How are you doing?

I'm fine. I'd like to say I wasn't worried, but I'd be lying.

Stop. I'm worried enough for the both of us.

Just take care of yourself.

You, too. BTW, pretty sure I don't have a job at BSP anymore.

They're probably clearing out your desk right now. I'll give you a good reference, though.

Gee, thanks.

Artemis walked to the lab cafeteria, grabbed a few snacks,

and then found his way back to the conference room to rejoin the HoloMeet. He opened up *The Coding Samurai*. There were only a few chapters left. He thought back to graduation, when the professor had given him Princess Di, and how much his life had changed with all the new people in it and the unbelievable situation he was now facing. He wasn't certain anymore what life was about or what he was supposed to do with it.

Artemis snapped back to the present and started reading.

Principles of Warriors

"My lady, I have a letter from your father," said Tama's maid, Kayo Kiyohara.

"Thank you, Kiyohara," said Tama, taking the letter from her maid's hand and breaking the seal.

"Daughter, times are quite dark since you've left. My army is positioned to defend against Toyotomi Hideyoshi and Tokugawa Ieyasu, who've returned to take Oda Nobunaga's place. I don't understand how such a great man fell so low, but the madness that people saw in him as a teen has returned with a vengeance. I had no choice but to end his tyranny and his plots against the Emperor.

"Today, I'm at the camp, surveying my men in the four areas of training: knighthood, weaponry, army principles, and combat principles. Knighthood involves taking care of one's affairs civilly, exercising cleanliness, and so on. Weaponry consists of training with the sword, bow and arrow, and other weapons.

"Most important to our victory are the remaining two: army and combat principles. Army principles involve planning, ranks, terminology, and preparation for combat. Combat principles involve the actions on the battlefield. I hope I have enough top-rank knights trained in all four principles to secure a victory. Very few samurai achieve this status.

"I don't know why I'm telling you all of this. I suppose I just want a few minutes to feel like I'm with you. I hope this note finds you well. You will be in my heart today as I fight for the future of Japan. Your father, Mitsuhide."

Lao's commentary

Most professionals aren't engaging in actual warfare. Nevertheless, knighthood, weaponry, army principles, and combat principles map directly to the workplace. Knighthood can be thought of as professionalism—dressing well and speaking and writing clearly. Professionalism also includes being respectful, prompt, and diligent.

Weaponry can be thought of as the knowledge and skill sets for your role. The Coding Samurai's main weapon is of course a computer. Those walking The Way of the Computer Warrior *are encouraged to build and maintain their own computers component by component. Understanding hardware leads to writing better software. Designing and building your own computer aids in achieving a better understanding. A programmer must also possess typing skills and the knowledge of one or more computer languages, as well as the programming patterns, applications, tools, and protocols they work with on a regular basis. Whatever the set of technologies and skills for a particular role, learning them in and out is equivalent to mastering weaponry.*

Army principles can be thought of as understanding how one's role fits into the organization. This allows you to do your job the best you can without crossing others or neglecting your own duties. Also, understand your team's purpose to the organization. Knowing what others in the company need from your team will help you communicate with them and write better software for the end users.

To become truly elite, knowing the company's market, products, services, systems, and personnel is a requirement. These are combat principles. If this understanding is deep enough, The Coding Samurai can find himself at the highest echelons of the organization.

At almost every place I've worked, someone had a copy of Sun Tzu's The Art of War. *Why? Business is a type of combat. Each role plays an important part on the battlefield. Professionals who master the four principles of warriors will become generals.*

****

The HoloMeet began and Artemis closed the book. The group gathered around the table and Professor Lao sat with one of his pet parrots on his shoulder. He was feeding it something and making baby sounds to it.

"I've sent everyone some software designs," said the professor. "We need to code these tools to go up against Deepak and the BSP network. Unless there are any questions, let's get started."

"What should I do?" asked Tilly.

"I've sent you some materials for your meeting with Jeff," said Professor Lao.

"Tilly, you shouldn't be sitting at home by yourself. Come over to my place," said Beyoncé.

"I'm taking care of Jef. Can I bring him too?" asked Tilly.

"If he pees on my Persian rug, I'm going to tear Artemis a new one," said Beyoncé.

"I'm coming over then," Tilly said.

"Tilly, when you get to Bey's, meet me in my home world. I need to talk to you," said Artemis before leaving the HoloMeet.

Artemis left the conference room and walked to the quantum he'd be using. He logged in to the group's network and switched to work-sharing mode. From Artemis' perspective, he was sitting in a small movie theater, with each team member's work area taking up a portion of the giant screen. Sitting to his right were Beyoncé and Mei; to his left sat Bits and Lukas.

"Has everyone looked over the professor's designs?" asked Artemis.

"I've never seen designs like this before, but it's nothing we can't pull off," said Beyoncé.

"Let's start dividing up the work," said Artemis.

"Who wants to work on this first design, 'Traffic Sniffer,' for data leaving Groundswell servers? He listed a bunch of patterns we need to look for," said Bits.

"I'll write that one," said Mei. "I've already started it."

"And I'll write the 'Crafty Back Door,' for *The Coding Samurai* to get into Groundswell's network," said Beyoncé.

"Hey, ladies, thanks for leaving us guys the scraps," said

Lukas.

"Don't feel left out, sweetie," said Beyoncé. "I'm going to need you guys to scrutinize the hell out of my code. I'll be lucky if I even get one shot to sneak it in."

"When's code freeze?" asked Lukas.

"They're saying tonight, but you know they always cram stuff in at the last second. I have a plan to make certain they do," she said.

"You sly woman," said Lukas, throwing some virtual popcorn at Beyoncé.

"So this next piece, 'Quantum Ion Cannon,' the ability to request billions of scenes from Groundswell server at once," said Bits.

"Hold up. Beyoncé, is Wei Wei working this weekend?" said Artemis.

"I think so. He still didn't have some of his tasks done yesterday," she said.

"He's already built something like this. He was using it for testing a bug he found in the reward system," said Artemis. "Can you see if he's online and ask him for a copy of it? It should save us some time."

"I'm on it," said Beyoncé.

"This is the last design, 'The Lasso of Truth,'" said Bits. "It says, 'This program must redirect infected packets from the BSP servers to a man-in-the-middle network. This code will redirect the quantum particles being sent to mind-fuck the world.'"

"He didn't write *mind-fuck*," said Artemis.

"I know, but it sounds hairier that way," said Bits.

"I'll do that one," said Lukas. "I know those protocols best— plus, we all know I'm an expert at man-in-the-middle."

"Really, Lukas?" said Mei.

"So what am I going to work on?" said Bits in a whiny voice.

"Your biceps?" said Lukas.

"Bits, once Beyoncé gets the copy of the script from Wei Wei, you'll need to get it in shape," said Artemis.

"See, right up your alley, big guy—getting things in shape," said Lukas, flexing his tiny arm muscles.

"Then what are you going to work on?" Bits asked.

"The professor never mentioned setting up the man-in-the-middle server," said Artemis. "I'm going to go set up Princess Di. Are you guys good if I take off for a little bit?"

"You're going to go cowboy coding on us?" asked Mei.

"No, I'm not going to do it by myself. Plus there's something else I need to do there," said Artemis.

"This is no time to watch porn, Artemis," said Lukas.

"Just go. We've got this," said Bits.

"I'll be back soon," Artemis said before logging off from the rest of the group.

He remoted into Princess Di. It felt like weeks since he'd seen her, even though it had only been a couple of days.

"Hey, Di."

"Hello, Artemis."

"Send Tilly a message that I'm waiting for her at my home world."

"Okay."

"Please load my home world."

Artemis arrived outside the biosphere. He wanted to change it into something else, like a sunny field with a creek flowing through it. He decided that when this was all over, that would be the first thing he did.

"Artemis!" shouted Tilly.

He ran up to her and hugged her. "I didn't know if I'd see you again," he said.

"Of course you would."

"I guess there's no point in worrying about that right now."

"We'll get through this," she said, hugging him harder.

"How?"

"By moving forward."

"One thing I didn't hear in the plan for going against BSP is what happens to the Groundswell signal if we can't destroy the quantum core," said Artemis.

"Honestly, I don't know."

"I have an idea, but I need your help."

"Of course."

"I pulled this out of the BSP offices when they refreshed me," said Artemis, stepping away from Tilly and holding up the vial he had hidden away during his trip to Europe.

"What is it?"

"It's the Reflux vaccine that they used to reverse all of the quantum effects on me."

"Ahh, I think I know where you are going with this," said Tilly, moving closer to him, locking her eyes onto his.

"When we saw the harpstones last, they were mimicking everything we did, including our sounds," said Artemis, fixing his gaze on Tilly.

"They have an uncanny ability for information replication."

"I saw it from the start, when they absorbed the mosses into their own bodies so they could perform photosynthesis themselves," Artemis said, now only inches from her face.

"So if we let the harpstones evolve with a mutation of the molecular structure of the refresh treatment . . ." Tilly wrapped her arms around Artemis.

"Then we can redirect the Groundswell signal to Princess Di."

"Pump the signal to the harpstone wormhole using the F.O.A.L. technology and let the harpstones refresh the signal completely."

"Exactly," said Artemis, holding Tilly close.

"Now let's get busy."

"I'd love to, but don't you think we should get all of the programming done first?"

"That's what I meant."

"Right."

"Wait, look up there," said Tilly, pointing up to the Martian sky.

"What is it?"

"Equuleus."

"And what is Equuleus?" asked Artemis, pulling Tilly even closer to him.

"It's the foal constellation. If you ever miss me, just look for it and I'll be there."

"I will," he said before pressing his lips against hers and feeling her body melt into his.

****

A few hours passed while Artemis and Tilly put the finishing touches on the harpstone signal relay.

"Tilly, you head back. I need to do something by myself."

"You sure?" she asked. Artemis nodded. "Well, you know where I'll be if you need me."

Artemis went to his home world, but this time he took a different path outside the Mars biosphere. He walked around behind the dome and followed a small path that led to a pile of orange rocks several hundred yards away. Arriving at the pile, he crouched down and crawled into a narrow crevice. Inside the small cave were all of Artemis' photos and videos.

Like everyone else, the amount of media available from Artemis' life was staggering. Most people had recorded moments from everyday life since the time they were born. The media took many forms: live streams, holograms, photos, videos. Once someone was tagged, even as a baby, the media was pooled together. Petabytes of seemingly mundane events were captured: breakfasts, dinners, signs along the road, squirrels. Occasionally, moments of meaning found their way into the ocean of media associated with each person. The constant stream of photos and video had become an adapted form of human communication for the modern era, like the chattering song of a bird in the forest, calling out and waiting for another bird to call back with a song of its own.

Artemis was interested in one particular moment from his childhood. He was eleven years old and in the sixth grade. He had to ride the bus from his house in the suburbs a few miles down the road from the elementary school. For several years, Artemis woke up every morning sick to his stomach because he knew what to expect. He was one of the last kids on the bus and his seat was near a group of several bullies. They would pick a target and torment that child horribly. One boy had boogers wiped on him for four weeks until the bullies grew bored. After him, they targeted a girl whose mother had died when she was four years old. They had taken turns blowing in her hair, an action which sounds harmless enough, but what they said afterward was so cruel that Artemis would never forget the words or their cackling laughter. "That's the ghost of your dead mother."

Every day, Artemis sat and read his comics—fearing that would be the fateful day they chose him. The morning the picture was taken—the one he was looking for—he hadn't been particularly preoccupied with the tormentors on the bus. He sat down in his seat and put on his headphones. After a minute or two, someone shoved his shoulder. He ignored it until the shoves became punches. He turned around and saw the menacing glares of the bus bullies. They were signaling him to remove his headphones. He took off the headphones and tried not to show the immense amount of fear he had inside.

"Hey, we don't like the kid sitting next to you," said the ringleader.

"Scottie? He's all right," said Artemis.

"All right? No he's not. He's a punk. We can't reach him," said the one with black hair and remnants of a cleft lip.

"What do you mean?" asked Artemis.

"We can't reach him and he needs to be punished. You're going to do it for us," said the ringleader.

"I—I don't know what you mean," said Artemis.

"*I—I—I don't know what you mean,*" said the third one, mocking Artemis.

"You're going to push his head into the window and punish him for being a punk or we're going to pound you every day for the rest of the year," said the ringleader, cracking his knuckles.

Artemis was terrified. He couldn't think. Suddenly, the third bully slapped him with his open hand.

"Do it, or that's what the rest of your year will be like," he said.

Without even thinking, he turned to Scottie, a small boy in fifth grade who always sat quietly reading his books, and shoved his head into the window. As soon as he did it, Scottie started wailing and Artemis heard the bullies laughing like wild animals.

"Did you get it? Did you get it?" said the ringleader to the black-haired bully.

"Yeah, I got it. Look," he said.

What he got was the photograph that was now in Artemis' hand—the photo of him pushing little Scottie's head into the bus window. Once they had the photo, they shared it with their friends and it quickly spread to the teachers and principal. Artemis was suspended for two weeks and almost expelled from school. He stared at the photo for a moment and remembered how it felt to hurt someone weak. Then he thought about Deepak and his plots.

I want to see that fucking smile wiped off your face, Deepak.

Artemis returned to the team. When he logged in, each one of them was feverishly coding and collaborating. They were testing the code in various configurations and under many different types of load.

"Try five billion requests," said Mei.

"That was five billion," responded Lukas.

"Really? It's holding up just fine then," she said.

"What about the packets? Did any of the packets get through with the signatures the professor gave us?" asked Beyoncé.

"Not a single one," said Bits.

"You've only used the mock server. Send them through Princess Di," said Artemis.

"Okay, here goes one hundred billion. I'm tired of wasting time," said Mei.

"How's Di doing?" asked Bits.

"Not even a hiccup," said Mei.

"So what else are we missing? What aren't we thinking of?" asked Artemis.

"I don't know. All of our code covers the professor's designs and scenarios. Our tests are solid. Should we contact Professor Lao?" said Lukas.

"I just messaged him," said Artemis.

"Were you able to take care of whatever you needed to do?" asked Beyoncé.

"I think so," said Artemis.

"Hello?" said Professor Lao, entering the team's shared work display.

"Professor, we're done testing the code," said Beyoncé.

"How much load?" he asked.

"One hundred billion requests," said Mei.

"How large were the packets?" asked the professor.

"An average of .34 moles," said Mei.

"What was the success rate of intercepting the signatures?" asked the professor.

"One hundred percent," said Mei.

"Create a checkpoint of the code and then keep testing it.

I've put together a few more requirements and test scenarios. Work on them as much as you can, but get some rest. Tomorrow, if diplomacy fails, we'll need all of our wits," he said.

CHAPTER NINETEEN
Officials

Artemis woke up on a cot in the corner of the lab to someone turning on the lights.

"It's almost ten a.m.," said the woman.

He didn't want to be here. He wanted to be with Jef, or even with his cousins. Mostly he wanted to be with Tilly.

"Live stream Bey's apartment," said Artemis.

"Good morning," whispered Tilly. Artemis watched her on the live stream tiptoeing into the kitchen to make something to eat.

"Good morning," said Artemis.

"Bey's not up yet."

"Good for her."

"How's Iceland?"

"Can we not talk? Can I just watch you make breakfast?"

"Sure," she said, smiling at him.

Artemis watched Tilly open the fridge and grab some orange juice and a couple of eggs. While trying to pull down a skillet hanging from the pot rack, she lost her balance; the skillet banged into the others, clanging throughout the apartment.

"Shoot!" Tilly said under her breath.

She continued to make breakfast, adding a couple extra eggs

to the batch. A few minutes later, Beyoncé staggered into the kitchen in her pajamas and slippers, barely awake. Tilly smiled sheepishly at her.

"Sorry," Tilly said. "I'm kind of a nervous wreck."

"It's okay. I wanted to see you before you left anyway," said Beyoncé.

"Well, here I am," said Tilly. "We're live streaming to Artemis. But he doesn't feel like talking."

"Good morning, Artemis," said Beyoncé.

"Good morning," he said, still sitting on the edge of the cot.

"I'm glad you came over last night. I liked having you here," said Beyoncé to Tilly.

"I liked being here. And so did Jef," she said, pointing to the ball of fur curled up on the couch.

"Aren't we supposed to dial the professor in a few minutes?" asked Artemis.

"Actually, a few minutes ago. Calling him on HoloMeet now," said Tilly as the holographic welcome screen emerged in the middle of the kitchen.

"Good morning," the professor said in a tired voice.

"Hi, Professor," said Tilly.

"I hope you slept better than I. Have you spoken to Artemis yet this morning?" he asked.

"We're live streaming. He doesn't feel like talking," said Tilly.

Artemis watched the meeting between Tilly and the

professor, pretending it was just a movie instead of his life. He wanted there to be a button he could press to move to the next scene, or a home world editor that he could use to just erase some of the setting.

"I've found a means to get you a meeting with Jeff. Have you the packet for him?"

"I have," said Tilly. "There's some code printouts, some summaries of your work together on DARPA projects, and—"

"Yes, it's all there," interrupted the professor. "But what we need to talk about is how you need to present yourself when you arrive."

"I don't understand," said Tilly.

"Jeff is . . . how can I explain him? He's been in positions of power and influence for much of his career and has taken a different path—quite a corrupt path," said Professor Lao. "Artemis, if you're watching, send us the next chapter of my book."

Officials

Tama walked with Kiyohara through the gardens outside the mansion where she lived in hiding. During the months they spent together, the two had grown close. The sound of horse hooves pounding the road interrupted their walk.

"I've finally made it to see you, Tama," said Hosokawa Tadaoki in the white jacket of a newly minted official, sitting atop his horse.

Tama said nothing as Tadaoki dismounted.

"It's a shame you've come all this way in that filthy jacket," she said, her arms to her side as he walked toward her to embrace.

"What do you mean? There's not a spot on it," he said.

"You've been so very conscientious with it, looking after every detail, tending to every tiny issue, to keep your jacket white. You must have exchanged many favors to obtain a jacket like that."

"You should change your tone with me," said Tadaoki.

"Do you remember why you wanted to become an official in the first place? Was it always so you could spend the day counting favors and making deals with those willing to give you what you wanted? That jacket will never be white. I wish you'd not come here," said Tama, turning away from Tadaoki and continuing her walk with Kiyohara.

"Don't turn away from me!" yelled Tadaoki to Tama, who continued walking away.

Lao's commentary

Most professionals are far removed from the positions where most corruption occurs. Developers tend to be of a different breed and make decisions not on who can do them a favor but on the merit and usefulness of something. Nevertheless, the Coding Samurai can learn a lot from the story of the white-jacketed official. Remaining conscientious and continuing to do work with the same attitude as when you first start your career is an epic achievement. Similar to how the official dirties himself over time, professionals can let their moral and ethical compass shift over time until they end up wearing the metaphorical gray jacket.

When we are young, it's easier to absorb everything we can. The world is wide, exciting, and rich with new things to learn. This is when we are wearing the white jacket. But our minds can lose luster over time. Those on The Way of the Computer Warrior *remember to remain consummate beginners. They avoid corrupting their spirit of learning and growing by keeping their minds open to new ideas and methods. Letting the jacket get dirty means losing this desire and the excitement about a world full of wonder.*

We also have to be careful not to slip ethically. When I was a contractor, I realized managers weren't necessarily tracking time closely. I along with other contractors took an extra fifteen minutes at lunch and didn't account for it on our invoices. A year later, I was taking an extra thirty minutes. Eventually it turned into two hours, and yet I was content to bill the client for those hours each week at lunch. I'd become corrupt and ashamed of myself.

****

"So Jeff's a shady sellout. Shocker," said Artemis.

"You've joined us, Artemis. Welcome," said the professor.

"If he's this type of person, why am I going and not you?" Tilly asked the professor.

"That's the part I need to explain. Jeff doesn't think you are going to meet with him to talk about how he needs to stop Groundswell's launch," said the professor.

"No? Then what does he think?" said Tilly.

"He thinks you're—how do I say this—an escort."

"What? I can't do that!"

"She's not doing that, Lao!" yelled Artemis, standing up from his cot.

The professor was silent for a moment. Tilly stood up and pressed her hands on the table, seething in anger. Beyoncé sat in stunned silence, both at Professor Lao's suggestion and at the burst of emotion from Tilly and Artemis.

"No one expects you to actually do anything with him. We just need to get you in the door. Jeff isn't going to meet with anyone unless he thinks he's getting something out of it," said the professor.

"Like a piece of ass?" asked Tilly.

"All you need to do is get in the room with him and then give him the packet. If you are afraid for any reason, just leave it and get out," said the professor.

"Why not just email it to him?" asked Tilly.

"Jeff doesn't read his email. His assistants handle it all," said the professor.

"Then why not send it to them?" said Tilly.

"To Jeff's pawns? They're just as likely to delete it as read it," said the professor. "Look, this is the only way I know to get the information to Jeff before the launch in a few hours. Can you help?" he said.

Tilly lifted her hands off the table and looked at Beyoncé.

"Do you really think the things you put together are going to change this guy's mind?" asked Artemis. "He doesn't seem to give a shit about anything."

"We have to try," said the professor.

Tilly looked back at Professor Lao and said, "I'll do it."

"This is a bad idea, Professor. You can't ask her to do this," said Artemis.

"Don't worry about me, Artemis. I can do it. Bey, will you help me with my makeup?" asked Tilly.

"Fine. I'll help you look like a ho, then," said Beyoncé.

****

Artemis and the group watched as Tilly's car parked on the street in the trendy warehouse district where Jeff maintained his offsite office. She checked her appearance in the mirror one last time, examining the bright red lipstick and heavy mascara Beyoncé had applied. Artemis thought she looked nervous.

"I look incredibly sexy, don't you think?" she said into the live stream.

"To say the least," said Artemis.

She rummaged through her purse again, checking that it contained the packet, breath mints, and pepper spray. After taking a few deep breaths and fidgeting with her sleeves and dress, she left the car and walked up to the door. She pressed the door buzzer, heard it unlock, and let herself in. There was no one in the reception area. She walked down the hall and heard music playing from one of the rooms. She tiptoed down the dark hallway until she stood outside the door of the room with the music, staring at it.

Artemis whispered "I'm here" into her ear, to give her the

strength to push open the door. He watched from her perspective as she regarded the man sitting at a desk with his face leaning over a vaporizer.

"Oh, wow. You're quite the cutie. I'm really going to have to thank Frank," said Jeff after lifting his face from the vaporizer. "What's your name?"

"Um, Bridgette," said Tilly.

"Welcome, Bridgette. I'm Jeff. Have a seat over here," he said, pointing to a small couch near his desk.

Tilly clutched her purse and took quick, short steps around Jeff's desk, avoiding getting close to him, and sat on the couch as far from him as she could.

"You're bugging out, baby doll. Relax," he said. "I'm not going to hurt you."

"Sorry. I'm fine. Really. I'm okay," she said.

Artemis cringed at the scene. He felt disgusted, wondering if he was about to see his girlfriend raped by a scumbag.

"Do you want a drink? I have a DIY Brew. How about a Triple Banger? On second thought, that drink makes people go crazy before passing out. Maybe some weed instead? My new vaporizer is unreal," he said.

"Um, water is fine," said Tilly.

"Water? Baby, you're killing me. If we're going to get to know each other, you're going to have to unwind a little," said Jeff.

Tilly jerked open her purse, grabbed the packet, and shoved

it on Jeff's desk into his little pile of cocaine.

"What's this?" asked Jeff, laughing. "A summons for a paternity test?"

"No. Just read it," said Tilly, her voice screeching.

"You're doing great, Tilly," whispered Artemis.

Jeff took the packet, opened it, and started reading it. He read carefully at first and then just started flipping through the pages. Finally, he set the packet on the desk and took another long pull from the vaporizer.

"So, I'm guessing you're not here to sleep with me," said Jeff.

"No, just to give you that," said Tilly.

"That is a shame, because you are one seriously foxy girl in that little dress," he said, scanning her body with his eyes.

Artemis winced.

"So, this Professor Lao—he wants me to stop Groundswell because Deepak put something in it that's going to mess with people's heads?"

"Yes. That's what's in there, right? All of the proof," said Tilly.

"We're in marketing. It's our job to mess with people's heads," said Jeff. "Some people invent things. Some people design things. Some people research things. Marketers make people want things, most of the time things they don't need, sometimes things that will actually hurt them. It's not our job to question whether something hurts someone enough to pull it from the market. That's for the lawyers to figure out. Are you a lawyer, pretty girl?"

"No," said Tilly.

"And neither am I. So what do you think I should do?" said Jeff.

"Hopefully the right thing," said Tilly.

Jeff erupted in laughter. "*The right thing*. That's a good one. You're still young and can afford to think about *the right thing*. It's good. Really it is. While you're judging me with my boner and pile of drugs, don't think that there wasn't a time when I didn't think about *the right thing*. But you know what happens?"

"No, what?" asked Tilly, scooting into the arm of the couch as much as she could.

"You see the people who are lying and conniving get promoted while you argue about doing *the right thing*. You see people making backroom deals while you sit in the cafeteria by yourself thinking about *the right thing*. And after seeing things go that way time and time again, you wake up one day and realize what *the right thing* actually is." He stared at her. "Don't you want to know what that is?"

"What?" she asked.

He stood up from the desk and walked over to where Tilly sat. He leaned down and put his face close to hers and said, "Whatever I can get away with," as he put his hand up her skirt.

"Get out of there, Tilly," yelled Artemis, pounding his fist against the wall of the lab.

Tilly shoved Jeff back, jumped up from the couch, and walked as fast as she could in her heels. As she left the room, Jeff shouted, "Don't you want your packet?" He laughed and threw it in the trash.

Artemis watched, his stomach in knots, as Tilly pulled off her heels and sprinted down the hallway to the door. She slid into her car and said, "Go to Beyoncé's." She started wiping off the lipstick and makeup. "So much for diplomacy. You guys need to get ready to do whatever it is you're going to do."

Artemis ran into the conference room and started the HoloMeet. Everyone else was already there waiting.

"You know, Professor, the next time you need some dirty work done, you can put on some lipstick and heels and sashay your lily-white ass into some creep's office and ask him to read a brochure yourself," said Beyoncé.

"Maybe it wasn't a good idea," he said.

"We agree. It wasn't a good idea," she said.

Bits and Lukas glanced at each other, conveying their familiarity with Beyoncé in this frame of mind. They both felt sorry for whoever ended up on the receiving end of her wrath.

Professor Lao finally responded, sounding genuinely confused, "I'm actually only half white."

CHAPTER TWENTY
Military Service

"Beyoncé, we need you to get the back door installed in Groundswell's codebase. I have an idea," said Professor Lao.

"Oh, I've seen your ideas, Professor. You stick to the equations. Trust me; hustlin' ain't your thang," she said.

Professor Lao, visibly annoyed and shamed, didn't respond to Beyoncé's rebuke. Bits and Lukas smirked at one another. Mei sat in stone-faced silence. Artemis felt that Beyoncé's anger was pulling the group apart.

"Bey, let's just take a breath," said Artemis.

"We don't have time for this. I'm going to go get this done," she said.

"Beyoncé! Don't go like this," he said.

"I know what I'm doing," she said, grabbing her bag and leaving.

"Damn, bull-headed . . ." muttered the professor.

"Professor, we need to keep an eye on her," said Artemis.

"I don't need a lecture from another young adult."

"Mei, please talk with your friend," said Artemis. "Professor, what now?"

"We need to prepare for battle."

Military Service

330

"What is it, Kiyohara?" said Tama to her maid as she entered her chamber. "You appear worried."

"Another letter from your father. It arrived by falcon. But Mitsuhide isn't on a hunt. I fear the worst," said Kiyohara.

Tama unrolled the letter and began to read.

"I spent today helping the men build defenses and digging latrines until I grew blisters on my hands. No man is exempt from this type of work during war.

"With this mundane introduction, I'm trying to avoid telling you what I must. Regrettably, if you're reading this letter, Tama, I've failed at my mission. I failed because your husband betrayed us. When you married Hosokawa Tadaoki, our houses entered an agreement that he would send aid if I needed it. Hosokawa abandoned me. No doubt he has sided with Toyotomi Hideyoshi, with whom he's found himself in financial servitude. It's too late for me, so do what you must to survive, even if that means remaining loyal to the man who betrayed your father. My only concern now is for your future. Remember all that I've taught you.—Your father, Akechi Mitsuhide"

Lao's commentary

Many times we look at our task lists and plan our time around accomplishing only those things. But in addition to assigned tasks, the Coding Samurai realizes the existence of additional responsibilities around the camp and willingly pitches in to help. Whether making tools for debugging common problems or improving test quality and code coverage, actively engaging in constructing things makes life easier for yourself and your team.

If work like this is continuously put off, the team will find themselves less efficient and less motivated when they realize that things have fallen apart through neglect. There are plenty of rewards from doing this type of work. Useful tools for debugging make production support problems easier to solve. Better testing improves code quality and lets developers focus on building out new features. Refactoring poorly written code makes the code more extensible and easier to maintain. Plus, many successful products have emerged from what started out as a tool or utility written by a developer who was trying to make life easier at work.

Making a fresh pot of coffee, updating the wiki, writing better tests, and other grunt work is similar to digging latrines, so there will always be team members who dodge it. Everywhere I've worked, there are people who don't make the next pot of coffee and leave messes for someone else to clean up. There will always be slobs and selfish people who dodge common work they feel is below them. In contrast, the Coding Samurai uses humility, ingenuity, and hard work to make the camp an environment that others want to respect and work in.

****

"Look!" said Artemis, pointing at a news stream that showed Beyoncé approaching the door of BSP headquarters as reporters milled about outside the entrance trying to conduct impromptu interviews.

"We're live streaming from outside the BSP offices in downtown Lepton Mountain, where the biggest consumer product in decades is about to launch. Excuse me, young lady.

Do you happen to work for BSP?" asked a middle-aged man staring at her with expensive streaming goggles.

"I don't have time for you right now," said Beyoncé, pushing past the man.

Back in the HoloMeet, Mei made an announcement. "I was able to reach her. Bey said she's turning on her feed."

The live stream broadcast through the HoloMeet as if on a screen hovering above all of their heads. The group saw Beyoncé walk past Brent, who was talking on the phone while doing something on his computer.

Brent turned to her and mouthed, "Good morning."

"Good morning, Brent," whispered Beyoncé as she walked past his desk. The work area was buzzing. All of the DOTs, even the ones who typically worked remotely, had come into the office for the launch. Beyoncé pushed through the crowds to her computer and logged in.

"You guys are going to love this," she whispered into the live stream as she shared an email she'd received.

Good morning, BSP employees.

As you know, today is the biggest day in Boom! Snap! Pow! Marketing's history, and perhaps the history of marketing itself. With the launch of Groundswell at 11AM EST, we will mark the start of a new era. Reaching consumers worldwide, we have innovated the most advanced product placement platform ever conceived.

We have high expectations! There's still a lot of work to do, so don't let off the pedal just yet. We're expecting a smooth ride, but if things get rocky, we'll need all hands on deck.

Also, per legal, if any media representatives ask for a quote, you are to say, "I work for BSP (make certain to fist-bump the air), the best company in the world. Today is an historic day." If they ask for more, say, "I have no further comment. Please contact BSP public relations."

Sincerely,

Jeff Rove

"What a joke," said Artemis.

"Mei and Lukas, are you set up?" asked Professor Lao.

"I've got Quantum Ion Cannon loaded," said Lukas.

"No, you don't. That's my position," said Mei.

"I thought we were switching."

"No, you idiot. You need to do something else."

"Mei, you need to keep the network up so we can support our team going for the quantum core," said the professor. "Lukas, get on that QIC. Blast away at the Groundswell servers to shift their resources to our region. It will also keep their engineers busy trying to handle all your requests. Once our region becomes the primary node, launch Lasso of Truth to funnel all of the traffic to the harpstone wormhole."

"Hold on, everyone! Bey's feed has gone black. Mei, bring it back up," shouted Artemis.

Mei's eyes locked onto her development environment as she started tunneling into Beyoncé's live stream. The screen lit back up to show Beyoncé sitting in a bathroom stall playing an old game called Candy Crush.

"Jesus," said Artemis, turning away from the HoloMeet.

"What the hell are you all doing?" she said, covering herself up.

"We thought we lost you," said Artemis.

"You did—for good reason."

"I see that now. What's going on?"

"I told Wei Wei I had food poisoning and had to run to the bathroom. He checked in the code for me. I figured Deepak would be watching check-ins from me."

"Brilliant," said Artemis.

"How'd you hide the actual code?"

"I put a header on each file so that the code seemed to be auto-generated."

"Let's hope it works."

"I've been in here twenty-five minutes. I think that's long enough to appear legit."

Everyone watching the live stream heard cheers erupt around the office.

"Groundswell must've gone live. I gotta go," she said.

"Keep streaming until you're out of BSP," said Artemis.

Beyoncé's feed showed everyone leaving the work area to attend the celebration party in the cafeteria.

"Hey, aren't you coming upstairs?" asked Tony, standing in the crowd of employees.

"I'll be up shortly. I need to do one more thing," she said.

"Groundswell! Groundswell!" said Tony, joining the chanting of the crowd.

Beyoncé walked by a monitor broadcasting a tech program covering the launch. Jeff was wearing the most outlandish suit yet and had what looked like at least a pound of pomade in his hair. He was standing beside a reporter.

"I'm Steph Judge, standing here with Jeff Rove, product manager of Groundswell, the marketing platform that will change the way consumers shop and even live," said the reporter. "Jeff, what can you tell us about your new product?"

"Well, Steph, our product is the effort of a great team of people at BSP Marketing."

"Sorry to interrupt, Jeff, but I noticed when you said 'BSP,' you enthusiastically punched the air. Can you please tell us more about what that means?" she asked.

"Well, Steph . . ." said Jeff before Beyoncé walked away. The office had cleared out except for Wei Wei, who stood outside his Mobipod, fidgeting and looking around nervously.

"Wei Wei, what's the matter?" asked Beyoncé.

"There you are. I need you to be a dear and look at something chop-chop," he said.

"Did you get my code checked in before the launch?" she asked.

"Yes, but I need you to verify the testing. Take a peek," said Wei Wei.

"Let me just send a message real quick," she said.

Artemis shouted at Beyoncé through the feed. "Just get out of there!"

"There's no time. If it's broken, we need to fix it quickly," said Wei Wei.

"Okay, okay. I'll look," she said before climbing into his Mobipod.

They all watched her face change to fear as she synced with Wei Wei's station. "What the hell is this?" she asked, reacting to Deepak's face appearing in her lenses through Wei Wei's quantum.

"He insisted I do it. I'm going now. Enough work," said Wei Wei, who then turned and left Beyoncé alone in the work area with Deepak.

"Hello, Beyoncé," the group heard Deepak say through her feed.

"Shouldn't you be at the party?" she asked.

"I have a few matters to tend to," he said.

"Like what?" she asked.

"Like you," he said, pausing to glare at Beyoncé. "Do you know we're using the first production release of Groundswell as we speak through this quantum?" said Deepak, flashing a toothy smile.

"Congratulations," she said sarcastically.

"Let's explore a little, shall we? How about a walk through SoHo? You like to shop, don't you?" asked Deepak.

"Just with my girlfriends," she said with a cold but pained look in her eye.

"Maybe today you'll make an exception. Look, some purses in this window. I think red is your color, isn't it?" asked Deepak.

"I'm not playing your game!" shouted Beyoncé.

"But you are," he said calmly. "Now, what's your favorite city?"

"I'm not answering your stupid question."

"What are you afraid of?" he said. "Tell me. It's a simple thing."

"Fine. It's Hyderabad," she said, then paused. "What the hell?"

"Oh, that's a fine city. The City of Pearls, some call it. I can see why it would be your favorite," he said.

"It's not my damn favorite. My favorite city is Hyderabad," said Beyoncé, her face showing fear and confusion.

"You've already told me what your favorite city is, my dear girl. It's Hyderabad. You needn't repeat yourself."

The group shouted over each other for Beyoncé to run.

"Go ahead. Talk to them," said Deepak.

"This sicko has me saying my favorite city is Hyderabad. Something is wrong with my head," she said as her eyes started to cross and spittle began to run from the side of her mouth.

"Get out of there!" said Artemis.

338

"I'm trying," said Beyoncé, struggling to get her words out.

"Artemis, I'm afraid your friend failed at putting in the back door. It was not well thought out to assume I wouldn't be looking at the underling's check-ins," he said.

"That's the one I wanted you to find, you dumb bastard. Artemis, do it . . . back door is wide open," slurred Beyoncé, about to lose consciousness.

CHAPTER TWENTY-ONE
Belief

"Mute the audio on her feed," said the professor in the team's holographic mission room. "Lukas, I hope you've begun firing that QIC."

"Yeah. Mei, how we doing?" asked Lukas.

"I've never seen this high of a gravity reading on a quantum network. But we're pulling BSP into our region. Maybe two more minutes," said Mei.

"I'm through Bey's back door," said Artemis. "But I'm stuck on a document server inside the firewall."

"We're inside the city gates at least. How long until you have the address of the wormhole for the Groundswell quantum core?" asked Mei.

"It looks like they deployed new clusters this morning. The document I'm seeing isn't up to date," said Artemis.

"I don't need a document to find it. Give me control," said Mei.

"Fine. Professor, are you there?"

"Yes, I'm trying to find where he has Beyoncé."

"Same here," said Artemis. "What have you got?"

Everyone vanished from the holographic display, leaving Artemis alone.

What have you done, Deepak?

Artemis checked the network settings but he couldn't find anything. He logged into the router and pored over the configuration as quickly as he could. Then he pulled the addresses of the quantums that had been on the network most recently.

"All right, let me try this," said Artemis, taking the first address and tunneling to it.

Lukas beamed into the seat next to him.

"What the hell happened?" asked Artemis.

"Doesn't matter," said Lukas. "I found the signature that's routing Groundswell back to the relay and away from us. Where's everyone else?"

"Working on it. Deepak must have done something to break us all up," said Artemis. "Okay, who's next?"

"I've found the service that's sending the infected packets," said Mei, who seemed so focused that Artemis wondered if she'd even noticed that the group had been temporarily disbanded.

"Kill it!" said Lukas.

"I can't," she said.

"C'mon, Bits. Where are you?" asked Artemis, cracking his knuckles.

"Guys, where'd you go? I've figured out how to strip the signature," said Bits. "Only problem is I don't know how to install my code."

"Mei, pass me control. I can do this," said Artemis.

"It's all yours."

"Almost there. One second. We're past the relay!" said Artemis, who continued typing away faster than anyone in the group had ever seen.

"What the hell is that?" asked Lukas, who noticed another display appear in the virtual movie theater.

"It's Princess Di," said Artemis. "She's on the left in the split-screen."

"It's that weird planet with those crazy Skittle mountains," said Bits.

"The harpstones," said Artemis.

"It looks like they're asleep or something. They aren't glowing like they were the last time," said Lukas.

"That's where I've sent the signal," said Artemis. "It'll be there in three . . . two . . . one . . ."

The signal reached the harpstones and they lit up like the sun. As the software continued to redirect the infected signal to them, the brightness and depth of the light they gave off grew. Soon, the mountains of harpstones were shooting off plumes of molten light in every color, as if a nuclear reaction were occurring inside them. The patterns flowed and swirled to unknown rhythms as the mountains grew formations of humanoid shapes along the ridge. First one or two, then hundreds, then thousands.

"They're dancing!" said Lukas. "Artemis, can we get audio from the harpstone screen?" asked Lukas.

"There you go," said Artemis, bashing away at his keyboard.

"What is that?" asked Mei.

"It's a Bollywood classic. 'Punjabi Mast,' from the mid-2010s," said Bits. "It's on one of my playlists."

The music filled Planet Heidi as the harpstones sang out. With their trillions upon trillions of synaptic connections, the harpstones were absorbing the signal and transforming the infected information that coerced shoppers to turn against their own tastes and desires—an alembic turning evil into art.

"The harpstones are doing their job," said Professor Lao. "Artemis, get to your home world. Tilly and Bits, join him there. As soon as Mei finds the wormhole, we need you to get in there and destroy the core. If we don't, Deepak's engineers will eventually wrest control from us. We won't likely have another shot," said Professor Lao.

"On my way," said Artemis.

"Don't expect it to be easy. Deepak will have protected the core well," said Professor Lao. "You're going to need to draw upon the strongest part of yourself to get through this, Artemis. Take these words with you."

Belief

"My husband has doomed us," said Tama to her maid, Kiyohara, as she looked out the window of the mansion.

"What is it, my lady?" asked Kiyohara.

"I see the sigil of Ishida Mitsunari approaching from the east. Tadaoki's debt became too large and he was forced to side with his lender, Tokugawa Ieyasu. Now Tokugawa's enemy, Ishida, is here to take us as bargaining chips," said Tama, turning away from the window.

"What would you have me do?" asked Kiyohara.

"You've shared with me much of what your husband learned from his Catholic friend, Takayama Ukon. I want you to baptize me," said Tama.

"But I'm no priestess!" said Kiyohara.

"I don't care. Do this for me, Kiyohara."

"I will do as you wish."

Kiyohara drew a bowl of water from the bucket in the kitchen. She came back to Tama, who sat on the couch in the reception room, the sound of hooves growing louder outside.

"Lay your head across my lap, my lady," said Kiyohara.

Tama let her head fall in Kiyohara's lap as her thoughts left the room. She remembered playing in the yard of her childhood home, swimming in the innocence of that time. Kiyohara took a scoop of water from the bowl and poured it across Tama's forehead, saying "This is Hosokawa Tama and she—"

"Give me a Christian name," Tama said.

Kiyohara nodded her head and resumed the ceremony.

"This is Gracia Hosokawa and she comes today to be baptized into Christ," said Kiyohara, as the sound of the outside gate being battered echoed through the room.

Lao's commentary

Necessary for a meaningful life, yet abstract, idiosyncratic, and elusive, belief is the most difficult lesson to master, whether one believes like Gracia Hosokawa or does not believe like an atheist such as myself. Much more than claiming a religion or possessing self-confidence, belief is the simplest of things, yet also the knottiest.

Far different than narcissism, believing in the inherent worth of yourself and others is an important requirement for a belief system. Even though sometimes The Way of the Computer Warrior *might seem to evoke a sense of self-denial, when considered deeply, it's revealed that the lessons protect the self in an impersonal world by teaching ethics, discipline, and restraint. Many lessons deal with how to present oneself in the external world while training the inner world to adapt and thrive. Without training the inner world of the self, you're a slave to external forces and circumstances.*

Belief systems must grow and adapt along with each person's life in order to retain power. Every system of belief requires daily conscious effort and practice to be of value. At its core, religion is the daily practice of one's beliefs. Religion isn't saying 'my book of reference holds the absolute truth' and then not thinking about it again for another week. Religion is what we do and think each day as well as what our intentions are. No matter if I claim a religion or not, by reverse-engineering my daily thoughts and practices, I can see what my beliefs truly are. If my spirit lingers in self-absorption, deception, bitterness, spite, and even hatred, violence, and oppression, then my beliefs are quite dark indeed—even if I wear a cross around my neck or kneel on the floor five times a day to pray or meditate.

No one can tell another the correct system of belief or the correct way to practice it. Nevertheless, history has taught us that beliefs without roots in humanity lead to fanaticism and extremism. Having no beliefs leads to nihilism and despair. A carefully constructed belief system, practiced daily, will provide each individual the meaning necessary to live life to its fullest. Finding and maintaining this deep meaning is the goal of The Coding Samurai *walking* The Way of the Computer Warrior. *This is why I say to train* kokoro, *or heart, above all else. When you're facing death and need to find the strength to live, you'll likely need to lean on something more than how many programming languages you know.*

****

Artemis couldn't stop thinking about his parents as he put on the modified haptic suit he'd need once they made it to the quantum core. It looked like a normal, white, stretchy suit, except at the wrists, where cobalt-blue metal gloves had been attached. He stared at the gauntlets while he clenched his fists.

Mom and Dad, I love you.

He arrived at the entrance of the biosphere in his home world just as the sun was setting. He felt sick to his stomach at the thought of Beyoncé stuck in BSP with Deepak toying with her. Tilly and Bits beamed in beside him.

"I'm so happy to see you," said Tilly.

"I feel like I'm surfing on a tidal wave and one mistake kills us all . . . no, kills everything," said Artemis.

"If we're going down, we're going down together," said Bits.

"The professor and I were able to make a few adjustments to our suits as well," said Tilly. "They can't destroy the core, but the other tech modifications might help."

"This F.O.A.L. tech is something else," Bits said as his suit created a quantum shield around the group.

"Don't waste it," said Tilly. "There are only five charges and it has a two-minute cooldown."

"What about your suit?" asked Artemis.

"Another thing you didn't know about me," said Tilly as she unsheathed a glowing red sword. "All-State Fencing Champion."

"What's that?" asked Bits, pointing toward the horizon as a faint light bubbled in the atmosphere.

"They found the wormhole to the quantum core," said Tilly. "Let's go."

The group approached the wormhole slowly as it continued to take shape. The faint bubbling light disappeared. Light bent around the red rocks in front of them, making the landscape deformed as if someone had hit it with a hammer. They walked to the right and saw a small slit in Artemis' home world leading into another wormhole. Artemis turned to Tilly and looked at her for a moment before slowly walking through.

The trio emerged into the middle of a field in the peak of summer. The sun was high and felt warm against their skin. Wind blew across the tall grasses, bending them toward the ground. Tilly looked at a device embedded in the forearm of her suit.

"It says the core is this way," she said, pointing toward the horizon.

They began walking side by side into the grasses and toward

what they believed was the Groundswell quantum core. The wind hissed as it blew through the grasses.

"I saw something," said Bits.

"Something other than grass?" asked Artemis.

"Something in the grass."

As they walked, the plants grew higher up around their waists. The wind buffeted them; the noise grew louder.

"Something just touched my foot," yelled Tilly.

"Let's pick up the pace," said Artemis.

They pushed forward through the field. The grasses continued growing higher around them.

"Is it just me, guys, or is this wheat getting really big?" asked Bits.

"It's not just you. It's getting tough to walk through," said Artemis. "Okay, something just brushed against my leg, too."

The group pushed forward, each step growing more difficult as the sturdy plants grew larger around them. Artemis looked around in every direction and saw nothing but open field.

"How far to the core now?" Artemis asked.

"It says five hundred meters."

"I can see for miles in every direction, and there's nothing but wheat."

"And whatever just slid across my foot," said Bits.

"Faster," said Tilly, pushing through the grass.

Artemis and Bits tried to keep up with her. With each step, the grasses grew higher and higher. The stalks were now so big that Artemis and the group could move in between individual stalks of grass the size of giant bamboo.

"Are we still going the right way?" asked Artemis.

"Four hundred meters away. But I can't see though the plants."

"Wait a second," said Artemis. "I'm starting to wonder—did the grass get bigger . . ."

"Or did we get smaller," said Bits, finishing his sentence.

Tilly, who had turned around to retrace their steps, bumped into Bits as she walked backwards.

"We shrank," she said as she turned around and shifted gears into a full sprint. "Run!"

Artemis and Bits turned around to see grass crashing to the ground as a train-sized cobra slithered toward them.

Artemis and Bits caught up with Tilly. They could hear the beast gaining ground on them.

"Stay close to me," said Bits.

"How far to the core?" said Artemis.

"I don't know, maybe two hundred meters," said Tilly.

Artemis thought he felt the heat of the snake's breath on his neck.

"There's a house!" said Tilly, pointing to an old farmhouse in the grass with the porch roof slumping under its own weight. Artemis recognized it as a decayed, dollhouse-sized approximation of Debbie's house in the outskirts of Lepton Mountain.

"We're not going to make it," said Bits. "It's right behind me."

"Faster!" yelled Artemis.

The snake lunged at them as Bits triggered the shield. Artemis heard the loud crack of a massive power discharge before a blue light surrounded them. He heard a deep thud. They ran up the stairs onto the porch, and he turned to see the snake coiling around itself from its strike being blunted.

"Let's get inside," said Artemis.

After they stepped inside the dark house, Artemis, Tilly, and Bits stood in a single room made of block walls. To the left, a set of stairs led to a second floor. To the right, light filtered down a hallway, along with the pungent odor of rot and curry. Artemis could hear a voice humming from down the hall.

"This way," said Artemis, leading them toward the singsong voice.

Bits and Tilly followed behind Artemis as he stepped slowly toward the light. He heard oil sizzling in a skillet. They entered a kitchen lit with fluorescent lights flickering above a stovetop. The headless figure of a woman in a nightgown stood stirring the contents of a skillet. Artemis looked at Bits and Tilly without saying a word. As he moved slowly toward the stove, he heard an alien yet oddly familiar sound bubbling up from the large pot boiling on the other burner. He looked at the stump of a neck on the woman and then reached for the spatula on the stovetop to probe the moaning pot.

"Would you like something to eat, sweetie?" said his mother's slimy head as it bobbed to the surface of the soup.

He dropped the spatula and fled the kitchen.

"Where are you going, sweetie? Artemis, come back!" yelled the head.

Artemis ran from the room as Tilly and Bits peered toward the bubbling pot.

"I'm sick, Arty. Don't leave me in here by myself!" the gory head said, continuing with its haunt.

"We can't go back outside. That thing is out there," said Tilly as they caught up to Artemis at the front door.

"What about the thing in here?"

"The core is close. Upstairs," she said, leading them to the stairwell by the entrance.

Artemis and Bits followed Tilly as she stepped carefully up each creaking stair. At the top of the stairwell, they were surrounded by total blackness. They activated the lights on their suits, but darkness still stretched in every direction. Their steps echoed deep into the cavelike chamber they had entered. The ground was like hardened clay or bedrock.

"Which way?" asked Artemis.

"It says thirty meters this way."

The group stepped carefully through the cold cavern. Water dripped into pools, and bats screeched and chirped. As they walked, Artemis began feeling squishy lumps under his feet.

"Do you guys feel that?" he asked.

"Yeah. I'm afraid to look," said Bits.

Tilly cast a light toward the cave floor. Littering the ground were the corpses of thousands of rats.

"Oh, god, I want to puke," said Artemis.

"What exactly are we looking for?" asked Bits.

"I suspect we'll know it when we see it," said Artemis. "How far now?"

"Twenty meters," said Tilly.

As soon as the words left her lips, light shone down from above, an array of intense beams piercing the darkness. In the center of the lights, a figure slowly dropped toward the cave floor. The humanoid shape reflected light into ten thousand shards. Long, broad wings flapped slowly and extended far from the figure. When the being finally made contact with the cave floor, the room shuddered and boomed.

"The quantum core," said Tilly.

CHAPTER TWENTY-TWO
Dying Loyalty

It stood before the three, its entire body a brilliant gold mirror. The massive wings bled where broken bones protruded from under the thick, white feathers. The tips of the humanoid's fingers extended into long, glimmering, golden claws.

"Kamikaze swarm," said Tilly.

Thousands of tiny drones peeled off the group's suits and targeted the creature. They circled around it and, one by one, detonated as they crashed into its body. Thousands of explosions echoed inside the cave, which filled with the stench of sulphur and smoke. The group stared into the cloud as the golden shape slowly emerged, smiling.

"You kids shouldn't have come—you aren't cut out for it," said a voice that, while clearly Deepak's, was deeper and more booming than his natural voice. "But that's your professor's weakness: his faith in the youth. Once they grow up, they forget what they are taught and succumb to the status quo they once fought against so passionately."

"And your weakness is that you only care about yourself. You don't have a soul," said Artemis.

"No, I don't. But I have something. Have a taste," said Deepak as a tendril shot from his hand.

When the tentacle made contact with Artemis' face, it split into four tips, which entered his head through his nostrils and ears. He immediately felt something tensing in his body. His heart raced. He tried to deal with the infected information being pumped into his nervous system but felt powerless to halt the assault. He heard individual leaves on the tree outside the F.O.A.L. lab scraping against the windows like fingers on a chalkboard. He sensed the subtle shift in the light leaking through the edges of his lenses as he squinted in agony. He became acutely aware of the immenseness of the universe and felt terror at his own insignificance, but he also felt connected to everyone in the world, as if he were part of a colony of inseparable souls swimming in a cloud, tumbling over each other in a hurricane. He could feel mankind's hopes, dreams, and terrors all at once. Then, in his bones, he only felt horror; his life was about to end.

Artemis, with all of the infected information surging into his mind, felt superhuman, one who was experiencing all of life condensed into one moment; yet he was also fragile like a baby who knew nothing, who had no tools with which to deal with the world. Overwhelmed by infinite decisions, he found himself unable to make a single one. He was confronted with his guilt over things he had done and things he hadn't done.

Why didn't I stop and help her? he thought as the face of his mother flashed into his mind.

Every memory he recalled was peppered with the fear of passing into the void, the nothingness of death, but he had an even deeper dread: that he might already be dead and in a permanent hell within Deepak's machine. His life had only been a test—and he had failed. He believed his life would continue now, not as a mortal in the purgatory of Earth, but as a slave inside this psychotic computer. He would be subject to chaotic cries of constant terror for all eternity, the signals subjecting him to every horrible experience written in the memory banks of humanity. Every thought became an image of death and a prelude to an inimitable horror.

"Help me!" he cried.

"I am," said Deepak, pulling the book from Artemis' pocket.

Dying Loyally

"They've broken through, Gracia," said Kiyohara, using her lady's baptism name."

"You know what must be done," said Gracia, standing up from the couch and leading Kiyohara to the innermost room of the mansion.

"I can't," said Kiyohara, pulling away from her.

"You must. I swore to my father that I would never let someone take my honor from me like Ishida Mitsunari no doubt will. Follow me, Kiyohara."

Gracia led her through the study, where they could hear soldiers yelling to one another in the entrance of the mansion. Gracia took a sword and dagger from the wall and hurried into the inner chamber. Once inside the tiny room, she had Kiyohara help her push a wardrobe in front of the door.

"Don't think about it; just do it," said Gracia, handing Kiyohara the sword.

"No!"

"Kiyohara, do it now!" said Gracia, turning the sword inward toward her stomach. She tried to push the sword into herself, but the blade cut into her hands, spilling blood onto the floor.

"I will help you keep your honor," said Kiyohara, pushing the blade into Gracia.

The daughter of Mitsuhide fell first to her knees and then onto her side as blood pooled by her body. She looked up into Kiyohara's eyes as she passed. Kiyohara let out a scream before turning the dagger on herself as Ishida's men bashed down the door and burst into the chamber.

Lao's commentary

There are moments of great significance in our lives where momentous choices will be made which will produce consequences that will determine how we define ourselves. For the samurai, dying loyally meant dying loyal to the lord. If the lord asked the samurai to go into battle to meet certain death, he would die on that command.

The Coding Samurai does not tend to live and die in such dramatic fashion. Nevertheless, death comes to all, and we must decide what it means to die loyally and with honor. Life and death are inseparable, the words only a convenience; so to live loyally is to die loyally. If you believe that we are a wasteful society, and that we should care for the earth, you can't die loyally if you're thoughtlessly generating pounds of unnecessary waste. If you believe in something deeply enough, your life will become a living testament to those beliefs. If the words are shallow, that will be apparent as well.

With that definition, how many die loyally? How many of us hold our convictions so deeply that they transform our life rather than let outside forces transform us so that we live in a manner counter to what we want in our hearts? To live in accordance with our beliefs—to maintain internal strength even when we are terrified and the world offers us every opportunity to sell out our convictions for pleasure, relief, or acceptance—is to live a spiritual life.

In any moment, we can opt out of selling our spirituality. We can resolve to live our life in harmony with what and who we care about most. To accept a job that you don't believe in, to spend years of one's life contributing to a company that causes more harm than good, to sell out the future of all humanity for the short-term benefit of "a good-paying job" is something many of us do every day to some extent. It's easy to sell out our beliefs and become just another cog in a technological machine that often feels like its perpetuation will lead to the eventual enslavement of humanity.

The very act of believing in a better world is the first requisite step in feeling powerful enough to act to create a better world. Even if we don't always live according to the ideals of our beliefs, it doesn't mean we stop believing in them and quit trying to embody them. I want to continue to believe in the qualities that lead to better lives for everyone, lives with more joy, less struggle, more kindness, less loneliness, more connection, and less alienation. The time to start living loyal to the life you want is now.

****

"So naïve," said Deepak, tossing the book to the ground of

the cavern.

"You're broadcasting a horror show," said Artemis, imagining his parents wearing Groundswell lenses and becoming zombies of the puppet master, Deepak.

"I'm about to make BSP the most powerful company in the world," said Deepak.

"You're addicted to power. Being kind and humble requires vulnerability, a quality that cowards like you lack. I used to think being strong meant I could handle a lot of pain. That's not strong. Strong is being brave enough to let go, to let people in and—" Artemis gasped as Deepak increased the power of the signal.

"I'm amazed that you can still make complete sentences," said Deepak. "What do you think your life meant, Artemis?"

Artemis, unable to answer, stared coldly at Deepak.

"You are merely a jangly puppet, pushed along through life by forces you never understood, by urges and instincts programmed into you before you were born to parents you never chose," said Deepak before taking a huge breath. "And you loved them," he said softly as he exhaled. "Not because of their qualities, but because you were compelled by billions of years of time to cling to them no matter what they did to you."

Artemis' body went into a spasm.

"Every aspect of you that you thought of as being real was just your own delusions, your own mistaken perspective," said Deepak, circling Artemis while hovering a few feet off the ground. "No one ever loved you because there's nothing within a person to love. No spirit, no identity, no being, nothing but illusion stacked upon illusion, the wants and desires of fleshy puppets, futilely burdened with the most dreadful of terrors—the loss of everything they ever cared for or loved—and for some an even more terrible burden, the awareness that they aren't even real." Deepak pulled on the tendril, forcing Artemis closer toward him. "Why should anyone suffer this way? You call me a monster, but I'm going to take away this burden from everyone. No more suffering from the horror of the consciousness of death. People will live and consume in perfect bliss. What's more humane, cleaning up the mistakes carved into the puppet or letting the puppet think it's something more while it knows in its wooden bones that it's all a lie—that there is no salvation, that all is vanity, that all is meaningless?"

In the flash of a moment, Tilly's sword sliced through the tendril extending from Deepak's hand. His golden face winced and Artemis pulled the flopping, spindly mass from his face.

"You're about to learn that the consequences in my place are quite real," said Deepak, fixing his eyes on Tilly. "I'm going to fuck you up."

Artemis slumped to the ground. Bits ran toward Tilly. Deepak leapt up and crashed down in front of Tilly just as Bits activated the shield. Deepak's golden claws reached for her but clanged against the blue bubble encasing the two. But Deepak simply chuckled as he stood over them waiting for the shield to expire. Artemis found the strength to stand up and began creeping toward Deepak from behind. Tilly stood with her feet planted, guarding with her sword.

"Stay behind me," said Tilly to Bits.

The shield evaporated and Deepak quickly raised his hand, bringing it down to slice through Tilly and Bits. Tilly caught Deepak's claws with the sword and pushed back his attack, then circled around him as he prepared for another attack. She caught his next swipe and Deepak smiled. His claws clamped around the sword, trapping it between his golden blades. With his other hand, he swung up, sinking the blades into Tilly's stomach, lifting her body toward the opening of the cave where Artemis could only see the outline of her body against the cascading light.

"No!" yelled Artemis, running toward Deepak and jumping onto his back.

When Artemis made contact with Deepak's metallic hide, he experienced pain unlike anything he'd ever felt. Since his memories and synapses had been restored by the refresh treatment, he suffered the entirety of the intense pain from Deepak's body burning his flesh. He took one arm and wrapped it around Deepak's neck, determined to let nothing separate them. With his other hand, he took the metal glove and pressed it against Deepak's back just behind his heart. Artemis discharged the glove and blue gel shot from his hand, coating Deepak's metal skin. Deepak screamed as the fluid began eating through his skin and into the quantum core. Deepak flung Tilly from his claws, and her body crumpled in a pile on the cave floor among the bodies of rats.

Bits, seeing Deepak recovering from the initial shock, ran to protect Artemis from Deepak's finger-knives. He charged and grabbed Deepak's left wing, near where Artemis was clinging to his neck. He grabbed Artemis by his waist and discharged the bubble defense, keeping Deepak's hand just out of reach. Artemis saw Tilly lying motionless on the ground and sank his hands deeper into Deepak's back, reaching in with determination until he felt the object in Deepak's body cavity in his hands. Artemis tore it from out of its golden shell and held the core between his hands, crushing it into dust with the metallic gloves.

Deepak fell to the cave floor. His wings folded over his body, encasing Artemis and Bits against him. Artemis shoved aside the demonic wings and ran to Tilly as blood streamed down his arms from his melted flesh.

"No," he said, taking off the gloves and running his fingers through her blood-soaked hair. "No," he said again, pressing his face to hers.

Bits walked over to Artemis' side and sat down next to him. He put his arm around him while Artemis rocked Tilly's body in his lap.

CHAPTER TWENTY-THREE
Friendship

"Mei, over here," yelled Artemis, stepping off the train, his burned arms in healing wraps.

Under the station lights, Artemis could see she was hesitant to approach him. He walked over to her and she reached out to gently hug him, being careful to avoid his burns.

"How are they?" Artemis asked.

"They're holding up," said Mei.

"Can we go there now?" asked Artemis.

"Of course," said Mei.

They walked to the parking lot in silence. Mei sat down on her scooter and said, "Climb on. Can you hold on to me?"

"I can."

The scooter took off under the night sky, heading for the Mother Mary Hospital at Lepton Mountain. Everything close to them rushed by while the stars in the dusky sky went nowhere—illusions. Artemis looked to the northern part of the sky and searched for Equuleus. Near Pegasus was a confusion of stars. When he imagined the pattern Tilly had shown him, one of the stars twinkled brightly. He began sobbing. He asked himself what was real: the night sky, his senses, his thoughts. Nothing definite remained. Maybe it was all an illusion after all.

Mei shifted on the seat of the scooter and pulled his attention from the stars to the person to whom he was now clinging.

No. My friends are real.

They arrived at the hospital, left the scooter, and hurried into the lobby. The receptionist greeted them. "Hello, how can I help you?"

"We're here to see Beyoncé Noel," said Artemis.

"Fifth floor. Take the elevators behind me. The nurses' station is to the left," she said.

At the station, an older nurse escorted them to room 505. Outside the room, a small screen displayed her name and a series of lighted codes. The nurse opened the door and then left. Artemis and Mei walked into the room, where Bits, Lukas, and Professor Lao were keeping Beyoncé company.

"I'm so sorry, Artemis," said Beyoncé tenderly when she saw him.

Artemis leaned over Beyoncé, holding her closely, and whispered to her, "It's so good to see you."

"It's good to see you, too," she said, kissing his cheek.

Artemis' attention shifted when he heard a reporter on TV say, "BSP." He watched intently as Jeff gave a statement to reporters in the lobby of the BSP office.

"We're working on determining the source of the outage. That's all I have to say," said Jeff.

"Then why is the FBI here?" asked the reporter. "And whose body was brought out earlier by the coroner?"

"The FBI isn't here. There are no bodies. No more questions," said Jeff, starting to turn away.

A group of five FBI agents pushed through the crowd and surrounded Jeff. One of them grabbed his arm and said, "Jeff Rove, you're under arrest."

"Federal agents are in the process of arresting Jeff Rove as we speak. It appears that the rollout of Groundswell is going far worse than BSP shareholders had hoped," said the reporter, following behind the agents as they led Jeff toward their vehicles.

"You're looking good, Artemis," said Beyoncé.

"Yeah, right. My mind isn't *that* far gone," he replied. "I look like hell."

"You're right. Put your head down here."

Artemis put his head in Beyoncé's lap even though he was confused at what she was getting at.

"Look here, you are getting so bald I can see what's on your mind. Bits, don't come over here. The shine is so bright on this guy's head that if you look, you'll be deaf *and* blind."

Everyone laughed at Artemis' expense before he made a request.

"The last night before Tilly died, I wrote this chapter for the professor's book. Can I read it to you all?" asked Artemis.

"Of course," said Beyoncé.

Friendship

"Why do you spend time with those girls, Tama?" asked her father,

Mitsuhide, standing in the doorway of their home as a young Tama ran under the thatched roof to escape from the cold evening rain.

"Do you not approve, Father?" asked Tama.

"A samurai shouldn't befriend just anyone. It's easy to find friends to carouse in town with. It's much harder to find those with intelligence and bravery," said Mitsuhide, standing tall in the doorway.

"I like them, though," said Tama, looking down while making a circle in the mud with her shoe.

"It has nothing to do with you liking them. It's about you avoiding disgrace. Go inside now and get dry," said Mitsuhide.

"That's what my father taught me about choosing friends," said Tama to Kiyohara, a week before the mansion was overrun.

"Your father cared for you," said Kiyohara.

"More than anyone or anything," said Tama. "You are the type of person my father imagined when he taught me how to pick my friends."

"You honor me with your words. I will try to never give you a reason to believe otherwise," said Kiyohara, taking Tama's hand.

Artemis' commentary

As coders, we mainly deal with analytical and quantitative thinking. This way of thinking is great for writing software that machines can understand but a terrible way of relating to people. People, the part of life that provides us with rich, deep, meaningful experiences—and also frustration and pain—are not machines or robots. We can't treat them that way.

At the workplace, we will be around people with starkly different beliefs, temperaments, histories, and personalities. We choose our attitudes toward them. We can reject those who are different than us, humiliate them or despise them, or we can choose to speak to them, listen to them, try to understand them, and occasionally even befriend them.

There's no one definition that can explain what friendship is or what it means. Like many things, you can feel it more than you can explain it. Friendship can't be weighed, packaged, or sold on the market. In life, but particularly in work environments, true friendship is a rare treasure. Anyone with an absence of friends can forge new friendships by remembering the old saying that the best way to make a friend is to be one first.

The people we choose to give our time to beyond what is required professionally have qualities that we hope will make us better people and better teammates. Seek out considerate, hard-working people who exude care and professionalism. These are the people to get coffee with. The Coding Samurai will hopefully walk a long time on The Way of the Computer Warrior. *This can be a lonely walk or one that includes the company of others. It's much easier to not get lost when surrounded by trusted people to call your name when you wander off. Plus, sometimes it's just nice not to be alone. The path still ends at the same place for all of us, but I encourage every young Coding Samurai to walk as many miles as possible with friends.*

****

"I really like that, Artemis," said the professor.

"I tried to sound like you," he said.

"I want you to know that I consider you my friend."

"I want you to know that I forgive you."

The professor nodded and stood silently.

"So, did you think about your favor?" Artemis asked Beyoncé.

"Yeah—would you bring me some lamb vindaloo and chutney?" she said.

Artemis smiled, but he wasn't sure if she was joking or being serious.

****

"One more bike ride before I go home to see my family?" Artemis imagined asking Tilly as he stood in the doorway of his apartment building the day before returning to Minnesota. His fantasy continued, thinking about the scene he wished were unfolding but never would happen.

"Sure, why not," she said, scratching under Jef's chin.

"How did Jef do on the bike ride over?" he asked.

"He really loved the air on his face," she said sarcastically.

"Okay, Jef. You have fun. We'll be back in a bit," said Artemis as he closed the door behind him and imagined walking with Tilly to the bike rack behind the apartment.

Artemis took off on the bike toward the city limits, still imagining Tilly riding along with him.

"Have you thought about what you're going to do next, after visiting your parents?" Tilly asked him.

"I don't know. I didn't think my life would feel like such a mess after just having helped save the world," said Artemis.

"I'm sure you could find a job back here in Lepton," said the voice of Tilly in his mind.

"Getting fired after three weeks on my first job doesn't look too good on a résumé," he said, chuckling.

"But you have the best recruiter in Lepton as your friend."

"That's true," said Artemis as they approached a familiar fork in the path.

"Which way do you want to go?"

"This way," said Artemis, pointing toward the farm.

"I've never been down here before," said Tilly.

The towering buckwheat had been cut down and baled since the last time Artemis biked through. A bass jumped in the nearby pond as the farmhouse loomed in the distance. He saw an indigo bunting on a limb of a weeping willow at the pond's edge. He felt like the bird was looking at him and trying to say something. The farm grew closer, and he smiled when he saw Debbie sitting on her rocking chair on the porch. He slowed down by the tree in front of her house.

"Hi, Debbie!" he yelled from the path.

"Hi there. Haven't seen you for a while," she said, taking a puff from a cigarette.

"No, I've been busy," said Artemis.

"Would you like a glass of lemonade?" she asked. "Real lemons, not that stuff from machines you kids drink."

"Sure," he said, laying down his bike by the tree. He

imagined Tilly following behind.

Artemis walked up to the porch and sat down by Debbie's rocking chair. He looked at the Lepton Mountain skyline in the distance.

"Here you are," said Debbie, handing him a glass of lemonade.

"Thanks."

"Been busy, have you?" she said, sitting back into her rocking chair.

"Very. What's new?" asked Artemis.

"Nothing really. We cut down the buckwheat. Not too much else," she said.

"Was it a good season?" asked Artemis.

"Oh, not too bad," she said, taking a puff on another cigarette. "I've seen better. I've seen worse."

"Has your grandson been by?" asked Artemis.

"Oh, yes. He checks on me often," she said. "What is it you say you do?"

"I don't really know anymore. I actually just lost my job," he said.

"Yeah, that sort of thing happens," said Debbie. "Got fired from my first job, too. My boss said I didn't fit in with the culture there—whatever the hell that means. I guess maybe I did have a pretty big mouth at that age."

"I don't believe that for a second," said Artemis, who felt a rush of emotions welling up inside him.

"What's the matter?" asked Debbie.

"I lost my friend. She died. She was killed."

"That's terrible. There's nothing better than a true friend and nothing worse than losing one."

"When I was here the last time, I didn't understand how you could believe that you weren't missing anything by living out here. I think I understand now."

"You do? Then maybe you could explain it to me because I still don't understand a thing. Flowers used to be flowers and sunsets used to be sunsets. Now I'm old. Flowers are the things my husband will never bring me again. Sunsets are the end to days I spend alone."

With that, Artemis' imagination lost its grip on Tilly, and she faded into the fields and the sky.

Artemis sat quietly as Debbie rocked in her chair. Several minutes went by and he just gazed out at the farmland and listened to the sounds of the natural world around him.

"Well, I should be going. I'm going back to see my parents tomorrow and I need to get packed. Thanks for the lemonade," he said as he stood up and set his glass down on the chair.

"Good seeing you. Don't be a stranger," said Debbie, smiling. "Stop by any time."

"Deal," he said, looking at her with a mix of joy and sadness while walking away.

"Remember, every day is beautiful," she shouted to him as he approached the edge of the yard.

****

Back at his apartment, Artemis looked at Princess Di sitting in the corner. He put on the haptic suit and entered. He found himself standing outside the biosphere, and he walked down the path to the obelisk and touched it. The wormhole flashed and he stood on the surface of Heidi, but it looked nothing like it had last time. In the distance, the harpstones had taken the shape of the Taj Mahal. There were still uncountable numbers of humanoid forms Bollywood dancing on the lawn in front of the monument.

"Di, change my home world to a sunny field with a creek flowing through it."

"Done."

Artemis heard furious scratching. He opened the door to find Jef staring up at him. "Okay, little guy. Let me get you some food, and then we need to get some rest. We have a long day tomorrow."

****

"You're home!" yelled Artemis' mom as he walked in the door of his parents' house.

"Hey, Mom," said Artemis, giving her a big hug.

"We missed you," said Artemis' dad.

"I missed you, too," he said, putting Jef down on the floor.

"He's gotten big," said his mom.

"And fluffier," said Artemis as Jef took off running across the floor to Buddy, who was sitting under the coffee table.

"Your room is just how you left it," she said. "I'm sure you're wanting to get your computer set up. Go ahead while I finish dinner."

"I didn't bring my computer," said Artemis.

"You didn't?" Artemis' mom said with a puzzled look.

"I brought a friend instead. This is Beyoncé," said Artemis as she walked through the door carrying a weeping willow sapling.

Artemis' mom and dad looked at each other, momentarily stunned, but his mom recovered quickly and welcomed Beyoncé. "So nice to meet you, Beyoncé. Make yourself at home. I'm Charlotte and this is Gunter," said his mom.

"Pleasure to meet you."

"You kids take a load off," said his dad. "We'll finish dinner."

"Dad, we aren't kids. We're Coding Samurai," said Artemis, making a karate-chop gesture with his hands.

"Are you okay, Son?" asked Artemis' dad before turning and following Charlotte into the kitchen.

Artemis led Beyoncé out to the backyard. He grabbed a shovel from the shed in the corner of the yard and began digging a hole in the center of the garden.

"So this is where it all started," said Beyoncé.

"I guess so," said Artemis.

The patio door opened and Buddy came running up to lick Beyoncé.

"He's a friendly guy," she said.

"Yeah."

"Arty, what are you doing?" shouted his mother from the doorway.

"I'm planting a tree, Mom!" shouted Artemis at his mother.

"Okay, well, dinner's almost ready," she said before going back inside.

After he finished digging, he took Beyoncé's hand and said, "Tilly, it took every moment since before beginningless time for us to meet. We love you, wherever you are."

"We love you, Tilly," said Beyoncé, wiping the tears from her eyes and holding Artemis close.

The two sat down in the yard next to each other and gazed deeply at the tree they had just planted.

ABOUT THE AUTHOR

Ian Felton has more than twenty years of professional experience writing software for organizations such as NASA, Mayo Clinic, Thomson Reuters, and many more. His poetry has been published in *Contemporary Haibun, Volume 12* (Red Moon Press) as well as in Contemporary Haibun Online. He lives in Minneapolis, Minnesota with his beautiful partner, Jen, and their cats. In addition to writing and wildlife photography, his interests include running his nonprofit organization, which puts musical instruments into the hands of children who need them, and practicing meditation and several Chinese martial arts. He's also a graduate student pursuing a Master of Arts in Psychology and Counseling Services.

Find out more and contact the author at http://www.ianfelton.com.